LIES

OF

OMISSION

LIES
OF
OMISSION

A Hanneke Bauer Mystery

Kathleen Ernst

First published by Level Best Books/Historia 2021

Copyright © 2021 by Kathleen Ernst

This novel is entirely a work of fiction. The names, characters and incidents portrayed in it are the work of the author's imagination. Any resemblance to actual persons, living or dead, events or localities is entirely coincidental.

Kathleen Ernst asserts the moral right to be identified as the author of this work.

AUTHOR PHOTO CREDIT: Scott Meeker

First edition

ISBN: 978-1-68512-027-6

Cover art by Level Best Designs

This book was professionally typeset on Reedsy.
Find out more at reedsy.com

For all the interpreters who, way back when,
shared those special days at Old World Wisconsin.

Praise for LIES OF OMISSION

"In her debut Hanneke Bauer mystery, author Kathleen Ernst takes readers straight into the perils of being a German immigrant in 1855 Wisconsin—particularly when no one believes newly arrived Hanneke as she insists she is married to the now dead Fridolin. Hanneke unravels the mystery surrounding the death of the man she knows to be her husband and digs deep to learn how to survive on her own amid anti-immigrant fervor of the day. This well-researched and compellingly told tale is a must-read for any fan of nineteenth-century American historical fiction and historical mystery devotees of any era."—Edith Maxwell, Agatha Award-winning author of the Quaker Midwife Mysteries

Characters

- Hanneke Bauer—Pomeranian immigrant
- Regina Gruber—Hanneke's acquaintance from the steamship
- Fridolin Bauer—Hanneke's husband, a farmer
- Christine Bauer—Fridolin's sister
- Josephine and Wilhelm Wiggenhorn—proprietors, Buena Vista Hotel
- John Barlow—deputy sheriff
- Asa Hawkins—nativist
- Angela Zeidler—proprietor, Red Cockerel Tavern
- Adolf—worker, Red Cockerel Tavern
- Clara and Charles Steckelberg—neighboring farmers
- Gerda and Oscar Muehlhauser—neighboring farmers
- Dr. Rausch, Dr. Jenkins—physicians
- Franz and Joe Rademacher—bricklayer and builder
- Lorenz Kiessling—yeast peddler
- Adam—barber
- Mr. Rutherford—supervisor, Vulcan Iron Works
- Theodor—Hanneke's brother in Pomerania
- Wilhelmine—Theodor's wife

Chapter One

As Hanneke Bauer watched the Milwaukee shoreline come into focus beyond Lake Michigan's choppy waves, she wondered if she would even recognize her husband. An unsettling thought, really. Gracious! This might be a most awkward reunion.

Frau Gruber, who'd elbowed through the other eager passengers, settled at the *Tempest's* railing beside her.

"Almost there," Hanneke said.

"Almost home," Regina Gruber corrected.

Yes. *Home.* Hanneke's grip tightened on the rail. It was May 1855, and at age twenty-eight she finally had a home of her own. That home lay beyond this lake, beyond the raw port city. God willing, she and her new husband would soon have children around their hearth as well.

She squinted against the glaring sun. There, somewhere on the docks stood Fridolin Bauer. Her husband. She knew him best from his letters, from the cramped lines of brown ink that suggested thrift and foresight. Eight months earlier they'd had two weeks of conversation, then just the one day and night as true husband and wife. But some things she remembered: blond hair parted on the right, worn long and combed away from his face. A thick beard. The hands of a provider, long-fingered but reassuringly broad and callused. A delighted smile when the first night star appeared, hinting at an inclination to dream of knowledge behind his trade. Hesitant speech; an endearing reticence that suggested not ignorance, but a shy respect. Warm hazel eyes that glinted with a promise: *I think we'll do well enough, you and I.*

And since Hanneke had cast her lot with Fridolin Bauer, she prayed he was right.

Regina sighed. "I wish your husband still lived in Milwaukee. Why he left a good job in the city to buy a farm is beyond my understanding. You'll be isolated out there."

Soon, Hanneke promised herself. Soon she would be free of Regina's endless criticisms. "Bookbinders are losing work to new machines," Hanneke said lightly. "But farmers will always be needed. Besides, I understand that there are many German families near Watertown. I won't be lonely."

Regina shook her head with pained resignation. "You must promise to accompany your husband if he brings crops to sell in the city. We'll have coffee and *kuchen* while you tell me all about the farm. You have my address?"

"Yes." Hanneke patted her valise. She'd written Regina's address on the back of her receipt for passage, and tucked it away with her legal documents and the letters Fridolin had sent during their months apart.

"Good." Regina flinched as a wave slapped the ship and sent a fine salt spray toward the travelers. "Well, all you can do is make the best of things. It's best to face the future without regrets."

"I have no regrets," Hanneke said firmly.

* * *

Milwaukee, hailed as the "German Athens" in Fridolin's letters, bustled around the swampy low ground where the Milwaukee River spilled into the Great Lake. Church spires poked heavenward. Gently rolling hills rose beyond the city. It does look like home, Hanneke thought, understanding in a more visceral manner why so many German-speaking immigrants had made their way to Wisconsin.

The waterfront was lined with warehouses, stacked barrels and crates awaiting transport, freight wagons hitched to sturdy teams of Belgian and Percheron horses. They flicked their tails at flies but otherwise waited patiently. One team reminded Hanneke of the dark draft horse her father had owned when she was a child.

And did Fridolin own horses? Had she even asked? Hanneke tried to think as she slid a hand beneath her bonnet, checking for loose pins. There was so much she didn't know about her new home. So very much.

Well, all would be known soon! She pressed her palm against an anxious flutter in her belly. None of that! she told herself sternly, and willed the flutter away.

When the ship docked the crew scrambled to secure it. The deck felt oddly still beneath Hanneke's feet. Gulls wheeled overhead, screaming, diving for scraps. Final plumes of smoke drifted from the steamship's stacks.

"There's Herman!" Regina cried, waving her handkerchief. "Do you see your husband?"

Hanneke squinted again, trying to turn the milling crowd into discernible individuals. "Not yet." Then she was jostled away from the rail by another immigrant eager for his first good look at Wisconsin. Hanneke didn't mind. Although she was excited to finally be close to the farm she'd spent the long winter trying to imagine, something told her to cherish these last few moments of the freedom she'd so enjoyed on the long trip.

When the captain finally decreed that passengers might disembark, Hanneke joined the throng funneling slowly onto the gangway. *To earn respect, it is important to dress well when in the city,* Fridolin had written. While on board the *Tempest* Hanneke had seen the derisive glances some travelers of British descent aimed at the German men in their broad-visored caps, heavy pants, oft-mended coats, and long beards; the women in their coarse skirts and kerchiefs. "More *Dutchmen,*" one Yankee had muttered. So today, in honor of her arrival and their reunion, and because it was Sunday, she'd donned a silk dress the color of sumac berries. She'd worn it to exchange matrimonial vows with Fridolin back in Treptow, in the region of Pomerania, Prussia. She also wore a lacy shawl she'd knit of her own hand-spun merino wool. After the wedding, when Fridolin had returned to America, she had whiled away many winter hours working with her smallest needles. She planned to wear this shawl, her very best work, to the Wisconsin wedding reception Fridolin had promised.

Even on shore, a brisk wind blew from Lake Michigan. The air smelled of fish and tar. Compared to the ports of Bremen, New York, and Albany, the

Milwaukee docks presented manageable chaos. Several steamships bobbed against their moorings. Dockworkers—mostly white, but a few free Negroes too, Hanneke noted—hoisted trunks and bales of goods with ease. Dock men hauled merchandise in wheelbarrows along trestle-and-plank paths laid over the river gullies. Yankee businessmen shook hands with colleagues. Boys played hide-and-seek amidst stacks of fresh-cut lumber and cordwood. The babel of various German dialects, English, and other languages she couldn't identify was overwhelming as friends greeted friends, captains shouted at their hands, merchants called for draymen. Cartmen lined the waterfront, yelling offers of their service. Runners from local hotels waited as well, bellowing the virtues of their particular establishment: "Here for the Hoffman House! Clean rooms, low price!" Hanneke also heard a dozen voices calling the names of their loved ones.

She did not hear Fridolin Bauer's voice, calling *her*.

Clutching her valise, Hanneke stepped away from the flow of passengers and carefully scanned the crowd. Had her premonition been correct? Were she and Fridolin both waiting, looking, not recognizing the other?

Regina Gruber shoved through the throng, her hand tucked in the elbow of a man wearing work clothes and sturdy boots. "Hanneke, this is my husband Herman."

"Frau Bauer." His smile was friendly. "Welcome to Milwaukee." Herman looked freshly scrubbed but the unmistakable blend of tannic acid and animal hide lingered. He worked in a tannery.

"How do you do," she said politely, trying to ignore the discomforting sense of being a woman alone in a world designed for pairs. Not here. She had not expected to feel that here.

Regina frowned. "Your husband hasn't come?"

Needing to busy her hands, Hanneke reached into her knitting pocket and pulled out the half-done wool sock dangling from four needles. "I'm sure he'll be along any moment."

"We'll wait with you," Herman said easily. "We're in no rush."

Which was a kind lie, no doubt. Hanneke couldn't imagine any tradesman feeling easy about taking time away from his work.

4

And so they waited. Herman lit a long *meerschaum* pipe and was soon puffing out smoke. Regina chattered about Milwaukee: the beer gardens, the Turners, the musical groups. Hanneke nodded, all the while watching for Fridolin. The single men who'd disembarked collected their luggage and trudged away. Some of the family men went to make lodging arrangements, leaving their wives and children sitting with feather beds and trunks.

As the minutes ticked by, Hanneke felt increasingly uncomfortable. She finally turned to Regina and Herman with what she hoped was a confident smile. "I can't hold you up any longer. Fridolin must have been delayed."

"You did wire him from Albany?" Regina asked. "He knew when to expect you?"

"I did." *I'll come to Milwaukee in advance of your earliest possible arrival,* Fridolin had written. *I'll be waiting.*

Herman rubbed one earlobe with fingers stained the color of tea. "We can't just leave you here."

"I'll simply proceed to the hotel," Hanneke said briskly. "My husband stays at the *Gasthof zum Deutschen Haus.* Do you know it?"

Herman's face cleared. "Yes, of course! They call it Hotel Wettstein after the owner. Other than Germans, the only people who stay there are Yankee businessmen wanting to learn the language."

Hanneke claimed her trunk, and Herman found a runner from Wettstein's who heaved it into his cart. Regina gave Hanneke a hug. "Contact us if you have any trouble," she called, as Hanneke climbed into the cart.

"*Danke schön!*" Hanneke waved. "I'm sure all will be well."

She wanted to believe that, but as the Grubers turned away, she stopped trying to hide her unease. After an eight-month separation, she did wish that Fridolin had not been delayed! The man who'd written such respectful letters would not have let something of little consequence keep him from the dock.

The driver snapped the lines and the cart lurched into the traffic of the city where Fridolin had lived for three years. Hanneke tried to place him on these streets, to imagine him striding to work, meeting friends at the *biergarten.* Beyond the marshes near the docks, small log cabins gave way to two-story frame and yellow-brick homes with gardens and henhouses and stables behind. Poles for gaslight stood at busy intersections. Telegraph lines tethered the city to places beyond.

They quickly reached the business and shopping district, crowded with pedestrians, buggies, and coaches. Hanneke wanted to enjoy this drive as she had, unexpectedly, enjoyed her brief visits to Bremen and New York. How exciting it had been to see the multicolored flags flapping from the forest of masts on the docked ships, and to imagine where their journeys had taken them! She had sucked in the newness of it all, satisfying a long-suppressed craving.

Now, though, uncertainty dulled the thrill of discovery. "Is it far to the hotel?" she asked.

The man's cheerful grin revealed several missing teeth. "No. Just to the market square. If you need anything during your stay, you'll find it there." He clucked suddenly to his horse, pulling the cart adroitly out of the path of a heavy wagon loaded astonishingly high with beer barrels.

"I won't be in the city long," Hanneke assured him.

"Where are you heading?"

"Northwest of here. My husband has a farm near Watertown."

He nodded. "I've heard it's good land around Watertown. They're growing a lot of wheat out there." He laughed. "Not the Forty-Eighters, of course."

"Of course," Hanneke murmured, to be polite. A revolutionary democratic movement had swept through the German states in 1848, led largely by well-educated men. After the uprising failed, many of those disappointed "Forty-Eighters" had felt compelled to emigrate.

Wettstein's Hotel was a three-story brick building. As the driver parked in front, two jeering school-age boys—perhaps ten—ran past the cart. Hanneke pulled her shawl more closely about her shoulders.

"Be off, rogues!" the driver barked.

One of the boys threw a handful of dust and pebbles at them, startling the horse. "Shh, boy, down now," the driver called, his tone soothing now, keeping the lines taut until he was sure the horse was calm.

The boys laughed, yelling over their shoulders. Only after they'd disappeared around a corner did Hanneke's brain belatedly discern what they'd been chanting, in an execrably accented semblance of her native tongue: "Dirty Germans! Dirty Germans!"

"Don't mind, ma'am," the driver muttered. His cheeks had flushed an angry brick red. "Most people are grateful for all the good things Germans contribute to the city. You'll be welcome here."

"Yes, of course," Hanneke murmured, although at that moment, she couldn't imagine feeling any less welcome. She remembered something Fridolin had said in one of his first letters: *A certain anti-foreigner spirit has simmered in some quarters here for years, and I am afraid it may come to a full boil in Wisconsin this year. But there is no need for alarm. Good German men won't allow themselves to be treated as something less than those who happened to be born on American soil.* The note had given her pause, for some in Treptow—those souls who knew everything about everything, and gloried in spreading their wisdom among those who did not wish to listen—said that immigrants were in danger of a cool reception…and mercy, was Hanneke sure she really wanted to travel all the way to America?

"Let me help you down," the driver said patiently.

Hanneke managed a smile and took his hand. She'd forgotten those comments when Fridolin's later letters had been filled with only affectionate descriptions of her new home.

The driver shouldered her trunk and led the way inside. She glanced at the people passing through the entryway; at those visible in the dining area beyond. No Fridolin.

She approached the desk clerk with a steady smile. "Herr Wettstein?"

"*Ja.* How may I help you?"

"I'm looking for Fridolin Bauer."

"Fridolin Bauer?" The proprietor blinked, then stroked his long beard as he considered her.

"Yes," she said firmly. "He should have arrived a few days ago."

"Fridolin often stays here," Herr Wettstein conceded. "And when he was here last—three or four weeks ago, I'd say—he did mention that he intended to return this month. But he hasn't come."

Hanneke's valise suddenly felt quite heavy. She set it on the floor. "He—but he intended to be here by now," she said, as if insistence might make Fridolin appear from behind the counter. "Perhaps…perhaps he arrived while you were away from the desk? Could someone else have noted his arrival?"

"I don't think —" the proprietor began, but something in her expression made him swallow the words. He dutifully thumbed back a few pages in the big ledger book, scrutinizing the scrawled names. Finally, he shook his head, not unkindly. "No, I'm sorry. Fridolin is definitely not here."

"I see." Hanneke took that in, turned it over in her mind.

"Do you wish to rent a room? It's six shillings a day, or seventy-five cents American. That's with three meals."

Six shillings. Keeping the exchange rates clear in her head was an ongoing struggle—francs, schillings, florins, kreuzers, cents. One thing was clear: the little reserve in her reticule had dwindled alarmingly. Almost all of her dowry money had been signed to Fridolin before he left Germany, as agreed in their marriage contract, allowing him to improve the farm before her arrival. He had instructed her precisely on anticipated costs, but on several occasions since leaving home two months before she'd been obliged to spend more than expected.

"Is there transport to Watertown?" she asked.

Herr Wettstein nodded. "It's a day and a half by stagecoach on the Watertown Plank Road. Next departure isn't until tomorrow morning, though."

"I see." Hanneke considered her options. Well, there was nothing for it. The afternoon was almost gone, and she was loathe to hire another driver and submit herself to the Grubers anyway.

The proprietor was waiting. "Yes," she told him. "Yes, I will need lodging for the night."

He reached for a steel pen and poised his hand over his ledger. "Your name, please?"

"I am Frau Fridolin Bauer."

Shock flashed in the proprietor's eyes, quickly masked with bland professional courtesy. So, Hanneke thought, last month Fridolin told Herr

Wettstein that he was coming back in May, but didn't tell him *why*. If Fridolin often stayed here, he must have more than a passing acquaintance with the proprietor. They were on a first-name basis, after all. Surely most any man would have announced with some pleasure the impending arrival of his wife.

So...why had Fridolin not done so?

* * *

"Watertown!" the stagecoach driver bellowed. "The Planters Hotel!"

God be thanked for that, Hanneke thought. The stagecoach trip had felt more interminable than her voyage across the Atlantic. Her bones ached and her eyes felt sandy. The feather bed at the Milwaukee hotel had seemed luxurious after the *Tempest*'s wooden berth; the stagecoach inn where she'd slept the night before, although plain, had been clean. But both nights, gnawing apprehension had robbed her of rest: Where is Fridolin? Why hasn't he come? What has happened?

In the coach, she'd been compelled to squeeze between a fat woman carrying a huge potted fern on her lap and an elderly man who snacked on garlic cloves. Hanneke had tried to study the dictionary Fridolin had sent her, but the coach's jolts and heaves made reading impossible. Instead, she strained to look at every passing farm wagon, buggy, and rider, hoping to recognize her husband.

Now Hanneke climbed stiffly from the coach. She took a quick look around, hoping to see her husband hurrying forward with an anxious apology: *My dear wife, I'm so sorry! My wagon broke an axle...I've just recovered from a terrible fever...my stable caught fire...we're together now, though, and all is well.*

But Fridolin was nowhere in sight.

Don't succumb to panic, Hanneke ordered herself. She blew out a long, slow breath. What next?

The plank road ended at a block of hotels, taverns, inns, and other businesses. The Planters Hotel, a three-story frame building, looked clean and comfortable. Fridolin had never mentioned it, though. She thought with unexpected longing of Regina Gruber's offer of hospitality. *You should not have been so proud!* Hanneke scolded herself. Having one friend in this new country would have been worth any dose of scolding or criticism.

The driver clambered to the top of the stagecoach, unlashed the ropes binding the luggage in place, and began tossing pieces down to his waiting assistant. Hanneke watched her fellow passengers collecting their luggage or directing porters. All right, then. She needed to find someone who could tell her how to reach Fridolin's farm.

One of the porters pointed to her trunk and said something in English. She recognized the word 'luggage,' but no more. *"Sprechen zie Deutsch?"*

"Ein bissen," he said. A little.

"I wish to go to the Buena Vista Hotel," she said. *It is a fine German hotel,* Fridolin had written. *A gathering place.* The man nodded, hefted her trunk, and set out, splashing carelessly across the street through the muck.

Hanneke followed more slowly, picking her way on an improvised walkway of planks. She knew from Fridolin's letters that the town had grown along the Rock River. That river powered mills and factories at the heart of the city. The main street was busy with buggies, workmen pushing handcarts piled with bricks or lumber, the occasional farmer driving stout wagons loaded with sacks of flour or baskets of spring peas and lettuce.

The porter dodged traffic with practiced ease but Hanneke was breathless before he stopped and gestured to a sign on a three-story frame building. The hotel was adorned with black, red, and gold banners—Germany's national colors. "The Buena Vista," he said, pronouncing it 'Byoona VISSta.'

Hanneke followed him inside. He set her trunk in the entryway, then turned expectantly.

Gott in Himmel. At this rate, she would be destitute before ever finding Fridolin. She fished a coin from her purse. *"Danke schön."*

A murmur of voices and the vinegar-gingersnap tang of sauerbraten wafted from the open kitchen door at the back of the hall. She put a palm against the entry wall to steady herself. She'd eaten nothing since breakfast, and she was tempted to search out the dining room before hunting for

Fridolin. She might fare better if she ate before facing—facing whatever news was waiting.

But…no. That wouldn't do.

She turned resolutely to the taproom on her right. Small tables crowded the room, with a billiard table in back. Mounted glassy-eyed stag heads adorned the walls. Several men were arguing enthusiastically. For a dazed moment, she thought she was hearing English, and wondered if she'd come to the wrong place after all. Then her brain sorted the sounds: Latin, surely. This was a place where educated men—scholars, professionals—came to socialize.

When she stepped into the room the argument paused. Other patrons glanced up from their steins or cards. She was glad she'd dressed well and demurely.

Hanneke stepped to the bar. The tender, a portly man, was spooning pickled eggs from a crockery jar onto a china plate. "Good afternoon," he said politely in High German. "The *Gesang Verein* is meeting on the third floor."

He assumes I'm here for a social club, Hanneke thought, feeling very tired. *"Danke schön, nein, Herr…Wiggenhorn?"* Yes, she was sure of it. *Wilhelm Wiggenhorn runs the place*, Fridolin has written. "I'm looking for Fridolin Bauer. He owns a farm near here. Do you know him?"

"Fridolin Bauer?" Herr Wiggenhorn's hands stilled as his jolly look faded. A man sitting at the closest table looked up sharply from his newspaper.

Hanneke felt her heart take on weight, like a wheelbarrow being loaded over-high with bricks. Any more burdens and she might not be able to trundle the load. *"Ja. Fridolin Bauer."*

The tavern keeper set down the spoon. "I am sorry. Fridolin…."

I am about to know, she thought. Whatever is wrong, whatever the problem—I am about to know.

"You see, you have come too late." The man spread his hands. "Fridolin Bauer is dead."

Chapter Two

A solar eclipse, Hanneke thought, as the light dimmed and a ring of stars blinked around the periphery of her vision. The air in the taproom seemed thick, unable to satisfy her lungs.

"I'm sorry!" Herr Wiggenhorn was saying. His words sounded distant and tinny.

Hanneke clenched the handle of her valise until her fingers ached, then squeezed tighter still. Sounds came clear again: muffled footsteps on the hall staircase, someone in the kitchen asking for sugar, a burst of laughter from the billiard table. The familiar smells of pipe tobacco and beer and pickled vinegar had soured, coating the inside of her throat.

She swallowed hard, willing down nausea and anxiety. "Are you sure? Perhaps—perhaps we're thinking of two different people."

The man sighed, bracing his hands flat on the gleaming bar. "I only know of one Fridolin Bauer in this area. He owned a little farm about three miles out of town on Plum Grove Road. Bought it about two years ago."

Which was exactly what *her* Fridolin had done. But it can't be true, she wanted to say. It can't be true because we were planning a life together. It can't be true because I left what little I had and traveled for two months to reach this strange place. To reach *him*. So, you see, he can't be dead.

Wiggenhorn leaned over the bar. "I'm sorry," he said again, his voice kind. "I can see this sad news is a shock."

"Please—can you just tell me what happened? It must have been sudden. His health was good."

The barkeep's brows drew in. He appealed silently to the solitary man at the nearby table, who'd been watching the exchange.

He frowned, but stood and joined them. "I'm John Barlow." His German was inflected with an accent she couldn't identify. "Fridolin Bauer was a neighbor of mine. And you are...?"

"I am Hanneke Bauer."

Mr. Barlow's face remained blank.

"Fridolin's wife!" she added sharply.

Herr Wiggenhorn took a step backwards. The desultory hum of conversation died in a ripple that spread from the nearest table to the back corners of the room. Hanneke felt the stare of every man there.

Mr. Barlow's eyes narrowed slightly. He pulled a chair over. "Perhaps you should sit down."

"I don't wish to sit down! I want to learn what happened to my husband."

"Well, you see," Mr. Barlow said, "that request presents us with a little problem. Wilhelm here and I both knew Fridolin Bauer well. And Fridolin Bauer was not married."

Hanneke's collar shrank around her throat. Her valise fell to the floor with a disconcerting thud. She left it there, needing every ounce of control to say, "Sir, you are mistaken. We were married last September when he traveled to Treptow, in Kreis Greifenberg."

"Fridolin *did* go back to Germany last fall," Wiggenhorn murmured.

"Perhaps," Mr. Barlow said, "you can explain why you didn't come with Fridolin when he returned to America."

"Because my mother was dying! I took care of her. We agreed, Fridolin and I, that it would be best if I stayed until she passed on."

John Barlow regarded her, bracing his chin in the cleft between thumb and forefinger. He was a lean man of medium build with the muscled look of a farmer. Dark hair was combed away from a high brow. Hollows beneath his eyes suggested weariness, but those eyes were alert, thoughtful. "If that's true, wouldn't Fridolin have told his friends upon his return?"

Hanneke wet her lips with her tongue, remembering Herr Wettstein's obvious shock when she identified herself as Frau Bauer. "I had assumed that he did. I—I can't imagine why he did not. He told me all about Watertown,

13

about how he was trying to improve the farm on Plum Grove Road. He promised that we'd have a reception when I arrived, and invite all of his friends and neighbors. I can't imagine why...." Her voice trailed away.

The taproom was silent. Even the billiard players in the corner were quiet. A fly buzzed at the window. On the street, the wheel of a passing wagon squealed rhythmically for want of grease. Hanneke forced herself to hold Mr. Barlow's gaze.

"I think," he said finally, "that we should see what Christine has to say about all of this."

"Christine?"

"You don't know Christine?"

Hanneke shook her head numbly. She felt as if she had somehow been thrust upon a stage while watching a play.

"Come with me." Mr. Barlow picked up her valise with one hand and gestured toward the side door with the other. In the entry hall, he put the valise on top of her trunk and turned to the staircase.

The juicy sauerbraten smell was stronger now. Hanneke fought away a wave of dizziness. She opened her mouth to ask for a few moments to sit and think, to just *be*—but he had already started up the stairs. Hanneke followed him, clutching the polished banister.

The first landing gave way to a short hallway of closed doors—guest rooms, no doubt. Hanneke became aware of voices as Mr. Barlow continued to climb. The stairs ended in a small landing on the third floor. A row of coat pegs lined the walls, with a shelf for bonnets and hats above. A full-length mourning veil trailed from one especially beautiful black bonnet.

"This way." Mr. Barlow ushered Hanneke into a large open room—the type used for balls or political meetings or musical performances. Chairs had been set out in rows. Men and women milled about in shifting knots of conversation.

"Wait here." Mr. Barlow scanned the room, then strode to a refreshment table in one corner. He paused by a small blond woman, leaned close, murmured something. The woman's expression became quizzical, but she amicably put down the ladle she'd been using to pour punch into crystal cups.

Mr. Barlow led her back to Hanneke. As they grew near, Hanneke felt the first stab of real grief pierce the shock. The woman looked to be a few years younger than Hanneke, which put her perhaps a decade younger than Fridolin. But her fair hair, her cheekbones, her warm blue eyes—these were the features Hanneke had clutched in memory for the past eight months. This was not Fridolin, and yet…it was almost Fridolin's face.

"Christine," Mr. Barlow said, "do you know this woman?"

Christine looked at Hanneke with mingled curiosity and confusion. She wore a black dress, relieved only with a mourning brooch made from a single yellow curl pressed neatly beneath black-edged glass. Hanneke pressed one hand over her mouth.

"I don't believe I've had the pleasure." Christine seemed fragile, like a hummingbird. "I'm Christine Bauer."

Her voice was expectant, waiting for Hanneke to introduce herself. Hanneke's tongue felt wooden. Stars began twinkling in the periphery again, pinpricks of light against gathering black.

"Fraulein Bauer," Mr. Barlow added, "is—was—Fridolin Bauer's sister. She kept house for—"

Darkness swallowed the stars, and Mr. Barlow's words, and Hanneke herself.

* * *

Hanneke felt firm hands rubbing her wrists; more hands supporting her shoulders.

"Give her air," a woman said.

A man's voice: "She needs water."

"Should we send for Doctor Rausch?" That was the woman again.

The urge to keep her eyes closed, to sink back into that blankness, was almost overwhelming. Had she actually fainted? Hanneke would not allow such weakness again, especially in front of strangers—most especially *these* strangers.

She opened her eyes and saw faces. John Barlow. Wilhelm, the barkeep. A middle-aged woman with a round face and concerned, red-rimmed eyes—probably his wife. Christine Bauer—Fridolin's *sister*?—stood behind those three, watching with one small, graceful hand curled in concern over her throat.

"Please," Hanneke said. "Please, I'm all right." She felt stiff hairs scratching the back of her neck and struggled upright. She'd been propped unceremoniously on an uncomfortable sofa with horsehair upholstery. Someone had carried her to the ladies' parlor on the ground floor. The room was small, cluttered with porcelain mementos and figurines. German mottos stitched with red thread on punched paper preached from the walls. "Just—if I could please just have a drink of water."

"Josephine?" Wilhelm jerked his head toward the door. The older woman hurried from the room and quickly returned with a pitcher and glass. Lemon water, cool and refreshing. Hanneke sipped slowly.

Josephine Wiggenhorn sniffled into a handkerchief—she evidently suffered from allergies—and leaned close to Christine. "Who *is* she?"

"I have no idea," Christine murmured.

John Barlow waited until Hanneke put the glass down before asking, "Do you require a doctor?"

"*Nein.*" Hanneke shook her head. "I'm a bit tired, and hungry, but I'm not ill." Although I did just learn that my husband is dead. And that he, for reasons I can't begin to imagine, apparently kept my existence a complete secret.

Mr. Barlow turned to the hotelkeeper and his wife. "Thank you, Josephine, Wilhelm. May we use the parlor for a few moments? We have a misunderstanding to sort through. Christine, please stay."

Christine Bauer and John Barlow sat in chairs pulled from the central marble-topped table. "You are feeling better?" he asked. His voice was flat, not solicitous.

"Forgive me," Hanneke said. Her hand fluttered first to smooth her skirt, then her hair. She pulled it to her lap and entwined her fingers to keep them still. "I never faint. It was just the—the shock."

Christine Bauer turned to Mr. Barlow. "John, what is this all about?"

"I'm sorry to bring you into this. But this woman—" his gaze flicked toward Hanneke—"appeared here at the hotel a short while ago. She claims…well, she claims to be Fridolin's wife. Widow."

"*What?*" Fraulein Bauer's eyes went wide and glazed with tears. "That's simply not possible! She—she must be lying."

Hanneke was tempted to accuse *her* of lying—this blonde woman who so resembled her husband. But in a strange way, Hanneke empathized with her. Fridolin had a sister, who lived with him here in Wisconsin, keeping his house! He had evidently kept a monumental secret from her as well. Why, why, *why?*

She rubbed her temples and drew a deep breath. "I'm not lying."

Christine wiped away a tear with a slender finger. "My brother has been dead for only two months, and you arrive without warning, claiming to be his wife—"

"I am not *claiming* anything that is not true."

Mr. Barlow thumbed his forehead for a moment, eyes closed, before regarding Hanneke. "Why don't you tell us what happened."

"Fridolin Bauer visited Treptow, in Kreis Griefenburg, last September. He conducted business at a bank where my brother works. When the two became friendly, my brother invited Fridolin to our home for dinner. We met, and—and we decided to marry. I was caring for my mother, who was very ill, and he had business appointments elsewhere, so we had very little time together. But we *did* marry, and made plans for my trip here."

Barlow's expression was skeptical. Christine rose abruptly and began to pace, her arms crossed tightly, elbows cupped in her palms. "This—I don't even know what to say! It's—it's preposterous!"

"It is truth." Hanneke pushed her spine against the sofa back. She felt hollow.

"Christine," Mr. Barlow said gently. "Come sit down."

"Surely you don't believe—"

"No, of course not. But we need to hear her out."

Christine took a moment to acquiesce. She perched stiffly on her chair, picked up a glossy seashell from the table, and began rubbing it with her thumbs. "How can it possibly be true that Fridolin would marry a stranger while on a business trip?" She darted a glance at Hanneke. "How could my brother have planned for a wife's arrival, and not *told* me?"

Hanneke desperately wanted to believe that Christine Bauer was lying. Looking at the anguish in the other woman's eyes, however, she could not. Hanneke swallowed something that tasted sharply of bile. "I don't know."

"And what did Fridolin tell you of me?" Christine turned the shell over in her hands, polishing it fiercely with the heel of one hand. John Barlow leaned forward in his chair, waiting.

"He...he did not mention you," Hanneke was forced to admit.

Christine Bauer looked at Mr. Barlow. "I won't hear any more of this." Her whole body was trembling now, and her eyes welled with fresh tears. "My brother barely cold in his grave, and...this is intolerable!"

"I'm sorry for your grief," Hanneke said. "But it is true."

Mr. Barlow swung his piercing gaze back to Hanneke. The man had a habit of twisting his mouth slightly to one side, a mannerism that conveyed both suppressed impatience and disbelief. "Fridolin's will has been read," he told her. "And there was no mention of a wife."

"We both had new wills drawn up in Treptow, leaving everything to the other. Right after our marriage."

"Do you have any proof of your claim?"

"Why...of course! I do!" Hanneke's shoulders softened with relief. She pushed to her feet and hurried into the entryway. How stupid she'd been to argue!

Her trunk still stood against one wall; her valise was on top of it. Hanneke crouched, opened the catch, scrabbled inside. She'd carefully tucked her precious papers into a thin pouch stitched of black oilcloth. Tears pricked her eyes when her fingers closed around the stiff fabric.

"Right here," she told John Barlow, who'd followed her into the hall. Her fingers fumbled with the pouch's closure. "I've got my marriage certificate, and my own will, and Fridolin's letters—" Her voice broke.

"I'd like to see them, please."

CHAPTER TWO

Hanneke stared into the empty pouch. Her precious papers were gone.

Chapter Three

"The papers?" Mr. Barlow asked impatiently.

Hanneke groped frantically among the other belongings in her valise: her toilette bag with toothbrush and hairbrush and comb, her nightgown, a work dress, and spare undergarments, the reticule with her beleaguered store of cash. But she knew the papers had been in the oilcloth pouch. They could not have slipped out or been mislaid.

Someone had stolen them.

Hanneke sagged onto her knees. She had cherished Fridolin's letters, reading and re-reading them when her loneliness threatened to swallow her whole; when her sister-in-law aimed sharp barbs with exquisite skill. This was new calamity, but also new grief.

She needed a moment to find the strength to rise and face Mr. Barlow. "They're gone. All of my papers. My marriage certificate, our contract, Fridolin's letters…they're all gone. They were right in *here!*" She showed him the empty oilcloth bag. "Someone must have taken them, while I was upstairs—"

"John." Christina's voice cracked from the doorway behind them. "I've had enough of this—this chicanery. Please *deal* with this person. For Fridolin's sake. And for mine."

Hanneke watched as Christine crept back up the stairs, clutching the banister. After a moment even her footsteps faded away.

"Fraulein," Mr. Barlow began.

"It is *Frau—Bauer.*" Hanneke kept her voice low but emphasized each word. "If we send word back to Treptow, we can get the proof you want."

"You may of course do that. But that will take time. Right now, you will remove yourself from the premises." Mr. Barlow grasped one of the leather handles on her trunk and swung it to his shoulder. He staggered, gained his balance, and walked out of the hotel.

Hanneke snatched up her valise and followed. Heat was beginning to sear through the numbness. She focused on that burning, glad of it, relieved to find fuel.

Mr. Barlow was already striding down the block when she caught up with him. "Where are you taking my trunk?" she demanded.

"Back to the Planter's Hotel. The stagecoach stop. You would be wise to leave Watertown on the next coach available. You can pursue your inquiries elsewhere."

"You presume a great deal of authority as a neighbor!"

"No. I assume authority as a deputy sheriff. I could arrest you for trying to perpetuate a fraud."

"A *fraud!*" Hanneke gasped as understanding finally dawned. *Gott in Himmel.* If Fridolin was dead, that left matters of inheritance, property rights, savings…

"I could summon the city marshal," Mr. Barlow was saying, "which would, I assure you, prove more unpleasant than our conversation has been. Instead, I expect you to purchase a stagecoach ticket and leave Watertown."

Hanneke followed, forcing herself to hold her head high, her back straight. This man was treating her like a stray dog, but she would not permit him to make her feel like one. "Mr. Barlow," she began as they reached the corner where she'd stepped from the stagecoach, "I must insist—"

She was interrupted by a man who'd been nailing a handbill to the hotel wall. He spoke in English, but Hanneke recognized the words "Barlow" and "*hausfrau.*" The man's gaze was sharp, cold.

Mr. Barlow unceremoniously dropped her trunk onto the wooden walk. "Asa Hawkins," he growled. Hanneke couldn't follow the rest, but she sensed a quivering anger beneath the words.

Mr. Hawkins stood a head taller than Barlow, and didn't appear to be intimidated. He looked like a lawyer or banker. His chestnut curls were carefully pomaded in place, his suit of brown wool was well-cut, his vest a lovely brocade the color of ripe wheat, his top hat a well-brushed glossy black and adorned with a long feather. But his left ear and cheek were badly scarred. A physical tension almost shimmered in the air around him. He held himself more like a boxer than a professional man, with feet planted widely and shoulders held back, as if daring—even welcoming—a blow.

He and Barlow exchanged unintelligible taunts, snapping at each other like bristling dogs. Then Barlow's fingers curled into fists.

"*Stop* it!" Hanneke cried, stamping her foot. "I just learned that my husband is *dead*. Aren't things bad enough without two grown men acting like petulant children on a public street?"

She was as shocked by the outburst as the two men. That strange sense of watching a play was back, as if nothing in this horrid afternoon was real. Barlow shot her a glare, but he did subside into silence.

Mr. Hawkins stared at her too. Then he smiled, slowly and deliberately, a wolfish smile on a hard face. It took every ounce of control Hanneke had left to hold the man's gaze.

Hawkins inclined his head slightly. "*Auf wiedersehen, Fraulein.*" He sauntered on down the street, whistling a tune Hanneke had heard the sailors sing during her ocean passage. *Yankee Doodle.*

John Barlow took a long, deep breath, watching his adversary disappear, before turning back to Hanneke. "Take my advice," he said curtly. "Leave on the next stage out. Don't come back. Unless you can produce proof of your claim—which, since I knew Fridolin well, strikes me as absurd—you are not welcome in Watertown."

Hanneke met his cold stare. "You are attempting to fulfill the obligations of your office, so I will say only this: I forgive you for your error."

Barlow's cheeks flushed a ruddy red. He opened his mouth, then closed it again. He settled his hat more firmly on his head and began to stomp away. Before taking more than two steps he stopped, ripped Hawkins' handbill from the hotel wall, crumpled it with a muttered curse, and cast it aside. He obviously wished he could do the same with Hanneke.

Her heart fluttered like the wings of a wounded wren, and hot tears stung her eyes. She blinked them away. Not yet, she ordered herself. She could not crumple yet. She was a widow. Someone had stolen her marriage license, her legal papers, her passport, and Fridolin's letters. She couldn't afford to purchase a stage ticket even if she wanted to. "Which I do not," she muttered. If she ran away, if she left this horrible place without learning what had happened to Fridolin, she would never know a moment's peace.

Late-day sun poked through the clouds and gilded the puddles. Hanneke sat down abruptly on her trunk. The initial shock was fading to fear, bubbling inside. Think, she told herself. *Think.*

But her brain refused to cooperate. She sat with arms clenched tight and numbly watched the afternoon unspool. The air sulked with the promise of more rain. A green-and-yellow dray wagon splashed down the street. A black woman wearing a blue paisley dress walked by, head bowed, a basket of laundry balanced on one hip. A skinny man with red curls knocked on the door of a nearby bakery calling "Fresh yeast today!" as he swung a pack basket from his shoulder. Two men in frock coats strode past, arguing in low voices about the need for a railroad line.

No one paused to say, Are you all right? Do you need help? Are you well?

Perhaps I should start shrieking again, Hanneke thought. Or tell Barlow to go ahead and arrest me. At least in jail I could rest. And I'd likely be fed something too. But Barlow was long gone.

A very fat man waddling by kicked the crumpled handbill in her direction. Hanneke picked it up and smoothed the paper open on her lap. The notice was printed in English on the top, followed by German.

Now is the time for Nativists to reclaim our city from the ever-growing presence of the foreign-born! Support efforts to keep the German and Irish elements from taking control. The emigrants from Europe are chiefly those classes who, discontented and oppressed at home, leave there filled with all the requisite materials to spread among our citizens anarchy, radicalism, and rebellion.

All Nativists of conscience must work together to gain legal protection for the following principles:

The naturalization law must be changed from the current requirement of five years' residence before gaining full citizenship to twenty-one years.

Only native-born Americans will be appointed to any state or local office or be permitted to legislate, administer, or execute the laws of this country.

Temperance must become the moral standard of the land. All taverns, the so-called 'beer gardens,' and other gathering places where spirits flow freely, must be shut down.

Hanneke crushed the notice again and tossed it into the road. Moments later a farmer, cursing in German, drove by in an oxen-drawn wagon. One wheel ground the notice into the sucking mud. Really, she thought, this is all simply intolerable. She pushed to her feet, smoothed her skirt, looked around.

Down the street, a woman in a faded honey-colored dress stepped outside with a broom. Standing in profile, the bulge beneath her apron was obvious.

A child, Hanneke thought, and felt another stab. She had the promise of children to grieve as well as her husband—the children she had already imagined with Fridolin's blond hair and intelligent eyes.

She tried to look away from the mother-to-be but something compelled her gaze to linger, as someone with a toothache might prod the pain with her tongue, needing to understand its depth. The woman moved the broom slowly, as if her day had already proved over-long. When she finished the top step she paused, pressing one fist against the small of her back. Then she took up the broom again and began whisking grit and clods of mud from the lower step.

Hanneke picked up her valise in one hand and grasped one of the trunk handles in the other. The wooden trunk scraped and thunked along the boardwalk as she dragged it toward the woman. The building was a tavern—much smaller than the Buena Vista, and only two stories. The frame building needed paint. The sign painted with a strutting red cockerel hung a bit askew. Hanneke's shoulders slumped when she realized that the small hand-lettered sign propped in one window was written in English. Then she scrounged up a few of her wits and made out the words: *English spoken here.*

So many Germans have settled in Watertown, Fridolin had written, *that bilingual merchants post signs to assure Yankee customers that they can conduct business.* Hanneke closed her eyes with relief. She hadn't lost Fridolin's words, his voice—the essence of who he had been, what he had thought.

She stopped in front of the steps and let her luggage rest on the sidewalk. "Pardon me. My name is Hanneke Bauer."

The woman glanced up, looking over her shoulder as if to be certain that Hanneke was addressing her before answering. "I'm Angela Zeidler." Behind the baby, Frau Zeidler was thin. She had high cheekbones, light brown hair captured dutifully behind her neck in a thick coil, and large gray eyes.

"I need a place to sleep tonight," Hanneke said simply.

"I don't have rooms." Frau Zeidler wiped sweat from her forehead with one forearm. "There's a boardinghouse across the way."

"I don't have money for a boardinghouse. I will gladly scrub, or cook, or do anything else that needs doing if I could just have a place to lay my head tonight. Tomorrow I will decide how to address my…circumstances."

"No, I can't—"

"Please."

The woman stood still, one hand holding the broom erect, one hand on her hip. Hanneke felt herself being assessed. Seconds ticked by. Finally, Angela Zeidler jerked her head toward the front door.

Hanneke dragged her luggage up the steps. *Danke schön, Gott.*

The front door opened directly into the taproom. The bar stood along the short wall to the left, with barrels and bottles behind. A dozen or so tables filled the room. No billiard table here, no framed prints or maps on the walls. The patrons slumping over steins of beer wore patched trousers and coarse Osnaburg shirts stiff with plaster or powdered with brick dust. A faint swirl of cigar smoke and pipe tobacco lingered in the air. The tables and bar were nicked and worn.

"Adolf," Frau Zeidler called to a young man lining clean steins on a shelf.

25

"Take the lady's trunk to the downstairs bedroom."

The young man nodded. He was thin as a whip, but had no trouble lifting her trunk.

Frau Zeidler stepped behind the bar and filled a stein with foaming amber beer. "Come with me," she ordered and followed Adolf into a small kitchen, where she added bread and cheese to a plate.

Then she led Hanneke into a narrow bedroom. It was spartan—a low bed with straw tick and linen sheets, a narrow dresser, a nightjar, a small Franklin stove. No chair. Nothing on the walls. Hanneke didn't care.

"You can rest here 'til morning," Frau Zeidler said.

"*Danke schön.*" Hanneke tried to convey the depths of her gratitude in her gaze.

"I can lay a fire," Adolf offered cheerfully.

"*Danke, nein.*" All she wanted—desperately—was solitude. Suddenly she thought about the proximity to the taproom. "Frau Zeidler—I'm not taking your bed, am I? I could make do in a storeroom, or—"

"It's Fraulein. And this isn't my room. It was Julius's. My brother's."

"I see." *Was* her brother's. Julius was dead? Or just gone?

It didn't matter. Hanneke held herself erect until Fraulein Zeidler and Adolf had gone, closing the door firmly behind them. She ripped her wedding shawl from her shoulders and stuffed it into her valise.

Then she sank onto the bed, curled into a ball, and cried as she had never cried before. She cried so hard she pulled the pillow over her head to keep Angela and Adolf from hearing. She cried so hard she could only gulp air in sharp, heaving gasps. She cried so hard her handkerchief was soon overwhelmed. She cried until she had emptied herself in the flood, and her insides felt cracked and dry and lifeless.

She'd believed that Fridolin Bauer was a good man. Had she been stupid? Had she been so hungry for a hearth of her own that she'd overlooked obvious clues?

The memory of his prediction echoed in the room. *I think we'll do well enough, you and I.*

Hanneke was furious at him. She pressed one arm over her aching chest.

I believed you! she raged silently. *I believed everything you said, everything you wrote—and it was a basket of lies!*

Wasn't it? Or were these strangers lying? She desperately wanted to believe that...and yet, that seemed impossible too. Christine Bauer, John Barlow, Wilhelm and Josephine Wiggenhorn, even Herr Wettstein in Milwaukee—a charade of that magnitude, with so many players...no.

She sat up slowly, breath still coming in little shuddering hitches, trying to think. *Someone* had stolen her papers. No one had known she was coming to Watertown, and yet someone who felt threatened by her arrival had been quick-witted enough to take advantage of her detour upstairs and rob her. Hanneke clung to that fact as a woman overboard would cling to the only bit of floating debris in a frigid, pitching ocean.

Abruptly she crouched beside her luggage, heaved open the trunk, and scrabbled beneath the clothes and linens and carefully chosen tools and mementos packed inside. Her fingers found three books that Fridolin had sent her: the German-English dictionary, a Bible, and a blank journal. *I am enclosing samples of my work,* Fridolin had written, *in hopes that you might find them useful.* She pulled the journal free and sat on the floor. The leather cover was soft. The endpapers inside were marbled with exquisite curves of green, blue, and purple. *The colors of the sea, chosen especially for you. Perhaps you will record your impressions of your journey to your new home.* Hanneke had filled half the pages already with tight script.

Now she flipped to a clean page and tried to capture thoughts flying around like moths:

> *Try to obtain copies of marriage certificate and will from Pomerania.*
> *Visit farm. Talk to Christine alone.*
> *Return to Buena Vista, inquire who had opportunity to steal my papers*
> *Talk with the physician who attended Fridolin.*
> *Find death notice.*
> *Talk with Fridolin's friends and neighbors.*

The scribbling helped calm her quivering nerves, just a bit. *I will not leave here until I know what happened,* Hanneke promised herself—and Fridolin too.

Chapter Four

Hanneke rose the next morning just as the first faint flush of dawn began pushing at the night. Someone had left a bucket of clean water by the door, and she washed her face and hands, scrubbing as if she might rinse away yesterday's tears and despair. She had no more time for those indulgences. She made the bed, and emptied and rinsed the nightjar in the alley behind the tavern. Then she fastened the belt with an oversized yarn pocket around her waist and pinned the hook she used to guide yarn near one shoulder. Nothing eased her mind like knitting. Now, with her world turned upside-down, she especially needed the comfort of yarn in her hands. More than that, she needed something, just a little something, that she could control. She desperately needed the ordered formation of stitches and a pattern that emerged exactly as she'd designed it.

Besides, in Pomerania, she'd occasionally sold some of her work. I am a skilled businesswoman, she reminded herself. She couldn't support herself selling socks and shawls and other woolen goods, but it was something.

The small kitchen was empty. The taproom was also silent: chairs turned up on tables, the floor swept. Retracing her steps, Hanneke built a fire in the cookstove and put water on to heat. After considering, she selected two brown eggs from the pantry to fry.

A small lump of lard was melting in the skillet when Fraulein Zeidler appeared in the doorway. "Finding everything you need?" she asked, eyebrows raised.

Hanneke wasn't sure if the question was sincere or sardonic. "I only thought to prepare breakfast for you. To repay your hospitality. I don't expect you to feed me." She swirled the grease around the skillet, then broke the eggs into it.

Fraulein Zeidler considered the eggs with distaste before turning away. "You and Adolf can share the eggs. If I have anything more than bread in the morning, I...." She spread her hands, palms up, with a small shrug.

"You're still suffering from morning sickness?" Hanneke eyed the other woman. Angela Zeidler was surely at least five months into her pregnancy, maybe six. "Perhaps you should...." Her voice trailed away, and she turned back to the stove. "Forgive me. It's not my business, of course. It's just that I...well, back in Pomerania, I helped quite a few women in your condition."

Fraulein Zeidler slid into a chair. "What were you about to suggest?"

"Ginger tea. If that's not effective, try making an infusion from the inner bark of slippery elm."

The other woman considered. "I do have a bit of ginger on hand. There, in that spice box."

Hanneke found what she needed, and soon had a small tin pot of tea steeping. She discovered half a loaf of dark rye bread wrapped in a towel, and cut a generous slice for her hostess. When she'd served the other woman, she pulled the skillet from the stovetop, spooned a small portion of eggs onto a plate for herself, and covered the remainder to keep warm.

She ate her breakfast while Fraulein Zeidler nibbled bread. Then Hanneke placed her palms on the table and caught the other woman's eye. "I owe you an explanation."

"You don't have to."

"I feel that I should." She pulled her knitting needles from their pocket. Tempted as she was to curl over the hurt and humiliation, not letting anyone else see, she also felt a need to make clear to Fraulein Zeidler that something more than carelessness or sloth had left her stranded and destitute.

After she summarized events of the day before, silence draped the room like a shroud. Fraulein Zeidler sipped her tea, expressionless. Finally, she asked, "Can you think of any reason why Fridolin would keep the news of his marriage from his sister and friends?"

Something small and hopeful lurched in Hanneke's chest. This woman *believed* her. "No. I spent much of the night remembering everything Fridolin told me. Every detail of his letters. I can't find any clue to explain why he would marry me, send letters that eagerly anticipated my arrival, and yet not tell anyone here."

Fraulein Zeidler broke a bit of crust from the bread and crushed it between her fingers. "Was there money involved? A dowry?"

"A small one." Hanneke gave a little mirthless laugh. "I had been living with my brother's family since our father died. Most of what little I had went to help pay my keep. But—yes." The word was sour as an old lemon. "And our marriage contract stated that what money I had went to Fridolin upon marriage. He said he wanted to use it to improve his farm, before I arrived. He spoke of having a summer kitchen built." *It will be more comfortable for you,* he had promised, a happy glint in those blue eyes. Or...had she only imagined that shine? Had she been so desperate for affection that she had fabricated what she had given up hope of finding?

"So it is possible that Fridolin Bauer lied to you in order to obtain your dowry."

Hanneke knit another dozen stitches and shifted needles before replying. "It is possible."

Fraulein Zeidler stared at the dregs of her tea.

"And yet, I'm not ready to accept that," Hanneke said. "Yesterday was...a nightmare. I wondered if Mr. Barlow was lying. I wondered if Fridolin was truly dead. I admit I didn't know Fridolin well, but usually, I am a fair judge of character. I would not have thought him capable of such duplicity." She sighed. "Then I met Fraulein Christine Bauer."

"And he had never spoken of his sister?"

"No." Hanneke pinched her lips together.

"So he *did* lie to you."

Hanneke groped for an honest answer. "He did not directly lie. But he was certainly untruthful by omission. Do—did you know my husband?"

"No." Fraulein Zeidler shrugged. "My customers are brickmakers and drovers and millhands. Gentlemen farmers—they don't come here."

No, Hanneke thought. Those people went to places like the Buena Vista.

31

"I did know *of* him," the other woman added thoughtfully. "His name was in the newspaper from time to time. For little things. Joining the *Männerchor*, or growing the biggest turnip exhibited at the county agricultural fair. Something like that."

"And you know of Christine Bauer?"

"I know she and Fridolin came to Watertown together. Fraulein Bauer keeps house for him. Did."

Hanneke rubbed a gouge in the table with her thumb. Fridolin's deception was stunning. Why? she demanded again of the man she had judged as good and decent. *Why?*

Fridolin did not answer.

"Fraulein Zeidler—"

"I think you may call me Angela."

Hanneke judged that a gift. "And you must call me Hanneke. Angela, do you know how Fridolin died?"

"Not in great detail. An accident on the farm, I think. I remember seeing the death notice in the newspaper. You might be able to get an old copy at the *Watertown Weltbuerg*."

The *Watertown World Citizen*. Hanneke nodded. "Yes. I'll start there. And perhaps Christine Bauer will talk with me."

"Perhaps." Angela's tone was dubious.

"She may refuse, but I have to try." Hanneke studied the scarred tabletop. "She knew Fridolin better than anyone. Certainly better than me." She sighed. "And...I want to see the farmhouse."

"What good will that do?"

Excellent question, Hanneke thought. "I just know I need to *see* Fridolin's farm."

Angela pressed one fist against the small of her back, giving Hanneke a long look. "You seem determined to break your heart all over again."

That, Hanneke thought, is quite possible. "It's hard to explain, but...I dreamed of that farm for months. It was Fridolin's home. And the place where he died."

Angela picked up her teacup, then put it back down. "Hanneke. What are

32

you planning to do?"

"Well, I'm going to cook, or scrub, or whatever else I can do to repay your kindness. With your permission, of course."

"I'll accept your help today. And I understand why you want to find some answers. But I suspect that you won't get very far. So, what then? Will you go back to Milwaukee? Or Pomerania?"

"My passport was stolen along with my other papers. And I don't have enough money for a stagecoach ticket to Milwaukee, much less fare back to Treptow."

"And I don't have enough money to offer you a job. You met Adolf last night—he's an orphan. In return for his help I let him sleep in the stable, and I feed him and give him a little cash if we have a good night. That's all I can afford."

"Of course," Hanneke said briskly. It would have been much too convenient if Angela Zeidler happened to be looking for domestic help. "But…might I trespass on your hospitality a short while longer? I can eat elsewhere, but if—"

Angela waved a dismissive hand. "I'm already cooking for a crowd. One more plate for a few days won't matter. And the bedroom was sitting empty. Although there are those in town who will think less of you for staying here."

Hanneke almost laughed. "After my reception yesterday, it's safe to say that my presence here will do nothing to improve your standing in the community."

"That's of no matter."

"Then I gratefully accept your hospitality. I won't intrude on your kindness a moment longer than necessary."

Angela eyed her. "You could earn ten or twelve dollars a month keeping house for a family in Milwaukee. I could find someone who would give you a ride there. I know people. Freight haulers."

"I'm grateful, but no," Hanneke said firmly. "I want to go to the newspaper office and look for the death notice. I need to go back to the Buena Vista and walk out to the farm. I also need to write to my brother, and ask him to send a copy of my marriage certificate." Humiliating thought.

33

"It will take weeks to hear from your brother. If he answers at all." Angela pressed her lips together into a tight line. "You've already caught the attention of a deputy sheriff."

"I've done nothing wrong. I will not be driven off as if I had."

Something flickered in Angela's eyes—admiration, maybe, quickly over-shadowed with worry.

"I can find work here as readily as in Milwaukee," Hanneke added. At least she hoped that was true. Or had Christine Bauer and John Barlow already poisoned her reputation? Possibly, but likely only among their own circle. Gentlemen farmers, scholars, bankers, and the like. It was much less likely that Hanneke's circumstances, her claim, would be of any interest to the laboring men and women in Watertown. And Hanneke was not afraid of hard work.

"You've been kind to a stranger," she added. "I'll find a situation somewhere. I simply can't leave Watertown until I know more about Fridolin's death. His secrets. And why someone felt so threatened by my arrival that they stole my papers. If I can't find some answers...." If I can't, she finished silently, I'll go mad.

Angela's forehead puckered. "And if Deputy Barlow doesn't want—"

Hanneke picked up her dirty plate and stood. "What Deputy Barlow does or does not want," she said, as she pulled a dishpan from its nail on the wall, "is of no interest to me."

* * *

When the dishes were dried and returned to their shelves, Hanneke settled down at the kitchen table to write two letters. She had paper and envelope in her valise, although she had to ask Angela for ink. When Angela brought the pen and inkwell, Hanneke slid a penny across the table. Angela quietly picked up the coin and dropped it into her apron pocket.

The first letter was addressed to the lawyer in Pomerania who'd helped her and Fridolin update their wills, asking for a letter attesting to the transaction.

The second was to her brother and sister-in-law. Hanneke wrote, *Dear*

Theodor and paused. "Good ink," she murmured.

"What's that?" Angela stood at the chopping block, mincing some wrinkled and musty-smelling potatoes and carrots she'd purchased from one of the farm wives who brought goods into the city to sell.

"Oh—nothing important," Hanneke said. "I just noticed that your ink is of good quality, nice and black. I went half-blind trying to make out Fridolin's letters. He must have watered the ink with tea."

"I'd think Herr Bauer could have afforded decent ink."

Hanneke stared at the vegetables. She couldn't tell if they had been wintered over in the ground, or were the last barreled dregs from someone's root cellar. "I expect he could," she agreed. "I chose to conclude that he was simply thrifty." She heard her own words ring in her mind: *I chose to conclude....* What else had she chosen to believe?

Resolutely, she picked up the pen again. Stared at the words for a few moments. Put the pen down.

"What's wrong?" Angela asked.

Hanneke rubbed her forehead with her fingertips. "I'm trying to decide what to say to my brother. My situation is...well, it's not an easy thing to explain." Or admit to. Not when Theodor and Minnie—especially Minnie—had gotten so practiced, these past few years, at listing all the reasons why Hanneke had not yet married.

"Brothers." Angela spoke the word softly, but with an edge of bitterness. Hanneke looked up, waiting for more. But after a few seconds of silence, Angela merely reached for another potato. She did, though, bring the knife down with a bit more force than necessary, sending half of the vegetable to the floor.

Hanneke wished Angela would confide in her. It would be nice to think about someone else's problems, if even for a short while. But she didn't want to intrude.

What she did want to do was finish the letter. Concentrate, she ordered herself.

Dear Theodor and Wilhelmine,

35

She put the pen down and leaned back in her chair. Just writing her sister-in-law's name brought back a flood of bad memories. Even the single good memory—marrying Fridolin Bauer—had, in the end, led to her current disastrous situation.

Hanneke had agreed to marry for want of a 'please.'

She and Wilhelmine had been dear friends as children, living on adjoining farms. "And now we are sisters," Minnie had said joyfully when she married Hanneke's brother Theodor. "You must find a good man to marry as well, and we will grow old sharing married women's secrets." But Hanneke had not found that good man—not among the farmers; not among the men who lived in town, where Theodor had managed to find a clerk position in a bank.

Instead, when her father died, she and her ailing mother relinquished the tired farmhouse and moved into Theodor and Minnie's house in Treptow. Hanneke told herself she didn't mind, and had made herself useful: caring for her mother, tending Minnie's babies, weeding Minnie's garden, scrubbing Minnie's floors.

And slowly, Hanneke and Minnie's friendship had faded. Minnie had first become critical of the way Hanneke sliced green beans or bleached linens or planted dahlias. Later came the barbs that hurt more: "You must try harder to find a husband," Minnie snapped in exasperation when her attempts to match-make came to naught. "You read too many books. You mustn't *think* so much."

"I don't believe I care to relinquish my right to thought," Hanneke said mildly, reminding herself that Minnie was pregnant with her fourth child and very tired.

But the final line had been crossed on the morning that Hanneke's niece Rosa, just five, had knocked an earthenware pitcher from the table. Milk splashed over Rosa's shoes and puddled on the floor among the shards of broken crockery. "Rosa!" Minnie had cried. She snatched the child up and carried her toward the dry sink to clean her shoes. Over her shoulder she'd tossed, "Hanneke, clean that up."

So, Hanneke had thought. I am no longer friend; no longer sister. I have become a maid.

That evening, Theodor brought a guest home from the bank. "Herr Bauer emigrated to Wisconsin several years ago," he told Minnie and Hanneke. "He's come back to Treptow to attend to some business affairs after the death of his father." Theodor occasionally brought colleagues and clients home, so the women were well used to cutting the chicken into smaller pieces, taking smaller portions of sauerkraut or salad themselves. Mr. Bauer was polite, and complimentary of the food, but spent most of the meal discussing politics in Pomerania and abroad. Later Hanneke had retired to one corner with a volume of poetry while Theodor and his guest smoked and played cards.

Hanneke was, therefore, astonished when Theodor came to the henhouse the next morning to find her. "Herr Bauer has asked my permission to offer a proposal," Theodor said.

"A proposal for what?" Hanneke asked, carefully sliding her hand beneath the red hen to retrieve an egg.

Theodor folded his arms. "Herr Bauer wishes to marry you."

Hanneke almost dropped the egg. "He does?"

"He does."

Hanneke's heart began to flutter, but she kept her voice calm. "I will accept."

Theodore's eyebrows rose. "I didn't expect such a hasty response. And—you don't have to marry Herr Bauer."

Hanneke felt a rush of regard for her younger brother's kindness. Still, they both knew that the proposal solved a problem. That's what she had become: a spinster aunt, an extra mouth to feed, an unwanted second opinion on domestic matters…a problem.

"*Danke schön* for that," she said quietly. "But I will accept." As she watched her brother walk away, the enormity of her decision almost took her breath away. Not only a new husband—a new country! But that's appropriate for a new beginning, she told herself. Hanneke wanted a hearth and family of her own.

Herr Bauer came to the kitchen half an hour later, where Hanneke was trying to calm tumbling thoughts by sorting twists of seeds saved from the early autumn harvest. "Your brother tells me that you might look favorably upon a betrothal." He clasped his hands behind his back, a gesture that reminded her of the village schoolteacher. "I know it is a great deal to ask you to leave your home and family and cast your lot with me in America. Still, I hope that you will please consider my proposal."

'Please,' Hanneke thought. He said 'please.' She took a deep breath. "Yes, Herr Bauer. I will marry you."

His eyes widened. Hanneke couldn't decide if he was delighted or surprised. "*Danke schön,*" he said simply. "I will endeavor to prove a worthy partner."

"I couldn't ask for more," she'd said. "I will do the same."

Now, sitting in Angela's kitchen, Hanneke found the thought of describing her public humiliation, her loss, absolutely unbearable. She imagined the long-suffering sighs and comments—"Oh dear, Hanneke has made quite a mess of things"—Theodor and Minnie would share upon learning the truth.

No. That would not do.

I am safely arrived in Watertown, Wisconsin. The final crossing of Lake Michigan, made by steamboat, was not too difficult. There were many Germans on board, some new immigrants like me, others well-settled residents traveling to conduct business or visit family. It was helpful to meet the latter and to gain their impressions.

Watertown is a young city, busy with new construction but surrounded by fertile land and scattered forests. There will be no shortage of hay or wood as in Germany.

I do need to trouble you with one request. My marriage certificate is missing. Please obtain a copy from the church and send it to me care of the Watertown, Wisconsin post office, as quickly as possible. It is very important.

I have chores waiting, so I must close. I hope this finds you and your children well and prospering.

Your sister,

Hanneke

As soon as the ink was dry, Hanneke folded the sheet into an envelope. Done.

Did Fridolin lie? He lied by omission. As now I have done, Hanneke thought. She rubbed her face with her palms.

Then she stood. She had too much to do to waste time on such thoughts now.

Chapter Five

By early afternoon Hanneke had scrubbed the tavern floor, plucked and gutted three chickens, and started two large iron kettles of stew simmering on the back of the kitchen stove. After promising to return to help with the dinner crowd, she changed into her favorite day dress of green and brown plaid—not fancy, just respectable.

When she scrabbled in her valise to find a new ball of yarn, she felt the soft merino wool of her wedding shawl. A thick cold ache settled under her ribs like silt after a flood. She drew out the shawl, letting it flow over her fingers. The single-ply yarn was whisper-thin, the intricate lace pattern her own design. She had imagined Fridolin beaming beside her at their Wisconsin reception, introducing her to his friends and neighbors; imagined their welcoming smiles and, because of the shawl, even admiring glances.

I indulged in pride, she thought, and here I am. There would be no reception.

She started to bury the shawl back in her valise. Then she lifted her chin. She would wear the beautiful shawl to remind herself that she was a capable woman. So resolved, Hanneke draped it over her shoulders. Then she put on her bonnet and left the tavern.

Angela had given her directions. After Fridolin's enthusiastic descriptions Hanneke had expected Watertown to feel like home. Instead, it felt foreign and strange. She'd never particularly noticed how *settled* Treptow was, with its mossy-cobbled streets, churchyards full of leaning stones, and timber buildings dark with age. Watertown smelled of sawdust. Huge piles of bricks and boards waited for masons and carpenters. Many of the wooden buildings she passed were still unweathered, pale as new cream. The air pulsed with the high whine of a sawmill, the clatter of freight wagons jostling back and forth, a rhythmic metallic clang from an iron foundry.

Hanneke heard a bewildering variety of German dialects spoken by some of the passersby—Prussian, Bavarian, Westphalian, Hessian, and others. She knew Yankee people, those born in the eastern United States of British stock, tended to lump people from all of the German states together. After meeting Asa Hawkins the day before she also knew that her own Germanness alone was cause for some Yankee residents' hostility. I need to ask Angela more about that, she thought. But first things first.

Hanneke mailed her letters at the post office building on Second Street, then walked to the local German-language newspaper and printing shop nearby. The newspaper office smelled of ink and tobacco smoke. She approached a man hunched over a desk, scribbling frantically.

When she told him what she wanted, he pointed to a table piled with folded newspapers. "We keep extra copies of recent issues on hand. Can't say if we've got what you want, but you're welcome to look. Back issues cost two cents."

Hanneke picked up the topmost edition and studied the masthead.

Watertown Weltbuerg
(Established in 1853)
Weekly German Paper
Has a large circulation in Wisconsin, especially in Dodge and Jefferson Counties, and is an excellent medium for advertising.

It didn't take her long to find the issue and article she was searching for. She pressed one finger against the smeary print as she read:

March 16, 1855
A Tragic Accident. Local resident Fridolin Bauer was accidentally killed yesterday while laboring to thresh the last of his wheat. He left the house he shared with his sister, Christine Bauer, after breakfast. When

he did not return for the noon meal Fraulein Bauer went searching, and found her brother unconscious and bleeding from a head wound, presumably suffered while swinging the flail.

Hanneke pressed a fist over her ribs. While swinging a *flail*? She remembered watching men thresh at home. Each grasped the staff of a flail and used the head—a short but heavy piece of wood attached to the staff with a leather thong—to beat kernels of grain from the stalks. Threshers quickly established a rhythm, walking around the splayed wheat or rye, the flail head swinging in heavy circles that easily cleared the workers' heads. Good threshers, anyway.

Hanneke blinked against tears. It mattered, somehow, that Fridolin had died such an awkward and ignominious death.

Unless, of course, the 'tragic accident' wasn't as simple as it seemed. She bit her lower lip, trying out that new idea, before returning to the article.

She immediately sent for Dr. Jenkins, who pronounced the wound fatal. Herr Bauer died within the hour.

Fridolin Bauer moved to the Watertown area in 1853 and purchased the Jaeger farm on Plum Grove Road. Prior to that time, Bauer had worked as a skilled bookbinder in Milwaukee, a trade he learned in his native Pomerania. After three years in that city, Bauer decided to try his hand at farming. He was aided in those endeavors by his sister, who kept house for him.

Herr Bauer will be remembered as a man of good cheer and firm resolve. He was a member of St. John's Lutheran Church, the Männerchor, and the Gesang Verein.

That was all. Hanneke snatched up the paper and hurried back to the man's desk, her heels clicking on the floorboards. "Did you write this piece?" She slapped the paper down, pointing.

The man sighed deeply but laid down his pen. He had stringy shoulder-length black hair. His shirt would have benefitted from application of potato starch and a hot iron. The eyes that met hers, however, were shrewd and assessing.

Hanneke tried again. "Forgive my impatience, sir, but—please. It's important."

He sighed again, but looked down at the newsprint. Then he nodded.

"Were you there? Did you see—"

"Of course I wasn't there." He settled back in his chair, folding his arms over his chest.

"Then how do you know what happened? It's not that I don't believe what you wrote," she added, seeing his mouth tighten. "It's just that—well, I knew Herr Bauer, you see. And I wasn't...I wasn't in Watertown when he died. I'm just trying to understand what happened."

"Ah, I see." His face lost some of the sharp angles. "I talked with Doctor Jenkins after it happened."

"And Fraulein Bauer? Did you interview her as well?"

The reporter raised and dropped one shoulder, as if shrugging both would take too much energy. "No need to."

"But didn't you wonder how Fridolin sustained a head wound of that severity while flailing wheat?" Hanneke gestured at the words he had written. "If no one was with Herr Bauer at the time, why was it assumed that the blow that killed him was accidental? Isn't there some reason to suspect that someone might have struck him?"

"Doctor Jenkins seemed certain that it was all an accident."

"But—"

"Look, ma'am. I'm sorry for your loss, but don't try to twist things. You're new in town?" He barely waited for Hanneke to nod before continuing, "Then you may not know what it's like out here. A lot of the men settling here have noble intentions of tilling the soil. They imagine a bucolic life—earnest endeavors, a bountiful harvest. And most of them have no *idea* what they're getting into. They excel at debating and making political speeches. Otherwise, these grand men—these divinity scholars and philosophers and professors of ancient literature—they fail. Fridolin Bauer was a bookbinder! What did he know of farm labor, or the tools needed to do it?"

"But—"

"You know what else? I've written too many of these." He jabbed his finger at the offending obituary. "There was the fellow last month who fell out of his own haymow. Broke his neck. And a few months before that a man bled to death after nearly severing his hand with an ax. And—"

"*Danke schön*," Hanneke said crisply. She turned to go, then faced him again. "Did you *know* Herr Bauer?"

"Know him?" The newsman gave that odd one-shouldered shrug again. "Not really."

And that must be my answer as well, Hanneke thought. Did I know Fridolin Bauer? Not really. Or...obviously not.

"Do you want to buy the paper?" he asked impatiently.

"No." She did, actually, but owning a copy of Fridolin's obituary wouldn't help anything. "However...I might like to place a notice. If it isn't too dear."

The newsman brightened. In short order, he'd taken both the particulars and another of Hanneke's coins. "We're going to press today," he told her, "so this will appear tomorrow."

"Excellent." Hanneke left him to his scribbling. Had she been reckless, spending money that would probably gain her nothing? Perhaps. But she had to try. She turned away, then paused, fighting an unexpected wave of dizziness. She pressed her fingers against her temples.

It is official, Hanneke thought, concentrating on slowly breathing in, breathing out. After seeing the official notice of her husband's death, she had to release any last shred of hope that Christine Bauer and John Barlow and all the rest of them were lying.

Still, the shock of seeing the harsh black type of Fridolin's obituary had not altered her sense that something about his death was *wrong*. She turned back to the reporter. "I wish to see Dr. Jenkins. Can you provide directions?"

* * *

Dr. Jenkins lived on Cady Street, on the west side of the Rock River. Hanneke found the address without difficulty—and kept walking. Don't be a coward! she scolded herself while trying to smile at a young woman pushing a baby carriage. Still...it was one thing to speak to a German newspaper reporter; quite another to speak with a Yankee man. She'd spent many hours on the trip across the Atlantic studying English, but she did not fool herself—she was nowhere near fluent, and her accent was likely horrid. And what if this Dr. Jenkins was a nativist? What if he took one look at her and—

"*Enough*," Hanneke muttered. There was nothing to be gained by dithering. A visit to the man who had proclaimed Fridolin's death a self-inflicted accident was in order.

She turned around and returned to the gracious brick house. Mature shrubberies studded its well-tended yard, and a cheerful fringe of red and yellow tulips grew along the front walk. A sign by a side door proclaimed "Dr. Wm. Jenkins, Homeopath and Physician."

Hanneke found the door open, rang the handbell provided, and had to wait in a small anteroom only a few moments before the doctor appeared and ushered her into his office. He was elderly, skinny as a split rail, and didn't look entirely well. His cheeks were flushed, and tiny red capillaries fanned from his nose. But his blue eyes were kind.

His German was as clumsy and halting as Hanneke's English. She'd brought her dictionary, though, and between them, they managed to communicate.

"Herr Bauer?" Dr. Jenkins said. "Yes. He died shortly after I arrived. A tragedy."

Hanneke, perched on a low chair beside the man's desk, clasped her hands decorously in her lap. "Are you sure it was an accident?"

"Yes. *Ja*." The man nodded firmly. "An accident." He mimed swinging a flail, aborting the motion to clap both hands to the side of his head, grimacing as if in pain.

Hanneke winced. "But someone else might have struck him, yes?" she asked.

The man sat back in his chair, looking shocked. "Who?"

That's what I'm trying to find out! Hanneke wanted to shriek. "Did you…" Floundering, she flipped through her book to find the right word. "Did you ex-a-mine the flail? Was there blood on it? The wound matched the shape of a flail head?"

The old man's expression of sympathy faded to something more reserved.

"There was no need to examine the flail."

This was getting her nowhere. "Thank you," she said, and let herself out.

She struggled with frustration as she walked away, and she stopped short when she noticed a sign in English: *J. Hawkins, Wholesale Drug Ware House.* Was the proprietor related to Asa Hawkins, the belligerent man who'd provoked Deputy Sheriff John Barlow's anger—the man who'd said something unintelligible, but clearly insulting, to her?

She started to walk on, but her attention snagged on a smaller sign propped in the window that provided information for German-speaking customers: "General Agent for most of the popular Patent Medicines sold in Wisconsin. Dealer in Drugs, Medicines, Paints, Oils, Dye Stuffs, &c."

Fridolin had needed pigments to make the marbled endpapers he used when binding books. Had he done business here? Hanneke hesitated, wondering if she should go inside and ask. But the memory of Asa Hawkins's sneers and hateful nativism made her move on.

Her final stop—the one she'd been dreading most—was the Buena Vista. She paused on the walk in front, grappling with bad memories. The afternoon was cloudy, and someone inside had already lit lamps and placed them in the windows as if to say, *Come inside, a warm welcome is waiting.* But not, Hanneke knew, for her. She allowed herself one deep sigh. Then she lifted her skirts and marched up the steps.

In the taproom, Wilhelm Wiggenhorn was tending bar again. Deputy Sheriff Barlow was nowhere in evidence. *Danke Gott* for small allowances, Hanneke thought as she approached the proprietor. "Excuse me."

The man's brow crinkled with dismay. "Fraulein. Why are you here? Go on, now."

"While I was upstairs yesterday, someone stole papers from a pouch in my valise," Hanneke began.

"You've got no business here—"

"—and I need you to tell me who might have had the opportunity to search my luggage."

"—and I don't want any more trouble."

The two stared at each other. Hanneke was aware that, once again, nearby conversations had faltered into silence. "I don't want trouble either," she said quietly. "All I'm asking is for you to tell me if you saw anyone lingering in the hall, near my luggage, while I was upstairs."

"I did not."

Hanneke turned to the other men. That man there, with the unkempt hair—he'd been here the day before, hadn't he? And the portly gentleman with the ruby-red cravat? She wished she had paid more attention to the patrons yesterday, and she tried to take careful stock now. Most were dressed as businessmen, in varying degrees of high fashion. Some were graybeards with furrowed faces, some little more than boys. It was their hands that united them. The hands holding steins, newspapers, and pipes were largely pale, unscarred, uncalloused. Fridolin Bauer had felt at home here, but he must have represented a minority of men actually trying to wrestle a living from the soil itself. She realized that the farm he described, that she had found so appealing, might actually have represented very different emotions to him.

"Please," she said. "If anyone was here yesterday afternoon... I'm trying to find out who might have stolen some important papers from my valise. It was left for a short time in the hall right outside this room."

No one spoke. A few of the men looked embarrassed. One or two had hard expressions, as if they believed she had killed their friend herself.

Then Josephine Wiggenhorn appeared in the doorway. For one moment Hanneke thought that the older woman had come to her aid. Then the tavernkeeper's wife stepped forward, grasped Hanneke by the elbow, and towed her from the room.

"Please," Hanneke said in an urgent undertone. "I'm only looking for someone to help—"

"No one here can help you." They reached the door and continued on to the front steps. "I'm sorry for whatever trouble you are in," Frau Wiggenhorn added. Her eyes were still red-rimmed and watery, but her tone was firm. "These people—all of us—were friends of Fridolin Bauer. We must take care of Christine in this time of grief." She released Hanneke's arm with a flourish, almost shoving her toward the street.

Hanneke stood her ground. "I do understand that, but—"

"I know Mr. Barlow told you to leave Watertown. You must do so."

A few passersby had stopped at the foot of the steps to watch the unfolding melodrama. "I cannot," Hanneke said quietly.

The other woman regarded her. "I can do one thing for you," she said unexpectedly.

Hanneke felt a tiny flicker of hope.

"I will purchase this." Frau Wiggenhorn reached out, fingering Hanneke's wedding shawl. "My daughter is getting married soon, and I haven't seen anything so fine in any of the shops."

The flicker died. Hanneke searched the other woman's implacable expression, hoping for some hint of sympathy. She found none.

Hanneke gently but deliberately tugged her shawl free. "Try bathing your eyes with a clean cloth soaked in tea made from stinging nettle leaves," she said. "It can only help."

*　*　*

"You had a difficult day," Angela said. The two women were ladling chicken stew onto tin plates. A long simmer had softened the stringy meat and plumped the tired vegetables. Hanneke had added pepper and thyme and parsley, and a splash of apple cider vinegar, and the stew smelled wonderful.

"No one admitted to seeing anyone near my luggage yesterday," Hanneke concluded.

"Perhaps it really was just a casual thief." Angela placed a final plate on a tray. "Someone who saw your luggage unattended took a quick look, and grabbed something that looked promising—"

"But the pouch itself was not taken," Hanneke reminded her. "Only the papers inside. The thief knew exactly what he was getting."

Adolf leaned in the door. "Hey, is dinner coming?"

"On its way," Hanneke promised. Now was not the time to ruminate on her own problems. What you need to do, she admonished herself silently, is help your hostess as best you can. She didn't like the pallor in Angela's cheeks, or the bruise-colored smudges beneath her eyes.

The taproom was filling with patrons, noise, and fragrant curls of pipe and cigar smoke. As Hanneke carefully carried her tray from the kitchen, she felt an unexpected surge of gratitude that Providence had brought her at least this much succor. Many of Angela's customers were tired bachelors, grateful to buy stew and rye bread and a mug of beer before trudging back to their bedroll in the attic of the factory where they worked, or to a rented bed at some cheap boardinghouse. They might not speak Latin, and they might toss peanut shells on the floor. But at that moment, the Red Cockerel felt superior to the Buena Vista in every way.

Adolf cheerfully manned the bar and helped Hanneke take orders for those few patrons who weren't German—a couple of Yankees, a handful of Irish; mostly men but a few women too. Even Adolf was stymied by a newcomer of undetermined background, whose limited English didn't seem capable of grasping the fact that he'd arrived just as the stew ran out. Finally, Hanneke fetched the kettle, showing it had been scraped clean. The man's face fell. "It smelled so good," he said sadly in broken German before shuffling away.

"I'm glad you're here," Adolf said to Hanneke, with a lopsided grin that made him seem more boy than man.

"I'm grateful to be here. Angela—and you—have been very kind."

Adolf shrugged and took a long swig from the tall mug of beer he kept behind the bar. "I know what it's like to be on your own. Angela does too."

"Yes. I see."

"You're good for her," Adolf added, throwing a sideways glance at Angela that was both affectionate and concerned. "She'd chop off her hand before asking for help. But she needs it."

Hanneke caught his gaze and held it. "I'm glad to do whatever I can for as long as I'm here."

Adolf grinned again. He was an endearing young man, hardworking and high-spirited. Don't grow too fond, Hanneke cautioned herself. You will not be here overlong.

When Angela began sidling among the crowded tables, reaching among shoulders for the cleaned plates the men had set aside, Hanneke did the same. The men were polite, even friendly, but they didn't greet her with the warmth reserved for Angela. Of course, they all *knew* Angela—in fact, most of the men spoke to her with affectionate familiarity. Hanneke suddenly realized that perhaps she needn't worry quite so much about her hostess. She was more than a tavernkeeper to these men, many of whom had no doubt left their families and struck out alone, trying to make a go of life in the new world. The Cockerel was a safe place, and even pregnant, Angela obliquely embodied all the mothers and sisters left behind.

There are worse things than working in a tavern, Hanneke thought. She'd never worked for wages before but really, this part wasn't much different than serving a harvest crew at home. Perhaps she could find work in one of Watertown's many hotels or taverns.

She was clearing a table by one of the front windows when she heard the distant thump of a bass drum. A mighty oath exploded from the man by her right elbow. Several men protested—"Not in front of the ladies!"—but all of them were stumbling to their feet, pushing back chairs, bumping into one another, caroming toward the door. Hanneke managed to get the tray safely down on the table before pressing herself against the wall until the crush had passed. In moments the taproom was almost empty. Even the factory girls straggled outside.

Hanneke met Angela at the open front door. Well-dressed men wearing top hats and red sashes were parading down the street. The torches many carried flickered wildly in the twilight. A bugler occasionally raised his horn to emit a two-note discordance that seemed intended only to attract attention. A drummer paced the procession with a dirge-like beat.

"What is it?" Hanneke asked, wondering if she had forgotten some American holiday.

"Know-Nothings." Adolf spat the words from behind them.

Hanneke frowned in bewilderment. *"Who?"*

"Damn nativists!" Adolf fumed. "They hate us! I'm going—"

"Adolf, no," Angela said sharply. She tried to grab his arm but he eeled between the two women, down the steps, into the growing crowd.

"Good heavens," Hanneke murmured.

The muttering tavern patrons clustered on the walk. The marchers ignored them. Many of those in the outer ranks held signs. "What do they say?" Hanneke asked.

"'We will not yield to a foreign hand.'" Angela's voice was flat. "'Beware the foreign influence.' 'America, our native land.'"

Hanneke suddenly felt chilly. "I see."

"The Know-Nothings started as a secret society called the Order of the Star-Spangled Banner," Angela muttered. "If anyone who wasn't a member asked a question about it, the answer was always 'I know nothing.' They are like children." But her tone was more wary than derisive.

Dangerous children, Hanneke thought. Suddenly she sucked in a quick breath. One of the marchers was Asa Hawkins. She abruptly started down the steps. "I want to see."

"You shouldn't!" Angela protested.

"I'll be all right." Hanneke felt a defiant urge to observe this clearly; to confront whatever menace these so-called nativists represented. She slid into the crowd. *"Entschuldigung!"* When the men watching heard a woman's voice, they instinctively made way until Hanneke reached the edge of the street.

Uneasiness tainted the air like smoke from a smoldering fire. The well-dressed men leading the procession exhibited a haughty superiority. Trailing the professional men came more marchers wearing shabbier clothes beneath the blood-red sashes. They didn't walk in lockstep but shambled in groups, sometimes pointing and jeering at the watchers. Hanneke's flicker of defiance faded as quickly as it had come, replaced with apprehension. It was all too easy for such people—weary, poor, struggling—to pin their disappointments and frustrations on others. She remembered the boys who'd taunted her and the hotel cart driver in Milwaukee. They'd already been taught to hate.

Fridolin Bauer. Why did you bring me to such a place?

He did not answer.

A whistle shrilled in the distance. A moment later several men on horseback trotted down the street, in opposition to the procession. Hanneke thought they meant to halt the parade but instead, they maneuvered along the walkways, keeping their nervous mounts between the marchers and the onlookers. Evidently, the march itself didn't concern them as much as the threat of a clash between self-righteous nativists and resentful immigrants.

The first rider on Hanneke's side of the street, riding a magnificent bay, carried a stout wooden baton. "Back! Back!" he bellowed.

"Police," someone muttered.

Hanneke didn't know if the arrival of the police was good or bad. The German men's anger grew sullen, either because they feared the police or because they resented the return of order. Something thrown—a rock?—hit the horse on the left flank. Marchers scrambled out of the way as the horse danced sideways, then broke into a canter.

Hanneke hugged her arms across her chest. It was time to—

The shove came so hard, so fast, that Hanneke was falling before her mind grasped the truth of a harsh hand slammed between her shoulder blades.

The road rose. Someone pinched her sleeve, trying and failing to grab her arm. A woman screamed. The approaching horse shrilled alarm as its rider reined hard. For a split instant, Hanneke smelled the animal's hot sweat, saw clods of mud explode from its hooves.

The next explosion was inside her head: pain, and fear, and a brilliant flash of fireworks. Then nothing at all.

Chapter Six

The pain returned first…throbbing in her head, stinging her hands, pounding her ribs. Hanneke groaned.

"She's coming around," someone said. A woman's voice. Familiar, although Hanneke couldn't find the name. She blinked and light seared the blackness. She clenched her teeth but another whimper of pain escaped anyway.

"Are you awake?" Another voice. Unfamiliar. Male. Groggy, Hanneke tried opening her eyes again. If only everything wasn't so blurry! An oil lamp sat on a nearby table. She knew that lamp, that table. Didn't she? Was she in her bedroom in Treptow? No…no, not there….

"Are you awake?" the man asked again. Hanneke worked hard to focus on the face: narrow, with a jutting chin, a sharp little beard, and round wire-rimmed spectacles pinched on his nose. A stranger.

"Yes," Hanneke mumbled. She was lying on something soft, and she tried to rise on her elbows.

"No, my dear lady, not yet," the man said, sounding not at all concerned. He thrust a hand a few inches from her nose. "How many fingers do you see?"

"…Three."

"Do you know where you are?"

Hanneke had already learned that the slightest movement of her head brought new waves of pain, so she searched with her eyes. The woman…of course, it was Angela, hovering anxiously. "The spare bedroom…at the Red Cockerel."

"And do you know your name?"

"Hanneke Bauer," she said irritably, seeing too late Angela's widened eyes, the quick negative shake of her head. At that everything came back in a rush.

"Um…ah. Yes, I see." The man, who was sitting beside Hanneke's bed, leaned back in his chair and stroked his beard. "I am Doctor Rausch. Do you remember what happened?"

"I was pushed in front of a horse."

Dr. Rausch wrinkled his nose and used one finger to settle his glasses more firmly. "What?"

"I was *pushed* in *front* of a *horse*," Hanneke repeated, bewildered by the man's confusion. German was his native language, surely. Was her accent so different than his own?

"Well…whether you stumbled or…well, yes. What matters is that you were quite lucky." Dr. Rausch pushed back the hair over her right temple, peering over his spectacles. "Amazingly so. If a rider any less skilled than Constable Peters had been in the saddle, you'd likely have been killed. As it is, you got no more than a glancing kick in the ribs. You knocked yourself unconscious when your head hit the street. Fortunately, it has not yet been macadamized."

"Fortunately," Hanneke agreed. She'd meant to sound docile but the conversation was so ludicrous that a gasp of hysterical laughter bubbled out. Dr. Rausch stroked his beard again, eyes narrowed, so much a caricature of a stereotypical physician that Hanneke had to suck in her lower lip and bite it—hard—to contain more inappropriate laughter.

"Thank you, doctor," Angela said. She took two steps toward the door. "We're grateful. Any instructions?"

"Primarily rest," Dr. Rausch said firmly. "Wrapping the ribs will help also, although I don't think anything is broken. But no matter what else…rest."

"I will." Hanneke watched him stand, wipe his hands on his trousers. "Angela?"

"Yes?"

"My reticule—it's under the mattress, by the wall." Hanneke gestured toward the foot of the bed.

Angela hesitated, then retrieved the bag. After leaning toward the lamp to examine its contents she handed the physician two coins. *Two more I hadn't planned to spend,* Hanneke thought.

"Danke schön." Dr. Rausch nodded politely at each woman before leaving. Angela followed him from the room. Hanneke heard their footsteps fade toward the front door. That was wrong... good heavens, what time was it? The taproom, usually a boisterous hum of conversation until well into the night, was silent.

A moment later Angela slipped back inside and sank into the chair the doctor had vacated. She planted her elbows on her knees and, for a few moments, buried her face in her hands. Finally, she drew a shuddering breath and raised her head again. "I was *terrified.* When I saw you fall—"

"I was *pushed.* I felt the palm of someone's hand land in the middle of my back and—and push. Hard. Deliberately, I'm quite sure of it."

Angela fretted her lower lip between her teeth. "The crowd was thick. Some of the men were ready to burst into the street, and I think others were trying to back away from the police. You may have been jostled...."

"I wasn't—ow." Hanneke winced, pressing one palm to her forehead. *Do not move,* she ordered herself. *Talk, but do, not, move.* She tried again. "I was not jostled."

"Gott in Himmel." Angela jerked to her feet and began to prowl the little room like a caged cat.

Hanneke stood it for as long as she could. "Please, Angela, I beg you—sit down."

"I'm all right."

"But I am not, and the sound of your heels—"

"Oh! Oh, of course." Angela abruptly dropped back into the chair. "It's just that—it's hard to believe it has come to this. Could someone be so brutal? Did you *see* the man who did this?"

"My back was turned."

"The crowd had grown so thick by that time.... Most of the men right there in front of the Cockrell had come *from* the tavern, but surely not all." Angela stared blindly at the wall. "One of the Know-Nothings must have slipped through the crowd. Did you speak? Could someone have heard you speaking German?"

Hanneke tried to remember, but her brain still felt like mud. "I might have muttered something to myself…but I don't believe I spoke loudly enough for another to overhear."

"Still, that must have been the cause. Oh! Those wretched *men!* Those nativists!"

"I am not convinced I was pushed simply because I speak German," Hanneke said. "Angela… what if it had something to do with Fridolin?"

Angela's eyebrows rose. "What could it have to do with—with that?"

"I don't know. It might, though."

"But…."

"I'm not ready to accept that Fridolin's death was an accident." Hanneke tried the idea out loud, hearing the words pulse in her aching head.

Angela's mouth opened in astonishment. "But—but—who would hate him enough to *kill* him? By all accounts, he was well-liked, friendly, a fair man to work for."

"I had no idea who might wish to harm Fridolin," Hanneke said slowly, "until tonight. He mentioned the Know-Nothings in one of his letters. '*A certain anti-foreigner spirit has simmered in some quarters here for years, and I am afraid it may come to a full boil in Wisconsin this year. But there is no need for alarm. Good German men won't allow themselves to be treated as something less than those who happened to be born on American soil.*'"

"So?"

"Well, what do you suppose those 'good German men' are doing?"

"I have no idea!"

"Perhaps because they meet in secret. Perhaps…." Her voice trailed off as she tried to corral what had been, up to now, stray thoughts. "Perhaps Fridolin was somehow working against these Know-Nothings. And if the worst element discovered that…."

"I—I—no. That's just…no."

"But why push *me* tonight?" Hanneke demanded, with a vehemence that brought another zigzag of white pain like lightning through her skull. She closed her eyes again, waiting for the worst to pass.

"They are cowards," Angela said. "It is not hard for me to believe that one would single out a woman to harm. There were very few women in the crowd, so…."

"Perhaps," Hanneke said, but only because her head hurt too much, her ribs throbbed too badly, to argue.

"You need to rest," Angela said. "May I help you change into your nightgown?"

The thought of such strenuous activity was unbearable. "I think not. I'm all right like this."

Angela got up and gently removed Hanneke's shoes, then pulled the blanket up to her chin. "Try to sleep. There's nothing else to be done this evening."

Sleep sounded marvelous, but another thought bounced back. "Angela—what about the tavern?"

"I closed for the night."

"*Closed?*" Hanneke was horrified. Angela would not make such a decision lightly.

"The police kept a riot from starting, but…everyone was angry." Angela patted her belly, as if trying to reassure the unborn child. "I was afraid that…well, by tomorrow, tempers will have cooled. I have enough problems without having trouble here. All it takes is one or two, drunk…."

"Yes." Hanneke could well imagine. "What about Adolf?"

Angela's eyes were shuttered. "Adolf has not yet returned."

"Oh." Hanneke wanted to find something comforting to say…but suddenly, even the simplest of assurances seemed beyond her ability.

"We'll talk again in the morning." Angela leaned over the lamp, and for a moment a wild pregnant shadow was thrown upon the wall. Then she blew out the flame.

I'll never have a child, Hanneke thought. For the first time that evening, she felt the hot salt of tears.

* * *

Hanneke didn't wake until dawn crept into the narrow room, dispelling the shadows. She lay still, staring at the ceiling, remembering what had happened. After a good night's sleep she was no less certain that she'd been deliberately pushed into the street...and no less frightened by that knowledge.

Finally, she scraped up the will to experiment with movement. Her headache was better. Everything else felt worse. Her hands were scraped and raw. Her side ached. Clenching her teeth, she inched upright and managed to stand. Only then did she see the strips of torn linen, waiting on the chair. Angela must have tip-toed in and left them. And I wouldn't have asked, Hanneke thought, knowing that she couldn't afford to repay her hostess for a ruined sheet. She remembered Adolf's cheerful observation—"You're good for her"—and suspected that Angela would not agree.

Twenty minutes later Hanneke made her way into the kitchen. Angela, an apron tied above her bulging belly, stopped stirring oatmeal long enough to pour Hanneke a cup of coffee. Hanneke accepted it gratefully, inhaling the rising steam, imagining it easing all of the tense hurt places inside. Then she sipped. "Ah," she sighed. "*Danke schön*. And for the bandages too."

"Did they help?"

"Immensely. I'm green and purple from here to here—" she gestured from waist to armpit—"but wrapping lessened the pain. And my headache is better." She watched as Angela slid the heavy kettle away from the hottest burners, then ladled oatmeal into two bowls. "Adolf is not back yet?"

"No." Angela dropped heavily into her chair. Her face looked drawn—gaunt, almost, as if she'd lost weight overnight.

Hanneke sat down as well, picked up a spoon, put it down again. "I don't know where Adolf is...but I'm aware that I've added to your burdens. I'm truly sorry, Angela."

"I can't help wondering about what you said last night. Your suspicions..."

"I should have held my tongue."

"That wouldn't have solved anything."

"I suppose not." Hanneke tried a bite of oatmeal. Angela made it thicker than she did, but today that seemed perfect, as if the hot mixture might help

58

patch her bruised ribs. "This is good."

Angela studied Hanneke across the table. "So…you think Fridolin might have gotten mixed up in the political troubles."

"I do," Hanneke said carefully.

"It's possible, of course," Angela admitted. "Watertown has only had constables for a year or so. I've heard that some of the German men have formed a secret society of their own—"

"Who?" Hanneke put her cup down so abruptly that coffee sloshed over the rim. "If I could talk to someone—"

"I don't know. I doubt that many of the men who come in here are involved. Men from the upper class would organize things. Free Thinkers. Men with political ambitions."

That did seem likely, Hanneke thought as she wiped up the spilled coffee with her apron. Such an organization had probably been birthed at a place like the Buena Vista, among scholars and political ideologues—likely some of the Forty-Eighters, who had fled but not forgotten the failed revolution in the old country.

Would Fridolin have been comfortable among such men? Hanneke had no idea. He had a good mind; had been a skilled craftsman and, lately, a gentleman farmer, but he had not spent time at a university. In the old country, many men of education and means considered everyone else peasants, beneath notice. Did that still hold true in America? She didn't know.

"But if Fridolin Bauer's death *did* come at the hands of Know-Nothings," Angela was saying, "I don't know how you could make a case now." She spread her hands. "What do you think you can discover after all these weeks?"

"I don't know," Hanneke admitted. "But I have to try."

Angela shook her head. "It was not always like this. I'm sorry you've come just as these Know-Nothings are rising to prominence."

"What is behind it?" Hanneke asked. "Surely there is room here for everyone."

"One would think. But in the last five years, Watertown's population has increased tenfold. Many of the new arrivals have been Germans. They say that German-speaking people now account for half of the people living here. Suddenly we are no longer a minority."

"Ah." Hanneke took that in, turned it over in her mind.

"And in the past year or so, a few German men have been elected to public office. Frederick Hermann is an alderman. Henry Mullberger is city clerk. And Ernst Off was elected city marshal."

"All of which no doubt terrified Yankees who want to keep political control."

"It's not *all* Yankees," Angela added judiciously. "But yes, some are afraid of losing power. And others, when faced with any kind of disappointment, need to point a finger and say 'It's their fault.'"

"Yes," Hanneke agreed quietly. "Although I imagine that's true in both directions."

Angela pushed her bowl away—still half full—and stood, then walked to the window overlooking the alley behind the tavern.

"No sign of Adolf?"

Angela shook her head. "I do worry for him."

"He's just a boy," Hanneke said gently.

"With a man's resentments." Angela sat down again, propped one elbow on the table, and rested her cheek on her palm. "It would be easy for someone on either side to take advantage of him."

"Surely this will pass, don't you think? The lawmen—Ernst Off, for example—won't let things get out of hand."

Angela shook her head. "Wisconsin is still a rough place. Last year, when a runaway slave was captured and put in jail near Milwaukee, a mob of abolitionists broke down the doors and spirited him away." She leaned forward. "I despise slavery as much as any decent person, but the point is, the law was not capable of keeping a violent mob from doing its will."

"Perhaps that was an isolated case...?"

"No. A few weeks ago a man was lynched—"

"Lynched?" Hanneke set down her glass heavily.

"In another small town, north of Milwaukee. There was some altercation between a German farmer and a Yankee neighbor. The Yankee was accused of burning down the German's pigsty and arrested. Put in jail. But before he could come to trial, a mob broke into the jail, grabbed the man, and hanged him. It was Germans who did it."

"*Gott in Himmel.*"

"So you see why I worry about Adolf."

"Yes," Hanneke murmured. Imagining Adolf being set upon by angry Yankee men was bad. Imagining him being swept up in some heinous act by angry German men was equally bad. She blinked to clear unwanted images from her mind. "Thank goodness he has *you*, Angela. You set a good example. Working here keeps him busy."

"I try, but he won't always listen to me." Angela traced one finger around the rim of her cup. "It was easier when Julius was here."

Angela's brother, Hanneke reminded herself.

"He was good for Adolf." Angela sighed. "Adolf had a hard time. His parents both died halfway across Lake Michigan on the steamship. When he and his younger sister arrived in Milwaukee, they were met by some cousin and his family. The cousin's wife was willing to take the girl in, but not Adolf. Told him to go out and make his way in the world. He was twelve."

Why is it, Hanneke wondered, that some women are given children they don't want, while some women who desperately want them are left without?

"Adolf ended up in Watertown. Julius found him scavenging for food. Brought him in and put him to work." Angela finally took a small sip of tea. "Adolf misses him. We both do."

Hanneke hesitated. "Julius is dead?"

Angela started, as if she'd forgotten she wasn't alone. Her expression became unreadable. "No. Julius is gone."

Before Hanneke could decide on an appropriate response a cheerful whistle sounded from the alley. A moment later Adolf walked through the back door. He grinned at them both, then made straight for the stove. "No sausage this morning? Well, no matter, I'm hungry enough to eat anything."

Angela and Hanneke exchanged glances. Adolf filled a bowl with oatmeal, poured himself a cup of coffee, added three spoonsful of sugar, and joined them at the table.

"Adolf," Hanneke said carefully, watching him shovel breakfast like a starving man. "We were worried."

"Worried?" His brow wrinkled, as if the suggestion was astonishing. "About me?" He looked from one woman to the other, indignation chasing away his look of confusion. "I'm not a child." He sounded petulant as a toddler.

"Of course not," Angela began. "It's just that—"

Someone rapped sharply on the back door.

"We're closed!" Angela called crossly. "Come back this afternoon."

The door opened. "My business won't wait that long," Deputy Sheriff John Barlow said, sounding just as cross. He held a newspaper, which he slapped down on the table in front of Hanneke. "What is the meaning of this?"

Chapter Seven

Hanneke's stomach muscles clenched. *You have done nothing wrong!* she reminded herself, but the combination of Deputy Barlow's official status and her experience the night before prickled her nerves. "What do you mean?"

"This," he growled through clenched teeth, and pointed.

Hanneke leaned over the paper. *Wanted: Information about the death of Fridolin Bauer. Leave any response at the post office, attention H.B.*

"What were you *thinking?* You foolish woman! I told you to leave Watertown!"

"And just where do you think—" She turned away, furiously blinking back tears. She wanted to throw her words like stones: I have nowhere to go! I have no money! I have nothing left, don't you see? And nothing to do but search for the truth.

She managed to swallow those bitter confessions. "What you have not done is tell me what law I have broken," she snapped instead. She was acutely aware of Adolf, following the exchange open-mouthed. Angela sat staring at her congealing oatmeal.

"Listen." John Barlow planted both hands on the table, leaning close. He wore a working man's coat of dark blue corduroy today, and dried manure caked the bottom of his trousers, but the intensity of his gaze spoke more of lawman than farmer. "All blazes might explode at any time, and I—we all—have bigger things to worry about than *you* causing—"

"Then do not worry about me!" Hanneke shoved to her feet. The movement caused a stab of pain in her side, and a sympathetic echo in her head, but those only honed her anger. "If I've broken some law, arrest me. If not, I suggest you address those pressing issues you speak of, instead of intruding on Fraulein Zeidler's breakfast!"

Angela bowed her head lower. Adolf's eyes had widened to almost perfect circles.

John Barlow's had narrowed to slits. A muscle in his jaw twitched as he turned to Angela. "Fraulein Zeidler, I beg your pardon," he said stiffly. Then he glowered at Hanneke. "As for you—the trouble you are stirring up is obviously beyond your understanding. If you have any shred of wisdom, or decency, you will leave Watertown. Today." He turned on his heel and left, slamming the door behind him.

"What did—" Adolf began, but Hanneke was already on her way out the door. By the time she got outside Barlow was striding down the alley. "Wait!" she called.

He turned impatiently.

"Pardon me," she said frostily. "I do hate to intrude upon your—your good graces. But you surely can't imagine that you might barge into Fraulein Zeidler's kitchen at such an hour, pummel me with vague threats, and leave without explaining yourself."

"I most certainly do not have to explain myself. But I will say this." His voice was tight, as if each word was squeezed out against his better judgment. "Yesterday I was called for the fifth time to a saloon frequented by railroad workers who seem more dedicated to trying to kill each other than laying track. I spent three hours riding all over the county trying to track down a man's stolen property. I was up for most of the night dealing with the aftermath of the Know-Nothing demonstration. I was, therefore, not pleased to read the morning newspaper and find that not only did you ignore my request to leave Watertown, you had the *impertinence* to place an ad—"

"Yes, yes," Hanneke interrupted. Her head was aching again, and she had little patience for his complaints. "How did you know where to find me?"

"Well, I had no idea where to find you for at least ten minutes," Barlow said caustically. "Then, before I could so much as get the milking done, Doctor Rausch paid me a visit. He had heard your name, and was...concerned that you managed to get yourself injured."

Of course. Hanneke's shoulders slumped as she remembered the good doctor's ill-hidden surprise when she told him her name; his flustered response to her claim of being pushed into the street. "Well, I'm glad someone was concerned," she retorted. "And *ja, danke*, I am feeling better this morning."

Barlow's cheeks flushed a ruddy red. He shoved his hands into his pockets as if afraid they might throttle her if left unfettered.

"I have done nothing wrong," Hanneke said. "I was attacked last night. I'm sure of it, even if you and Dr. Rausch and everyone else in this city chooses to label me a madwoman. I *should* be turning to you for help! I am not, but still, you have gone out of your way to insult me!"

"I—"

"Since you *have*, I would like you to explain yourself." Hanneke grabbed her elbows; the alley was too narrow to admit direct sunlight, and the morning was cool. "You said something about all blazes exploding, and troubles I did not understand. What troubles?"

John Barlow wiped a hand over his face. The dark circles under his lower eyelids were more pronounced than Angela's. His posture, the set of his jaw, the shadows in his eyes spoke of an inexpressible weariness. "They are none of your concern."

"I disagree. My husband felt compelled to keep remarkable secrets. He died in an accident that I find both ridiculous and suspicious—"

"Fridolin Bauer was a good man. He was not a good farmer."

"—and yesterday evening I was shoved directly into the path of an oncoming horse. *Shoved!*" Hanneke saw a torn curtain flick in a nearby window, a curious face appear, then disappear with apparent disinterest.

"You were in the middle of the crowd," Barlow said.

"Yes."

"A crowd that was growing by the minute. A crowd filled with angry men who are willing to tear this community apart because of politics and immigrant conflicts. And you want me to believe that someone took advantage of the situation to push you."

"I—"

"Maybe you stumbled. Maybe you tripped. Maybe you were jostled. How can you insist that none of those are possibilities?"

"I..." Hanneke began, but her voice trailed away. She was sure! And yet....

Satisfaction flared in his eyes. He'd succeeded in planting doubt in her mind, and he knew it.

The man was galling. I will not admit to uncertainty, Hanneke thought, and had to content herself with that stalemate.

"Fraulein...whoever you are." John Barlow folded his arms inexorably across his chest. "I know you were on the street last night. You saw the procession. Surely you realize the volatile nature of the tensions that have been growing lately."

"You mean the Know-Nothings. Angela said they act like children."

His mouth twisted in that already familiar manner. "Fraulein, there is nothing child-like about them. A few years ago, in Philadelphia, Know-Nothing nativists provoked riots that left thirty-some people dead. After operating as a secret society for years, the Know-Nothings have organized themselves into a political party. I do *not* want those party members to spark violence in Watertown."

"Well, why don't you arrest them?" Hanneke demanded. "I saw dozens of them marching down the street! Why don't you just—"

"Those men broke no law," Barlow growled. "And besides, are you so simple-minded as to think that every member of the local Know-Nothing lodge marched last night? We're trying to identify the leaders. I need to know what judges and aldermen and policemen slip to their secret meetings at night. Those men incite riots, but they rarely appear in them."

Hanneke nodded slowly. A small rat sidled along a gutter, sniffing hopefully, finally disappearing beneath a loose board on a neighbor's stable. Barlow shook his head, looking disgusted, and started back down the alley.

"Deputy Barlow!" Hanneke cried. Then, remembering the face at the window, she lowered her voice. "Please—just a moment, if you will." She waited until he, with a look of long suffering, turned back again. "I am well aware that you hold a low opinion of me. But I must ask—is it possible that Fridolin was mixed up in this political trouble? I've heard rumors of German men creating their own secret society—"

"What have you heard?" he asked sharply.

"Well, I—just that," she stammered. She'd brought enough trouble to Angela's door without implicating the poor woman further. "But please, for the sake of your friendship with Fridolin Bauer, won't you please consider that he might have been killed by one of these nativists?"

Barlow closed his eyes, rubbing his temples as if his head ached too. A door opened nearby, and someone emptied a dishpan into the alley. Two small birds descended immediately, pecking at sodden crumbs. The last burst of Hanneke's anger sapped away, leaving her anxious and tired.

Finally he opened his eyes. "Just leave—things—*alone,*" he muttered. Then he walked away.

Hanneke walked back to Angela's door slowly. Had she been unwise to mention her fears to Deputy Barlow? She certainly had been unwise to lose her temper. He knew things, things that might help unravel whatever knot Fridolin had tied before his death. Screeching at Barlow like a gull would not earn either his sympathy or his confidence.

Back in the kitchen, she found Angela still seated at the table. Adolf was shoving another log into the stove, but he turned as Hanneke came back inside. "I thought you were going to get arrested!" he cried.

"And I may yet," Hanneke said, trying for a smile. "But so far, Deputy Barlow has evidently not found just cause. I imagine he's tried." She slid back into her chair and picked up her coffee cup. Only then did she realize that her hands were trembling. She set the cup down quickly.

"Adolf, pour Hanneke some fresh coffee, will you?" Angela asked. She waited until that was done before turning her attention to her guest. "Hanneke…."

"I know. I'm sorry." Hanneke allowed herself a bracing sip before going on. "I did put a notice in the paper, asking for information about Fridolin. But I asked responders to leave a note at the post office! I didn't even mention this place, or you. Deputy Barlow would never have known where I was staying if Dr. Rausch hadn't told him."

"I know. I read the notice." Angela cocked her head at the newspaper Barlow had left on the table. "But the thing is…now he *does* know where you're staying."

Hanneke felt a sinking sensation in her stomach. "And that's a problem."

"I lost business when Julius left. I've built things back up, but in these times everyone is tense, upset…I simply can't invite more trouble." Angela sounded resigned. "Yankee sentiment against foreigners is rising. And John Barlow is a Yankee."

"Deputy Barlow is married to a German woman," Adolf objected.

"That may be," Hanneke said quietly, "but he's a lawman who has ordered me to leave Watertown." She spread her hands, palms up. "He may come back here if I stay, and if your customers saw him…well, it would make them uncomfortable."

"Yes, it would." Angela cupped her elbows. "Watertown is split between Dodge and Jefferson Counties, and with the new city marshals…there are more lawmen than people are accustomed to seeing. It makes some of them anxious."

"And that would hurt business," Hanneke said. "It wouldn't be fair for me to intrude here any longer."

"But…." Adolf began again, then let his voice trail away. The dismay on his face was so sincere that Hanneke reached out and patted his arm. "I'll be fine," she told him.

"But where will you go?" he asked.

"Well, I had planned to walk out to Fridolin Bauer's farm today. I'll start with that, and then—then figure what comes next. Although…." She sipped more coffee, trying not to panic, trying to think. "I will have to find a place to leave my trunk."

"She can leave that here, can't she?" Adolf asked Angela. "In the stable, maybe?"

"Certainly," Angela said at once, adding for Hanneke's benefit, "It came with the building, but we use it primarily for storage. It's right across the alley." She smiled—grimly, but a smile nonetheless. "And if Deputy Barlow returns, I can say with complete honesty that you left with your luggage."

"I'll take your trunk out for you," Adolf offered.

"And my valise as well, I think," Hanneke added briskly. After the theft of her papers, she was loathe to leave what little she had left behind—the three volumes Fridolin had given her, her wedding shawl, her silk dress, her favorite teacup. Well, nothing for it. She could carry her knitting in her pocket and her money—such as was left—in her reticule. Everything else would have to stay.

Adolf lugged Hanneke's trunk out to the stable and put it in a back corner, out of sight from the doorway.

"*Danke schön*, Adolf." Hanneke heard a quiver in her voice and cleared her throat. Sometimes the smallest acts of kindness meant the most.

Adolf glanced over his shoulder and lowered his voice. "It's hard for Angela to trust anybody. Please don't think unkindly of her."

"I couldn't possibly."

He leaned even closer. "And I think she's in debt."

"To whom?"

"There's a man named Hawkins—"

"Hawkins?" Hanneke hissed. "Asa Hawkins?"

Adolf looked startled. "I don't know his first name. He's an auctioneer. He buys goods in big quantity, freights them in, then resells at a profit." The boy shrugged impatiently. "*Anyway*, he's come around here a few times to talk to Angela. She sends me off, so I can't hear, but she's always upset after he leaves."

Hanneke was all too familiar with Hawkins's sneers and derogatory remarks. He'd shown himself to be the worst kind of nativist even before she'd spotted him marching in the Know-Nothing parade. He was an odious man, and if Angela was somehow indebted to him... Horrid thought. Hanneke pinched her lips together. How bad was the situation? Was Angela in danger of losing the tavern?

"Don't say I told you!" Adolf's gaze was pleading. "I just wanted you to understand."

"Of course," she assured him. "She's lucky to have a good friend like you."

After Adolf left on an errand, Hanneke went back into the kitchen. Angela was still sitting at the table. "I am sorry, Hanneke."

"You have no need to be."

"If you do end up staying in Watertown, it's just as well that more people don't learn that you were here with me." Angela gestured at her belly. "My child has a father, but I do not have a husband." Her voice was steady, but those gray eyes were shadowed.

Hanneke chose her words carefully. "I regret that you face hardships, Angela, but they are none of my business. You've been generous and kind. Should anyone ask, I'd be proud to call you a friend."

Angela reached out and squeezed Hanneke's hand. Then she lumbered to her feet and began washing the breakfast dishes. Hanneke fetched her bonnet and shawl and made ready to visit Christine Bauer.

* * *

Hanneke didn't need directions to the Bauer farm on Plum Grove Road. *I purchased from a Pomeranian fellow a farm three American miles northeast of town,* Fridolin had told her. *It is a short drive if I need to take the wagon, and a pleasant walk if I am seeking only conversation and news....* Hanneke was glad to leave Watertown behind, and tried to forget about being shoved into the street. Right now, she must concentrate on talking with Christine. Perhaps something unexpected, something helpful, would come from that. Everything else would have to wait.

Soon she left the busiest streets behind. Her spirits inched up, just a bit. Sunshine warmed her shoulders. Her ribs still ached, but walking eased stiff muscles. She pulled her knitting from her pocket. She was starting a new shawl today, which required only two needles. With one needle set in the sheath on her belt, she had one hand free to keep the yarn flowing smoothly while she walked.

Once past the city she passed acres of stumps, and cutting crews beyond, working to satisfy the ever-present need for railroad ties and building lumber. Beyond those, the landscape rolled from forest to what Fridolin had called "oak openings"—meadowland dotted with ancient trees. Delicate white shooting stars bloomed along the roadsides, and blue spiderworts too.

It was a marvel. Such rich land! The openness, the abundance of timber and fertile black loam, patches of swampy land promising marsh hay for the taking—it was overwhelming. She passed farms with barely a pumpkin patch cleared and others with acres already green with grain. No wonder so many people from crowded, hard-scrabble, exhausted patches of Europe had chosen to risk their futures here. This land represented brutal labor, but also the promise of better things.

Hanneke felt a new ache take seed in her heart. She imagined pausing with Fridolin at the end of a busy day on *their* farm to take stock, pleased with each improvement. She imagined riding to town on the wagon seat beside Fridolin, taking pumpkins or geese to sell at the market, or perhaps hauling a new rocking chair or mirror home....

"This will not do," she said aloud, startling a bright bluebird up from its branch on a glossy-leaved shrub beside the road. She began walking again, more briskly.

She passed several farms before finding the turn onto Plum Grove Road, which veered left near the skeleton of a huge tree that had been split by lightning. As she gathered her bearings, a boy and his cow emerged around a bend. *"Guten tag,"* he called. He carried a thin branch but it trailed on the road behind him, evidently not needed.

"Guten tag," Hanneke answered. "I'm looking for the Bauer Farm. I believe it's just up ahead?"

"The Bauer Farm?" The boy paused, looking puzzled. Then he nodded. "Oh, you mean the old Jaeger place. Yes, just up ahead. Third farm on the north side of the road." He whistled to his brown cow, who politely ambled on.

"Danke," she called after him, but her memory was re-visiting another letter: *Neighbors still call it 'the Jaeger Place.' I suspect that you and I will need to till it for a few more years before it is known as our own. It is not as well established as some, but I was able to purchase eighty acres at a good price, ten acres of which have been improved.*

Hanneke walked on, hurrying now, as if some invisible cord was drawing her on. Not this farm… nor this one—the Steckelberg place, wasn't it? But soon, beyond this stretch of woods. A few moments later she rounded a bend in the road…and there it was. Fridolin's farm.

Her hands stilled, and she shoved her knitting away. No, she thought. *Our* farm.

Despite the abundance of local wood, a German builder had constructed the home in the Old County *fachwerk*, or half-timbered, style. A straw-and-mud mortar had been packed between an open framework of squared beams. The house was modest, one story with, most likely, a loft beneath the roof. A narrow front porch ran the length of the house, providing a shady place to snap beans or card wool. A vegetable garden extended from road to porch—Americans might waste such space on lawns, but Frau Jaeger had not. Someone had woven slim boughs through the rails on the garden fence, creating a barrier to rabbits with a minimal expenditure of precious lumber or expensive nails. It all felt very European. Very Germanic.

Grapevines had been trained along the fence. Hanneke paused at the front gate, surveying a cloud of delicate red columbine blooming in one corner, parsley and thyme and dill weed along the walkway, squares sprouting green with new growth—kohlrabi, kale, onions, potatoes, leeks. The layout was tidy, but her palms itched with wanting to take a hoe to weeds poking up here and there. And were those beetles on the broccoli? She'd have to….

"*No,*" she muttered. She swallowed hard, trying to quell the salty lump in her throat.

Then she took a deep breath and squared her shoulders. She checked for stray locks of hair beneath her bonnet, picked a bit of lint from her skirt. *I am a respectable working-class woman,* her clothing said. *I am not a woman who puts on airs or tells fantastic tales.*

She let herself in the gate, strode down the path, mounted the steps, wiped her palms on her skirt, and knocked on the door. After a few moments, she heard muffled footsteps. Then the front door opened and Christine Bauer appeared. "Oh!" she exclaimed. She wore the same dull black dress today, with a black crocheted pelerine around her shoulders and the mourning brooch with one yellow curl entombed beneath glass.

Hanneke managed only with difficulty to look away from that pin. "I beg your pardon. I know you didn't expect me to call—"

"You are not welcome here." Christine started to shut the door.

"*Please.* I don't mean you any harm. I—I'm just trying to understand what has happened."

The two women stared at each other. Christine's gaze darted over Hanneke's shoulder, up and down the road, as if looking for assistance. A goose honked from somewhere behind the house, and a breeze riffled the grapevine leaves.

"I beg you," Hanneke said quietly. "Just a moment of your time. May I come inside?"

Chapter Eight

Christine pursed her lips. Smudges of fatigue showed beneath her eyes. Her cheeks were hollow. Hanneke reminded herself that this woman was grieving Fridolin's death as well—and that she had known him far better and longer.

"No, you may not come inside," Christine said finally. But she did step out onto the porch.

As she did, Hanneke caught a quick glimpse of a closed interior door, just beyond a small entryway. The door was wide, and a thin curl of smoke wisped beneath it. "Is—is that a *schwartze Küche?*" she stammered.

"Yes," Christine said shortly, pulling the front door closed behind her. "What is it you want?"

Hanneke pulled her attention back from the house that should have been hers, but was not. "I want to understand why Fridolin kept my existence a secret from you, and yours a secret from me."

"I have no reason to believe that you even knew my brother." Christine twisted the fingers of one hand through her pelerine's openwork.

"Fridolin Bauer traveled to Treptow last September." Hanneke spoke quietly but quickly, trying to forestall more objections. "He liked ham but not mutton. He ate bread dry, without butter or grease. He loved going outside on clear nights to study the stars."

"So, you…you might have met my brother. It does not prove that you married him."

"He had a bad scar on his right thigh. He told me he got it as a boy, when he jumped from a haymow and landed on a scythe."

Red spots appeared on Christine's cheeks, harsh against her pallor.

"His—your—mother died in childbirth when he was six," Hanneke continued. "The midwife smelled like peppermint and had a withered foot. He said he hid in the pantry behind a cabbage crock and—and listened."

Christine hugged her arms across her chest. Hanneke thought she saw the actual moment that a crack formed in the younger woman's disbelief. Something new flickered in her eyes. Fear, perhaps, or simply shock as she allowed herself to wonder. Her indignation seemed to flow from her bones like corn from a sack.

We've both been duped, Hanneke wanted to say. She wanted to reach out in commiseration. But the moment felt fragile, and she feared that either response would be rebuffed.

Finally, Christine said, "I came to America to keep house for my brother. I did so for three years in Milwaukee before we came here and started over. I cooked his meals, I darned his socks. I was the only person he had to talk with on long evenings. How could a man keep such a secret from his sister?" Her voice trembled. *"How?"*

"I don't know." Hanneke thought of her own brother Theodor; how she would feel in similar circumstances.

"I am sorry for your distress, but there is nothing for you here."

"This isn't just about Fridolin's secrets," Hanneke persisted. "Something strange and—and terrible is going on. Someone stole my marriage papers and will while I was upstairs in the Buena Vista. And yesterday evening, someone shoved me into the street." Hanneke waited for a reaction and got none. "Did Fridolin act in any unusual manner in the months before he died?"

"No."

"Was he...do you know if he was involved in politics? I understand that some Germans are working to defeat the Know-Nothings. Was he involved in that effort?"

"No. Fridolin had all he could manage to keep this farm limping along."

"Was he truly such a poor farmer? I was shocked to learn the manner in which he died—"

The tears overflowed, tracking down Christine's cheeks. "I will not revisit that painful day! My brother's skills, or lack thereof, are none of your concern!"

Hanneke struggled to find some new line of inquiry, something that might turn Fridolin's sister from an adversary to an ally. "I am not raving mad, and I am not trying to cheat anyone. But we are not entirely unalike, you and I. We are both women responsible for our own welfare. For reasons I cannot imagine, Fridolin Bauer did both of us a great injustice. Perhaps, if we work together, if we shared—"

"I have nothing to share with you!" Christine looked incredulous. "Why should I? What *possible* motive could you have except stealing from me what my brother left behind when he died?"

"That is not true! I don't want money. I just want to understand what—"

"Fridolin left me with very little. Can't you see that? I could end up at the city's poor farm! My brother's bank account was almost empty when he died. In fact, I can't help wondering if he gave money to *you*."

"Quite the contrary. I gave *him* my small dowry, which leaves me destitute. He said he wanted to build a summer kitchen."

"Oh!" Christine gasped softly. She looked away, one slim hand over her mouth.

"I'm sorry," Hanneke said quietly. "But if we could just—"

"No more. You must *go*. Leave Watertown. I know that Deputy Barlow already ordered you to do that."

"I am not able to simply—"

"Wait." Christine turned abruptly and disappeared into the house, slamming the door behind her.

Several long minutes ticked by. Perhaps the woman isn't coming back, Hanneke thought. Perhaps she intends to leave me standing here like a leper, barred from comfort and company.

Then the door opened again. "Here." Christine thrust a small piece of paper toward Hanneke.

"What's this?"

"A note. Take it to the Bank of Watertown on Main Street. You'll receive enough money to get you back to Milwaukee—"

"This is *not* why I came here!" Hanneke made no move to take the note. "Fridolin must have had some reason for keeping secrets from both of us. All I want is the truth! That's *all!*"

Christine was trembling. A little sob hiccupped from her throat, and she needed a moment to find words. "I think I know that," she whispered finally. "Perhaps we are more alike than we can even imagine. Perhaps…perhaps if things were different, we might have even gotten along—"

I think we'll get along well enough, you and I.

"—but things are *not* different. They are as they are. I have nothing left but this farm, and I have to provide for myself. So please—just *take* this!" Christine forced the note into Hanneke's hand, closing her fingers over it. "Take it and *go.*" Then Fridolin's sister darted back inside. When the door slammed this time, Hanneke heard the metallic clang of a bolt sliding home. A moment later the muslin curtains hanging inside over the front windows were jerked closed.

Hanneke stepped stiffly from the porch and walked back down the garden path. She opened the gate and latched it carefully behind her. She looked in both directions. The road was empty, east and west. There was nothing left to do but plod back to Watertown.

And I'll do that, Hanneke thought. Soon. Right this minute, that seemed impossible.

A woodlot stood across the road from the house. She spotted a fallen log, half-hidden behind a thicket. She waded into the brush and sank down upon it.

It was quiet among the trees. Peaceful. Hanneke gazed through the branches, across the road to the house. She felt light-headed, almost dizzy.

And what did you expect? she asked herself. Had you really hoped that Christine might have softened? That she might help?

Yes. That's exactly what she had hoped.

"*Mein Gott,*" she muttered, pressing the heel of one hand against her forehead. This place—Wisconsin, Watertown, Fridolin's farm—it was all both so much less and so much more than she had imagined.

Focus on the less, she tried to tell herself. Fridolin had not mentioned a *schwartze Küche*! Black kitchens, the enlarged walk-in chimneys designed to allow women to heat bake ovens, cook, and smoke meat overhead with the wood of a single fire, had been designed to minimize wood use. They were also so dangerous and unhealthy that they had fallen from favor in the Old Country. It had never entered Hanneke's mind to wonder if a *schwartze Küche* had been built here in the New World, certainly not in the house Fridolin had spoken of. No wonder he had wanted money to build a summer kitchen.

Another lie of omission.

But it hadn't *all* been lies. The woods, the space, the fertile soil…the abundance was staggering.

"I could tend it," Hanneke whispered to a large gray squirrel scrambling up a nearby tree. She stared toward the garden, remembering the promise now hidden beyond the fence. She would move the compost pile farther from the porch, and take a scuffle-hoe to the weeds, and mulch the strawberry patch with marsh hay. It was time to set out lettuces, tomatoes, eggplants. She'd brought seeds for her favorite watermelons and muskmelons, and it wasn't too late to get them into the ground. She'd plant squash… move the asparagus so the plants would get more sun…set out bee skeps…add a cheery marigold border to help keep beetles from the broccoli.

Hanneke felt a searing heat beneath her ribs that made it hard to breathe. She'd dreamed of this farm for a long time, imagining little ways to make it her own. But she would not pluck weeds from the garden, or sweep dirt from the porch, or anything else. Oh, Fridolin, she thought. Surely, *surely*, you could not have been so cruel as to promise me this, and not mean it. What did you do? And why did you do it? *Why?*

Fridolin did not choose to send an answer from the heavens. The birds that had scolded her entry into the woods went about their business of securing food and shelter for another day.

Hanneke sat…and faced the hard truth. If she proved her case, Christine might find herself with nothing. I would not cast Christine out with no means! Hanneke thought. But there was likely nothing she could say to induce Christine to believe that and help her.

As if summoned by thought, Christine appeared in the driveway beside the house, walking toward the road. She'd again put on that beautiful black bonnet with ruching and flowers expertly crafted from silk ribbon. The long mourning veil flowed down her back, and a shorter one covered her face. Hanneke had chosen not to wear black crepe for her parents, for a single drop of rain or perspiration made the fabric shed its dye, staining the wearer's skin. But Christine obviously cared about proprieties and fully expressing her loss. She walked with her head down. Everything about the woman's posture spoke of immense sadness.

Hanneke held her breath. Christine walked past without glancing up and was quickly out of sight. Was she headed to a neighboring farm? To Watertown?

It's not your business, Hanneke told herself. She needed to return to Watertown herself. There was nothing to be gained by sitting and lamenting the farm Fridolin had promised her. It simply would not do.

She waited a few minutes more, giving Christine time. But when Hanneke finally stood, the world wobbled and she put her hand on a tree trunk to steady herself. She should have slipped some bread and cheese into her pocket before leaving the tavern that day. If nothing else, she needed water.

Well, Christine was gone. There must be a well in the farmyard. Surely no one could begrudge her a drink. Hanneke left the woods, crossed the road, and walked down the drive to the farmyard.

She was met by a *Vierkanthof*—a four-cornered square formed by out-buildings. There was a *fachwerk* stable on the west side. At the back stood a huge *Scheune*—a grain barn built of weather-silvered planks and thatched with straw. On the eastern edge, an abandoned foundation was surely the start of her summer kitchen. This *Vierkanthof* was also very Germanic, but in an apparent nod to Wisconsin's immense space, the buildings didn't connect at the corners.

Two hogs dozed in a muddy wallow. An ox and several sheep grazed in a fenced field beyond the stable. Cotswold sheep, Hanneke noted—large animals with fleece that, when shorn, could be combed into a lovely worsted roving. Cotswold wool was so strong that she sometimes added it to merino wool when knitting the heels and toes of socks.

The rest of the farm was surrounded by grain fields. One field was already dotted with tidy rows of green—probably winter wheat sowed last fall. The rest were barren. Beyond the fields, woods.

Hanneke oriented herself. Besides the Steckelbergs, Fridolin had written of other neighbors along Plum Grove Road. He had not mentioned John Barlow, even though the deputy sheriff had said his land abutted Fridolin's. The Barlow place must be north, beyond the field and forest, fronting another road. Thanks to the sheltering bulk of Fridolin's grain barn, the narrow woodlot, and geography, it was unlikely that Barlow might glance from his labors and spy Hanneke in Christine's farmyard.

The well was off to one side, with a dipper hanging from the housing. The cool water tasted of minerals. Hanneke felt better after slaking her thirst. All right, then. She should head back to Watertown.

Except she didn't. She stood staring at the tidy green rows of knee-high wheat in the field. She didn't know who would harvest that grain, but Fridolin had planted it. Fridolin. Her dead husband.

She glanced toward the *Scheune*. A ramp led to its main entrance, double doors wide enough to permit a farmer to drive his team onto the threshing floor. Those doors were closed and no doubt barred from within, but a smaller entrance was situated to their right.

Fridolin had died in that building.

Hanneke walked toward the barn. One of Christine's geese ran forward, hissing and beating its wings. Hanneke flapped her skirt at the bird. "You," she said, "are the least of my worries." The goose gave ground.

The small door was not locked. Hanneke slipped inside. As her eyes adjusted to the dim light, she inhaled the familiar sweet-musty smell of straw and hay. She poked her head into a small granary where barrels and sacks held threshed oats and wheat and rye, and a few tools had been piled in one corner. Then she moved on.

The threshing floor bisected the barn, separating two big storage bays. The west bay held a few piles of straw, probably forked there by Fridolin, and a butchering cauldron, a plow, and some other odds and ends. Bundles of last year's wheat still lay piled knee-high in the east-side bay—far more than one would expect to find in an industrious farmer's barn in May. Or even in March, when Fridolin had died.

But...*oh*. The central threshing floor itself was not empty. Why under Heaven had Christine not asked someone to clear the floor? A worn tarpaulin lay on the floor, loosened sheaves of wheat still spread in a circle on top. A flail lay nearby. A farmer might have simply stepped away from his task for a moment, pausing to wipe his forehead or take a drink of switchel. But that wasn't what had happened here.

Hanneke pressed one fist against her stomach, fighting a lurch of nausea. She imagined Fridolin working here, building a rhythm. Swing, beat, step. Swing, beat, step. Swing, beat...*what*? What had happened?

She stepped closer, crouched, studying the tarpaulin. Fridolin must have circled the stalks at least once, for some wheat kernels beaten from the stalks now lay with bits of chaff, waiting to be scooped up and winnowed. Did he do the winnowing too, or had Christine helped? A winnowing tray waited off to one side, made of wood and wide as a man's arm spread. Not even a fanning mill? Winnowing would have been a heavy task for Christine Bauer.

Hanneke picked up the flail gingerly, as if it might somehow strike her too. The staff was stout, with no cracks or other signs of structural weakness. The leather thong holding the two pieces together was sturdy, intact, and well-knotted. There was no chance that it had somehow given way, causing the flail head to lurch mid-swing.

Finally, she grasped the flail head with her other hand. The edges were dulled from use. A dark stain blotted the wood. She dropped the thing with a shudder.

Her disappointment was palpable. She realized how dearly she'd been clinging to the hope that Fridolin had not truly died in such a forlorn and absurd manner—that someone had managed to club Fridolin from behind while he was working.

Fridolin, she thought, *how did you manage to do this to yourself?*

He may have been relatively new to farming, but he'd owned the farm for two years. Anyone still threshing in March had spent a long winter whittling away at the huge chore. Threshers usually developed an even, almost hypnotic rhythm. She'd never heard of anyone injuring themselves in the process.

So, had something startled him? She looked around without spotting anything unusual. Anyone flailing grain alone on a March day would probably not open the big doors—only winnowing required wind—so it was unlikely that a bird had swooped through the breezeway. Perhaps a bird in the rafters had startled him? This afternoon, the rafters were empty of doves or swallows. The thatched roof looked unusually well-constructed—new, in fact, the golden rye stalks not yet weathered brown. Had some creature wriggled into the barn and startled Fridolin as he worked? Possible, Hanneke decided, but extremely unlikely.

So what had happened? *What?*

The air inside the barn felt too close, too thin. There was nothing for her here. She abruptly shoved to her feet, let herself out the small door, and crossed the yard. The goose made another run at her, neck weaving snake-like, but gave up as Hanneke strode toward the house.

She climbed the back steps without conscious forethought.

The door was, to her surprise, unlocked. Her skin tightened as she stood with hand on the latch, some measure of caution poking through. No one was in sight, but Christine might return at any time. If she found Hanneke inside, Deputy Sheriff John Barlow would surely do more than order her from town.

But this house should have been *hers*. She felt compelled to see exactly what she had lost; to look for something of Fridolin left behind.

Just a quick peek, Hanneke told herself. Very quick. Holding her breath, her pulse pounding at her temples, she stepped inside.

Chapter Nine

Once inside Hanneke stood for a moment, arms crossed tight over her chest, ears straining for any sign of Christine's return. The air smelled of smoke and onions, and held more chill than the farmyard. She shuddered with cold—or fear, or grief.

"Well, then," she whispered in the silence. "Get along with it."

A small bedroom was in the house's northwest corner on the ground floor. Hanneke briefly considered the neatly made bed with a blue-and-white woven coverlet, a Sunday dress of blue silk hanging on a peg beside two work dresses, one of cotton and one of wool. Four exquisite bonnets sat on top of the wardrobe. The needlework on display—a motto stitched on punched paper hanging on the wall, a crocheted silencer embracing the nightjar lid, *C.B.* embroidered on the pillowcases—was adequate, but not of the caliber of those bonnets.

Moving on, she stepped inside the huge central chimney. The bake oven was empty. A few coals glowed in the cooking pit beneath a cast-iron kettle dangling from a trammel hook. Smoke still hazed the chamber, stinging Hanneke's eyes. Countless fires had blackened the interior bricks, and several salted hams hung overhead. Hanneke regretted the impulse to enter the *schwartze Küche*. The stink of stale smoke would cling to her hair and clothing.

Besides, if there was any clue to Fridolin's secrets to be found, she wouldn't find it inside the chimney.

Hanneke retreated and shut the black kitchen door. She peeked out the windows again. No one was in sight.

She learned from a skillet in the kitchen area that Christine had recently eaten sausage and potatoes. Two plates sat in the dry sink, waiting to be washed, suggested less than ideal housekeeping. The partial loaf of wheat bread remaining was high and good-textured and a perfect golden-brown—not easy to accomplish in a brick bake oven, Hanneke noted with grudging respect. That bread, and the lone sausage and handful of fried potatoes left in the cold skillet, were so enticing that Hanneke's hand twitched. But I am not yet a thief, she thought. She slid her hand into her knitting pocket, taking comfort from the soft wool.

Further survey indicated that Christine wore wooden clogs when doing outside chores, that she had made wine and sauerkraut and apple vinegar last autumn, that she had enough time and energy to keep her kitchen shelves tidy but not enough to keep them dusted. About Fridolin, Hanneke learned nothing.

A trapdoor in the floor of a small pantry probably led to a storage cellar. Hanneke darted to the back door and listened again—silence. She hurried back to the pantry, heaved the door open, and started down the steps. Her mouth felt cotton-dry and she tried to force away the image of Christine Bauer returning to find her rummaging in the cellar.

There was little to rummage through, actually: some empty barrels that smelled of old potatoes, a few bins holding wrinkled carrots and kohlrabi and onions, a few rugs rolled up and stored against one wall, a couple of tin pails. She climbed back to the main floor and eased the heavy trap door back in place.

Two rooms fronted the house, a large workroom and a sparsely furnished parlor. The workroom showed evidence of Christine's handiwork: a sampler on the wall, a spinning wheel, and a table spread with pieces of glossy silk, spools of ribbon, a roll of heavy buckram. Hanneke poked through a wooden sewing box holding thread, buttons, bits of lace wrapped around blue cardboard, packets of needles. A high shelf held crocks and labeled bottles. Starch, and sulfur for bleaching linen. Oxalic acid and cream of tartar for removing black stains that damp mourning veils left on skin.

There were dyestuffs too: black walnut, logwood, madder, quercitron...

84

Hanneke had only read about quercitron, a dye made from the bark of an American oak tree. But many of the others were familiar from her own experience of preparing mordants and dyes for her knitting. Her knowledge of dyestuffs came from books and from trial and error. She'd often wished for a friend who shared her interest—someone to talk with about making color fast or what produced the richest hues.

I might have found that friend in Christine, Hanneke thought. If Fridolin had been honest with us both, and given us a chance....

A muffled shout sounded through the window. She flattened herself against one wall, heart thudding wildly, and dared a peek. A man and a boy were driving a team of oxen down the road. She held her breath until the lumbering animals and their tenders disappeared.

In the front parlor, Hanneke quickly scanned a tiny woodstove, a daybed, two wooden chairs beside a table, a shelf with a Bible and several books—nothing unusual. She turned hopefully to a small desk. An oil lamp sat on one corner; an inkwell, pen, and penwiper rested on the blotter beside an account book. Surely this was Fridolin's handiwork! The front cover was tooled in a handsome design, and the inside binding stitched from marbled paper. Several pages had been filled with slanted, narrow script: *Received from Anna Schmidt, $3.50, for one spring bonnet; spent, $1.76 for three plumes, thread, and a yard of cream-colored lace.* Another page contained recipes for dyeing feathers, silk, and cotton.

Ah. No wonder Christine's bonnets were exquisite. She was a professional bonnet maker.

Beneath the account book were two sheets of paper. The first was a notice in draft form.

> *Miss Christine Bauer, Fashionable Milliner,*
> *And ~~Flowerist~~ Artificial Flowerist*
> *~~Would like to inform~~ Respectfully informs the ladies of Watertown*
> *That ~~she is ready her services~~ she will create*
> *the latest and most Fashionable Styles*
> *Of straw, silk, and lawn, Hats,*

> *together with ribbons, ~~flowers, leaves~~ and a general assortment of*
> *Milliner's goods,*
>   *and a great variety of French and American Flowers.*

That's exactly what I would do, Hanneke thought. After the loss of my financial protector, I would take pains to build up my business. She picked up the second paper.

> *For Sale – ~~Eighty acres of~~ Fertile farm, eighty acres, on Plum Grove*
> *Road one hour north of Watertown. Ten acres cleared. Stable, threshing*
> *barn, ~~summer kitchen~~ room for additional outbuildings. Livestock*
> *(oxen, 14 Cotswold sheep, 2 hogs, 6 geese) can be included in terms.*
> *House constructed ~~with~~ in Pomeranian manner.*

Hanneke felt a dropping sensation in the pit of her stomach. Christine was selling the farm that Fridolin had described with hope and pride. The farm where Hanneke had planned to plant dahlias wherever she wished, and design her own kitchen garden; to scrub her own floors, raise her own sheep and geese, sit by her own fire on cool evenings. The place where she had planned to make a home, raise children, care for her husband. *I think we'll do well enough, you and I.*

Obviously, Christine and Fridolin had barely managed to scrape by; there was no way Christine could manage alone. Hanneke knew she was a fool not to have considered that. Still, she had not.

Fridolin left this farm to me! Hanneke thought. But the will found after his death had been an old one, and it would take months to get a response from her letters to Treptow. If Christine sold the farm before those responses arrived, it would be *very* difficult to get it back.

Hanneke felt something ratchet up between her ribs, as if someone was winding an internal clock. *Hurry! Hurry! Hurry!* She needed to find the truth behind Fridolin's secrets—*before* Christine could sell the farm.

But...what will you do then? Hanneke asked herself. Turn Christine out on the street?

Hanneke considered the two pages in her hand. How desperate was Christine? Things couldn't be *too* bad, for she had not written cross-wise when drafting her two advertisements—filling a page with cramped writing, then turning it sideways and writing over it again to save paper. Perhaps Fridolin had brought an ample supply of paper from his bookbinder job, for Christine hadn't even used the backs of the pieces of paper. And the ink was a glossy black.

Black. Hanneke's forehead furrowed. She picked up the glass inkwell and held it in front of the window: pitch black. Quickly, she opened the three small desk drawers. No other inkwells.

Now, that was odd.

The desk also held another small ledger where Christine kept household accounts—also in black ink. Hanneke skimmed the recent entries for groceries, a haircut and shave, a new ax, toothache medicine purchased from a druggist, six yards of calico.

Having completed the ground-floor circle around the central chimney, Hanneke found herself beside the back door again. She'd found few signs of Fridolin, informative or otherwise—no clothes or personal effects. Had Christine already cleared them out? Or... Hanneke contemplated the stairs that led to the second floor.

Once again, she made a quick circle of the house, peering furtively out the windows. The road was deserted. Hanneke picked up her skirts and hurried upstairs.

The air smelled musty with rodent nests and old fruit. Round slices of dried apple and squash hung on knotted strings dangling from the rafters, protected from flies by flimsy muslin drapes. On one side of the big chimney, Hanneke found a chair with a broken leg and several large trunks. The only trunk that wasn't empty held what appeared to be tools of Fridolin's former trade: stitching machine and trimmer, a variety of stamps for decorating leather covers, several long-handled finishing wheels, scissors, awls, pens, stacks of plain and marbled paper, a flat bone likely used for creasing. Hanneke gently closed the trunk, imagining Fridolin's feelings as he watched new machines take over the work he had so painstakingly mastered.

On the other side of the chimney, a low daybed stood against the western wall by the single small window. And—there, Fridolin's prized possession, a small telescope.

A pair of maroon slippers sat beside the bed. A silk top hat hung from a peg, good quality, but so worn that the brim showed a dull spot right where his thumb and knuckle would have pinched each time he tipped his hat. She touched the spot with a gentle finger, picturing Fridolin smiling politely to friends and acquaintances on the street.

A low table held a pair of reading glasses, a prayer book, a candle, a *meerschaum* pipe, a folded copy of the German-language newspaper. She also found an English-language magazine and was satisfied when she was able to translate the title: *The Wisconsin Farmer.* She flipped to several pages that had been flagged. Fridolin's interests had ranged from *Twenty-Four Best Varieties of Apples for Orchard Culture* to *The Value of Carrots for Milch Cows.* He'd also flagged an advertisement for *J.H. Manny's Patent Adjustable Reaper & Mower Combined.* Apparently, Hanneke thought, Fridolin had indeed dreamed of mechanizing the farm. She wished they could have discussed that dream together.

Hanneke had grown up on a farm. Since her only brother to survive childhood had no interest in agriculture, and she *did*, her father had taught her what he knew about raising crops and livestock. He'd encouraged her to read widely as well, and the unusual upbringing had left her often feeling somehow apart from other girls. After her father's death, when Hanneke had moved into Theodor and Minnie's house in Treptow, neighbor-women came to trust her advice about curing children's earaches or treating mastitis in goats. They did not, however, develop close friendships. Hanneke had thought that she'd found such a friend in Fridolin—someone as curious about the world as she was.

Now she willed away a fresh wave of loss. Then she turned to the final page with the corner folded down…and found herself staring at an illustration titled *Full Blood Merino Sheep, Imported From France.* In one margin he'd penciled an *H,* and circled it.

She sank onto the edge of the daybed. He'd remembered her favorite breed of sheep.

Her throat felt thick, and she pressed the magazine against her bodice. This attic corner had been Fridolin's place—the place where he'd thought of the wife he'd left in Pomerania. Hanneke imagined him settling down after a weary day of farm labor, perhaps even after a convivial evening with his sister…. Or had he and Christine not gotten on well? I'll never know, Hanneke thought. She replaced the magazine.

The bedside table had one drawer, and she eased it open. Her throat thickened as she stared at a volume of Annette von Droste-Hülshoff's poetry. She had given it to Fridolin before he left Treptow.

Two weeks they'd had between meeting and marrying. Just two. They'd both been shy at first. Often Theodor or Minnie was with them, and conversation was polite and superficial. But on the occasions when they'd been able to go for a stroll, or when he sat on the garden bench while she weeded her herb plants, how they'd talked! Even debated, at times. He'd challenged her to defend her beliefs, but never with rancor, whether the topic was inconsequential or of profound importance. They both abhorred the notion of slavery, and the recent Wisconsin law that demanded that citizens help return any runaways they encountered, but disagreed about the most effective strategies for bringing relief to the poor. (She argued for government-provided work, while he advocated taxing landowners to build poor farms.) Fridolin believed they should sow only wheat in Wisconsin, but she wanted to grow some rye for their own use. (*It's less laborious to grow*, she'd argued, *and is much heartier!*) Fridolin believed that Johann Wolfgang von Goethe was the greatest German writer; she assured him that he must read von Droste-Hülshoff's work before making that assertion. To be sure he did, she'd purchased a copy at the bookseller's stall on market day. "Something to read on the journey," she'd said, and his eyes had twinkled with pleasure.

And he kept it, she thought now. That knowledge was a comfort.

Still, it was dangerous to linger here. Resolutely she set the book aside to see what else had been tucked into the drawer. She found a ribbon of red, gold, and black, printed with the words *American Turnverein, Milwaukee,* on top of some papers. Hanneke was familiar with the organization, which promoted physical activity and camaraderie. Fridolin's apparent membership, however, was much less important than the correspondence stacked in the drawer. Letters! Three of them, still in their envelopes, addressed to *Fridolin Bauer, Watertown, Wisconsin*.

She slid one free and hastily scanned the cramped lines. A friend from the Old Country had written of the weather, a good harvest, a sick aunt. Nothing helpful there. The second, also written in German, seemed to be from a friend looking for advice about immigrating. Where should he settle? Was Wisconsin too crowded? Were land prices too dear? What should he bring; what should he leave behind? No help there, either.

The third letter was short and written in English. Hanneke squinted, struggling to make out at least some of the words. *Dear Fridolin...Milwaukee... mail....* Oh! Hanneke sucked in her lower lip with vexation. It was maddening not to know what—

A man's voice came from the drive below the gable window.

Hanneke jerked away from the window and dropped to the floor. She heard the back door open below. Christine's voice drifted up the stairs: "Yes, I'm just getting home. I would be grateful to have more firewood chopped."

Hanneke's skin went clammy with sweat. Her heart pounded like a runaway horse. *Gott in Himmel,* she had lingered too long and now Christine *would* find her, Christine and her hired hand or helpful neighbor or *whoever* he was, and they'd summon Deputy Sherriff John Barlow who would arrest her and put her in jail, and—

Stop! Hanneke ordered herself, just before rising panic burst free in a sob. Be calm. Be still. You haven't been caught. Not yet. She waited, holding her breath, cheek pressed against the loft floor, wondering if she had left anything amiss downstairs, anything that might give Christine alarm.

No outcry came, no angry footsteps on the stairs. Eventually, Hanneke began breathing again. She heard an ax splitting wood, sometimes banging the length when the blade got stuck. Well, then. She was probably safe. Fridolin had been dead for two months and Christine had not found the emotional strength to pack away his belongings, so it was unlikely she'd be inspired to do so now. And chances were at least fair that she would not decide she needed the last of autumn's dried apples or squash for supper.

I just need to wait her out, Hanneke told herself. Sooner or later, Christine would leave the house again.

For a while, that idea kept her calm. As the minutes—or was it hours?—crept by, though, the bizarre blend of anxiety and boredom left her damp-hot and shiver-cold in alternating swings. Her mouth felt dry as hackled flax. She needed to use an outhouse or nightjar. One of her legs began to cramp. Worst of all, dust on the floor tickled the back of her throat, her nostrils. Hanneke clenched her teeth. A sneeze, a creaking floorboard—either would lead to disaster.

She tried to distract herself by focusing on other things. Really, Christine was a mediocre housekeeper. Mouse droppings were visible beneath the table. Several blobs of wax as well, as if Fridolin had once blown out his candle with unnecessary force. Furry balls of dust had taken up residence in the crack between floor and wall. And what was that, lodged behind one table leg? A flat disc, tan—a cheap wooden token of some sort. No telling how long it had been there.

Just as there was no telling how long she would have to lie on the floor staring at it. The frenzied fear ebbed, leaving room for recrimination. How could she have acted in such a shameful manner? I should just march downstairs and confess my sins to Christine, she thought.

But she didn't. Instead, she watched an oblique diamond of light from the gable window creep across the floor. She might have even dozed, only to jerk to wakefulness by another murmur of conversation from below, or a clank of sound. Was Christine fixing supper for her guest? The smell of fresh wood smoke drifted to the attic, and sometime later the unmistakable aromas of frying bacon and coffee. Hanneke's stomach growled with longing. She went rigid again, afraid that the audible evidence of her growing hunger had reached below, but there was no sign.

In fact, there was no sign of anything for a while. Then Hanneke heard a muffled thump, low voices. A few moments later the back door opened, slammed. Hanneke didn't dare move until she heard another burst of conversation. That had drifted through the gable window…hadn't it? Not through the floor?

Hanneke eased to her knees, clenching her teeth against the pain of cramped muscles. She peeked out the window and caught a glimpse of Christine and a man in a worker's clothes walking down the road, heading west. The man was probably a neighbor who'd stopped by to help out. Perhaps he was walking Christine to his home to visit his wife. Or…perhaps a bachelor farmer was already trying to make himself indispensable.

What does it matter? Hanneke thought as she scrambled stiffly to her feet. The urgency was back now, pounding in her brain: *Get out! Get out now!* Fridolin's third letter was still clenched in her hand, and she thrust it into her pocket. She grabbed the token and secreted it away as well. Then, limp with relief, she hurried across to the floor, down the stairs, to the back door—

Where she almost sagged to her knees. Christine had locked the house behind her.

Hanneke frantically rattled the door against the padlock outside. Then, "Stop it!" she muttered. She had to calm down.

She paused, then whirled. The front door! *You're a fool*, she scolded herself, as she ran back through the workroom. She remembered hearing Christine slide the latch before opening the door earlier.

But when Hanneke reached the door, she stared in horror at the padlock Christine had looped through the two door handles on the *inside*.

Hanneke was locked inside the house.

Chapter Ten

W hy on earth would Christine feel a need to add an interior padlock to the latches on the front doors? What was she so afraid of? "Me, probably," Hanneke muttered and felt a surge of hysterical laughter rising in her throat.

That would accomplish nothing. She cast about, trying to stave off panic.

Windows! Herr Jaeger had ringed the house with double six-over-six windows. They locked by a simple peg mechanism that would make raising the lower frame impossible from the outside.

Hanneke had one knee on the nearest window's sill when she paused. Herr Jaeger had also built his house so close to the road that both gable ends and the front were in clear view of any passersby. In the gloom of twilight, someone might walk quite close before she saw them.

All right, then. One of the back windows. She replaced the peg and ran to the kitchen area. There were two windows in the back wall…but a large dry sink was under one, and a cluttered table beneath the other. It would be impossible to exit through either of those windows without leaving clear evidence of her visit.

That left only the pantry. Herr Jaeger had cut a pass-through in the back wall, about waist height, to make it easy for Frau Jaeger to dump potatoes and onions and kohlrabi in from the garden, and from there take them down to the cellar.

Hanneke unhooked the simple latch and the door swung open. She tossed her reticule through, and her shawl and bonnet. Then she scrambled through herself. She landed hard, first on her hands, then on one hip. Pain stabbed through her ribs.

Someone had left a low garden stool against the back wall and Hanneke crawled onto it. Her body began shuddering violently, as if needing to rid itself of the long afternoon's worth of fear and upset. The blasted goose came running again, squawking. *"Go,* you stupid bird!" Hanneke hissed, so fiercely that the bird subsided.

Hanneke sat for a moment, hidden from the road by the garden fence, listening. Nothing but the goose's fading honks, and the whisper of a breeze through the wheat. Finally, she managed to stand. Her fingers trembled as she dusted off her skirt and straightened her clothing. Her cheeks felt flushed with humiliation and the fear of discovery. But she was *out*.

Hanneke shoved the pass-through door closed. She couldn't latch it again, but it stayed put. With any luck, Christine would simply think she had forgotten to hook the latch the last time she'd used it.

Then she walked quickly around the house and down the drive, striving to look as if she belonged there. She reached the road before anyone appeared. All she wanted to do was get far, *far* away from there, but her knees suddenly felt quivery as clabbered milk, and her stomach twisted with nausea.

Hanneke was ashamed of herself.

She plunged into the woods again, found the log she'd vacated...when? Hours earlier, certainly. It felt like days. It's not as if I have somewhere to go tonight anyway, she thought. And at least she hadn't been caught hiding inside like a thief. She imagined again that horrible scene: Christine summoning Deputy John Barlow, his disgust, the sound of the door to a jail cell clanging closed behind her.

A tiny voice somewhere inside answered: But if that had happened, you would have had a place to lay your head for the night. And perhaps a plate of bread and jam.

The relief Hanneke had felt plummeted into something darker, something approaching despair. She folded her arms on her knees, buried her head, and for quite some time tried not to think at all.

When she finally raised her head, twilight had deepened into full night. She sat quite still, letting her eyes adjust to the gloom, taking in the tiny rustles and flutters among the trees. She hadn't had occasion to experience true night since she'd arrived in Wisconsin. But on the ships...oh, there she had come to love the early dark hours.

She'd heard enough tales about ocean crossings to plan for her own trip across the Atlantic with little enthusiasm. To a large extent, the gloomy predictions were true. Her days onboard were tedious. The steerage hold was fetid with vomit and sweat and baby linens. Only two stoves were provided, and people waiting for their turn were sometimes so aggressive that she relinquished her chance to boil water for coffee or macaroni, and made do with zwieback and prunes and bits of the dried ham she'd brought. After two weeks at sea, the drinking water had gone so stale she could only sip it if doctored with white wine.

But the nights! Those Hanneke would remember with joy for all of her days. Sometimes she wished Fridolin was there to point out some of his favorite constellations. She remembered his voice tinged with wonder as they contemplated the glittering canopy of stars one chilly night shortly before their marriage.

But there were other distractions at sea. The few Yankees on board kept to themselves so the Germans gathered to sing hymns and old folk songs to the accompaniment of guitars and harmonicas and even an accordion. When a quartet from Schleswig-Holstein performed, even the ship's captain lingered in the shadows. Sometimes the sailors chimed in with their own jaunty songs. On these evenings Hanneke wrapped in her warm cloak and soaked it all in, knowing that this time at sea was like no other.

And sometimes she had dared to wonder if her deepest, most secret desire was this freedom—to be not beholden to father or brother *or* husband.

Now, sitting in the woods like a common beggar, having trespassed into Fridolin's farm, endured the agony of narrowly escaping detection, and debasing herself by crawling through a vegetable pass-through, she felt quite differently. She had spent a lifetime preparing to be a respectable wife and mother, to tend a farm. She'd believed that she had finally found what she'd yearned for. And it was all gone.

Eventually, she stood and made her way back to the road. The house was largely dark, but a soft light glowed from the workroom. Christine had returned.

Hanneke turned away from the house. A chill was creeping into her bones, and her stomach cramped with hunger, but there was nothing to do but to walk back to Watertown. The moon was waxing, and the road shone pale among the shadows. Perhaps she could creep into Angela's stable and sleep there. Surely Adolf wouldn't mind. She set out: past the fields, through the woods west of the Bauer farm. The going was a bit harder there, and a little spooky with the rustlings of unknown New World creatures in the underbrush.

She was almost through the woods when a tiny light pricked the night somewhere ahead. She froze, but the light disappeared. Without the hushed thrum of her own footsteps, though, Hanneke heard a whisper of a new sound. *Thud-thud-thud.* Pause. *Thud-thud-thud.* Pause. She recognized the sound, but it made no sense. Perhaps I *am* losing my wits, Hanneke thought.

As she crept from the woods' gloom the light blinked back again, then coalesced in the field near the road—a candle shining from within a glass-sided lantern. A shadowed figure nearby was bent with the work of hoeing: strike-strike-strike, step, strike-strike-strike. A sound and cadence as familiar to Hanneke as, well, flailing grain. But who would work his field at such an hour? Certain urgent chores demanded moonlit work—harvesting or haying, especially if rain threatened—but hoeing was usually not one of them.

Before Hanneke could puzzle that further, a dog leapt to its feet with one sharp bark. The worker straightened at once. "Hush!" A woman's voice, stilling the dog. They were a good distance away from the dark house and outbuildings, but she kept her voice low as she faced the road and called, "Is someone there?"

"*Ja*," Hanneke called, matching the woman's tone. "My name is Hanneke Bauer—"

"*Bauer?*"

Hanneke drummed one fist against her thigh with frustration.

The worker dropped her hoe, picked up the lantern with one hand and her skirt with the other, and made her way to the edge of the field and lifted her lantern. "You're that woman."

Hanneke returned the perusal with as much dignity as she could summon. "My name is Hanneke."

"You're the one claiming to be married to Fridolin."

"And you must be Clara Steckelberg. Fridolin told me that the Steckelbergs were his closest neighbors to the west. You and your husband married... what, a year ago? Two? A second marriage for you both."

"Anyone could have told you that."

"Fridolin also said that your sour cream-apple pie is the crowning glory of every harvest supper. And that he once borrowed a scythe from your husband when his own blade snapped mid-harvest. By the way, is your husband well? He was struggling with a cough when Fridolin last wrote. February, that was."

Clara Steckelberg put the lantern on the ground. She was stocky, with stooped shoulders. Hanneke felt some grim satisfaction as she watched the older woman digest what she'd heard.

"All that suggests that you knew Fridolin," Frau Steckelberg said finally. "It doesn't prove that he *married* you."

"No. But he did."

"I heard you went back to Milwaukee."

"Obviously I have not."

The hound poked his nose at Hanneke, sniffing violently as if to say, *Who on earth is she?* Frau Steckelberg shifted her weight from one foot to the other. "What are you doing out here at this time of night?"

It felt surreal to be interrogated in the moonlit world of dark and darker shadows. "I walked from town this afternoon because I wanted to speak to Christine Bauer. I did not come to upset her, but only to try to get some idea of why Fridolin would marry me without mentioning his sister to me, or me to her."

"Did Christine give you any answers?"

"No. She's as shocked and bewildered as I am."

The woman folded her arms. "If Christine didn't give you the time of day, why are you still about?"

"After Christine turned me away, I found a log in the woods across from her farm and sat. For quite a long time. I don't even know how long. Being there...actually seeing the farm I'd heard so much about, been dre—" Hanneke stopped abruptly; she would not confide her dreams to this woman. "It was a bit overwhelming. So I sat, and thought, and grieved. Now I am walking back to Watertown." All of which was true, but.... Another lie of omission, she thought. How easy it was to do, once one got started. Had it been that way for Fridolin?

"Hmmn." Clara Steckelberg absently scratched her dog's head. An owl called from the woods.

"You were his closest neighbor...did you notice anything odd about Fridolin's behavior in the past months? Anything unusual? Anything that might make a man act as he did?"

"As you *say* he did."

Hanneke almost turned around then, too tired to argue. But something held her still, waiting. Some last slim hope that Frau Steckelberg might have something helpful to share.

Finally, the older woman said reluctantly, "Well, I guess there's no harm in saying that there have been some strange goings-on over at the Bauer place."

Somewhere deep inside, Hanneke felt a butterfly burst from its cocoon.

"I've seen men coming and going at all hours of the night," Frau Steckelberg muttered. "Sometimes on foot. Sometimes in a wagon. Once or twice on horseback. Never with a lantern, even on moonless nights."

Hanneke kept her voice even. "Do you know who thevisitors might have been?"

"No. And I didn't ask Fridolin or Christine either. I don't want my own husband to know how much time I spend out here at night. But that's why I started bringing the dog out with me. And I've a pistol in my pocket."

Something iced down Hanneke's spine. She tried to take measure of Frau Steckelberg's expression, but the lantern at her feet threw long, hideous shadows that made that scrutiny impossible. "Well," Hanneke said lightly, "perhaps they were just travelers."

"Not likely. Plum Grove Road doesn't go anywhere to account for that much travel."

"Is it possible that political meetings were being held somewhere out this way?" Hanneke asked, thinking of the big threshing barn where Fridolin had died. A hundred men could sit inside; if the doors were closed, no one would be the wiser. "Germans gathering to discuss the rise of these Know-Nothings I've heard about?"

"Could be," the older woman allowed, but her tone was grudging. "Although I haven't heard about it."

"Ah. Not likely, then," Hanneke murmured. But she wasn't convinced. Might Fridolin have been bludgeoned by a Know-Nothing who despised him for being German? Or...might Fridolin have argued for moderation in the German response to the spread of hateful nativisim, and angered some zealot determined to pursue a violent path?

Well, those were not questions for Clara Steckelberg. Hanneke brought her mind back to the moment. "Aren't you afraid, then? Being out alone at night when strangers are skulking about?"

"No one's ever bothered me. If I'm near to the road and see someone, I always ask—as I did when I heard you. You're the first person to answer! Usually whoever it is starts to run, or kicks their horse up. Fools," she added, like a curse. "Their business may be their own, but they've no call to risk a good horse."

Hanneke turned all that over in her mind. Was Fridolin one of the men organizing the anti-Know-Nothing movement? She wanted very much to grab this woman's arm and plead, Please tell me everything you know about Fridolin Bauer. *Everything*. I know so little, and you know so much.

"I need to get back to work," Frau Steckelberg said. "Even I need *some* sleep."

"Yes, of course," Hanneke murmured. "I've been selfish to keep you from it. I thank you for your time. And your kindness."

"You're...welcome." Frau Steckelberg sounded startled.

Hanneke wondered again what picture had been painted of her. She'd surely been depicted as brazen. Greedy. A liar, and a potential thief. Perhaps worse. And perhaps, she thought, I have become all of those things.

"If you've been out from town since midday...are you hungry?"

The very word made moisture spring to Hanneke's tongue. "A bit."

Frau Steckelberg wiped her hands on her sleeves, reached into her pocket. "I always bring a snack with me. It's not much, just a piece of *kuchen*."

Hanneke accepted it gratefully. *Kuchen.* She broke off a chunk, careful to catch the crumbs, and popped it into her mouth. The pastry was light with wheat flour, topped with crunchy crystals of sugar that perfectly complemented the tart goodness of diced rhubarb.

She was poised to gobble the slice whole, but at the last moment she paused, broke what was left in two, and handed half back. "Why don't we share."

The women stood in silence, savoring simple pleasures: a bit of food, clear skies, an unexpected moment of companionship. Hanneke felt something in the air between them change. Suspicion had been replaced...if not with trust, then with at least a vague sense of normalcy.

"Might I ask," she dared, "why you are out here so late? It sounds as if you often do field chores by moonlight."

Frau Steckelberg shrugged. "My husband is a good man. A good husband. But he is a Latin farmer."

"You mean...he was not born to it." Hanneke wondered if Charles Steckelberg had been one of the men in the Buena Vista the day she arrived

"No. He was a professor of classic literature in Prussia, and left after the troubles in '48. Now he spends half of his time arguing the merits of some translation or whatnot with a few of the other displaced men, and the rest of it here, trying to earn a living." She made a small gesture toward the field. "I haven't read the books he so treasures, but I know how to farm."

"I see."

"Charles does not want me to do fieldwork." Frau Steckelberg's tone was both rueful and proud. "And I don't want to cause him any concern. I've reached an age where sleep often doesn't come easily, so...."

"You come outside and do what needs doing."

"*Ja*," Frau Steckelberg said simply. "I often come out after dark to fix...

well, to do chores."

Would it have been such with Fridolin and me? Hanneke wondered. By all accounts, Fridolin had struggled to prosper as a farmer. If he'd lived, would she have started creeping outside at night to correct his mistakes too?

Clara Steckelberg gestured broadly. "Charles thinks we're done here. He thinks the only purpose of plowing is to kill weeds and so create a seed bed for sowing."

Hanneke nodded. "He doesn't understand the soil."

A quick flash of white in the shadow may have been a smile. "Exactly!"

"I've always believed," Hanneke said, "that the best preparation for seeding is to pulverize the soil."

"Yes indeed! Good soil is *loose*."

"We have to allow for air circulation—"

"And water—"

"And a texture that makes it easy for the tiniest roots to grow," Hanneke finished.

Frau Steckelberg nodded. "Tonight Charles was exhausted by sundown, and he sleeps like the dead. So I came out to work at the clods."

Hanneke smiled—and realized, with a start, that for a moment she had actually forgotten recent events. Clara and I would have been friends, she thought. If things were different, Clara and I might have become great friends. She imagined them sharing work, sometimes at one farm and sometimes at the other; whispering affectionately about their husbands' foibles; debating the merits of this seed or that tool over cups of steaming black coffee and warm, fragrant *kuchen*—

From the woods came a sudden huge ruffle of sound—wing beats, two short squeaks. The dog shot silently into the blackness.

Something just died, Hanneke thought. The moment of camaraderie did too. She and Clara Steckelberg were no longer destined to become friends. "*Danke schön*. I'm grateful for the *kuchen*. It was good to meet you, but I must let you get back to work now."

She'd started walking when Clara said, "Wait."

Hanneke turned around.

"I think...I think I should tell you," Clara began, sounding hesitant for the first time, "that things...well, things aren't always what they appear."

Hanneke's skin prickled. "I've found that to be true," she said carefully. "Are you referring to something that has to do with Fridolin?"

Frau Steckelberg had picked up her hoe, and now she twisted the handle in her hands. "I don't know if you're telling the truth about your wedding or not. But if you *did* marry Fridolin Bauer, well, I'll just say that you may be better off without him."

"What do you know?" Hanneke asked urgently. "What haven't you told me?"

"Strangers aren't the only people slinking about at night. I've also seen Fridolin."

Hanneke stifled the urge to grab Clara Steckelberg by the shoulders and shake her. "What do you mean?"

"From the direction he was heading, Fridolin Bauer wasn't heading toward any political meeting." Clara sounded disgusted. "He was headed toward a woman."

Chapter Eleven

ock-a-doodle-do!

C Hanneke jerked upright and awake, blinking. Only the faintest wash of gray lightened the night's shadows. Her head felt fuzzy, her tongue as well. The air smelled musty with a sharp undertone, like manure. She was sitting in straw....

The rooster crowed again from his perch on top of the stall wall. Ah. *Ja.* She had, at Clara's invitation, spent the remainder of the night in the Steckelberg stable. At the time, it had seemed like a gift from Heaven.

In the light of a dawning day, it felt like considerably less.

Hanneke pressed her palms over her face. Recent events flashed through her memory like some fiendish magic lantern picture show: sneaking into another woman's home, crawling through doors intended only for cabbages and turnips, sleeping in a stable like a cow. All to learn the truth about, and defend, her husband—a man who may have been spending time with another woman.

The night before, when Clara had insinuated that Fridolin had been engaged in something clandestine and inappropriate, Hanneke had been too stunned to respond. Fridolin Bauer! she'd thought. Are your sins against me even greater than I know? But Frau Steckelberg had refused to say more. "It's not my place to gossip. I just thought you should know that you may have had the wrong idea about Fridolin Bauer all along."

Now Hanneke thought, I simply cannot continue like this.

All she'd wanted to do was find the truth. With every effort, the answers became more elusive. And really, why should she keep trying? Fridolin was dead, and nothing she discovered could bring him back. Christine was going to sell the farm. It was time to give up.

Admitting failure left a bitter taste on her tongue, but the idea of leaving Watertown brought a physical flush of relief. Angela would be glad to see her go. Angela had also said she could arrange a ride to Milwaukee with a freight hauler. Once in the city, Hanneke could stay with Regina Gruber until she could find work and a room of her own. She would turn her back on Fridolin Bauer and his lies and empty promises. In time the frozen lump of grief and anger beneath her ribs would fade. At least a little.

With an effort, Hanneke roused herself. Lethargy simply would not do. Daylight was filtering through the cracks and Herr Steckelberg would soon be at his chores. She scrambled to her feet, slapping away bits of straw clinging to her dress. Her stomach growled in sympathy with her parched tongue and throat. As she tiptoed to the door her muscles felt stiff, her bruises felt sore, and her ribs ached. Tears stung her eyes when she saw, just inside the door, a pitcher of water covered with a heavy cloth and something rolled into a scrap of canvas. She swished the stale feeling from her mouth before drinking deeply, then splashed what was left of the cold water on her face. The canvas revealed two pieces of cold bacon and a thick slice of rye bread spread with goose grease.

She gobbled every crumb. Bless Clara Steckelberg.

Then Hanneke crept outside and darted—as Clara had directed—through the western field to Plum Grove Road, praying that Charles Steckelberg was lingering over his own breakfast. She waded into the woods so she could relieve herself unseen, then re-pinned her straggling hair into a knot behind her head. She grimaced, hoping she'd meet no one on the road before she could tidy herself. If I must wander homeless, Hanneke thought, I should at least tuck a toothbrush and hairbrush into my reticule.

She strode quickly, eager to leave Fridolin's farm far behind. She decided to leave Clara Steckelberg's supposition behind as well, for now, and focus on facts. *Something* mysterious was taking place along Plum Grove Road. Did those secretive nocturnal travelers Clara Steckelberg saw have anything to do with Fridolin's death? Perhaps, perhaps not, but Hanneke no longer felt safe wandering the near-deserted country roads alone.

By the time she reached Watertown, the morning's bustle was well underway. Her steps slowed as she made her way back through the city. Hearing voices or footsteps behind her made her skittish. She cringed away from workmen and gentlemen alike—even from an aggressive woman selling fresh fish from a basket. When footsteps pounded close behind her Hanneke's heart seemed to skip a beat. She whirled. *"Nein!"*

A young man skidded to a stop with an astonished look. He said something in a language she didn't recognize before sidling past, keeping her in view until he was out of reach, as if afraid she might attack him. A few moments later he caught up with another man. They greeted each other with claps on the back and the hearty laughs of old friends.

Hanneke stood still long after the two had disappeared. She scarcely noticed other pedestrians' annoyed glances as they swerved around her. Finally, she gave herself another mental shake. Her jittered anxiety only reinforced her decision to abandon the search and leave Watertown.

She walked briskly back to Angela's tavern and cut around to the back. She glanced first into the stable and saw her trunk and valise sitting exactly where Adolf had left them. She pressed one palm over her chest, taking one long, grateful breath, before turning to the tavern.

As Hanneke let herself in the back door, she called, "Angela? It's me…." Her voice trailed away. Something smelled scorched. Adolf was alone in the kitchen, stirring a boiling pot of oats over the stove. When he saw Hanneke he dropped the spoon. A string of emotions chased across his face—joy, relief, worry.

"Adolf?" Hanneke closed the door behind her. "What's wrong? Where's Angela?"

"She didn't come down this morning, and when I went upstairs I could hear her groaning—"

Dear *Gott*, Hanneke thought. The baby.

"—but when I knocked on the door she told me to go away, and when I asked if I should fetch a doctor, she wouldn't let me." Adolf ran out of air and sucked in his lower lip.

"I'll go up."

"What should I do?"

"Put a kettle of water on for tea," Hanneke tossed over her shoulder. "Fill the wood box. Add more water to the oatmeal. And wipe up the spill before that spoon mortars itself to the floor."

The second story was mostly unfinished storage space, with a trunk and a few odds and ends shoved beneath the eaves. A small room, obviously Angela's, had been partitioned off in the corner. Hanneke knocked softly on the closed door. "Angela? It's Hanneke. Adolf said you weren't feeling well."

A pause, then, "Come in."

Inside, Hanneke tried not to show her dismay. Angela lay on the bed. Her eyes seemed sunken. One hand lifted from the quilt in a gesture that seemed to indicate futility.

"Forgive me for intruding." Hanneke perched on a chair near the bed. "Adolf was worried."

Angela looked away. "I know. I didn't mean to...."

"What happened?" Hanneke looked around for any sign of miscarriage—bloody bedding, an ill-used nightjar. None of that.

"I had some pains in the night and some spotting."

Not good, Hanneke thought. "Are you still seeing blood?"

"No. This morning my back aches. Nothing more."

Tense muscles in Hanneke's shoulders began to unclench. "The best thing for you is bed rest, then. If you'll permit me, I'll bring up some hot tea and toast. And I'll make a boiled custard pudding for later."

Angela pleated the edge of the sheet. "I'd be grateful."

Hanneke started to rise, but a dawning sense of guilt made her reconsider. "Angela, I must beg your forgiveness. I know that my argument with Deputy Barlow upset you. I fear that had something to do with your distress."

"It may have. In the Old Country, my parents were terrified of the police. I admit I...well, I panicked when Barlow barged into my kitchen." Angela gave her a wan smile. "But I think I owe you an apology as well. The better part of my distress last night was caused by guilt. I was ashamed that I let you—*asked* you—to leave."

"You have nothing to feel ashamed of! I've brought you nothing but trouble in turn for your kindness."

"Hanneke…." Angela abandoned the sheet in favor of picking at a nubbin of yarn on the blanket. "I'd be most grateful if you'd stay. At least for a bit."

Stay. So much for going to Milwaukee. "For as long as you'd like," Hanneke managed, hoping her tone held more reassurance than hysteria.

Perhaps it did not, for a faint frown drew Angela's brows together.

Hanneke held up a hand. "For as long as you'd like," she repeated. "I appreciate the opportunity to make myself useful, especially since you absolutely must rest. Now, first things first. I'll be back with some hot tea."

Once in the hall, Hanneke leaned against the wall for a moment, pressing the pads of her fingers over her eyes. Then she went downstairs to make Angela's breakfast.

* * *

Within thirty minutes, Angela had consumed two cups of ginger tea, eaten some toast without ill effects, and drifted back to sleep. "I think she'll be all right," Hanneke told Adolf.

Patches of scarlet stained his cheeks. "And…did she lose…."

"The baby is fine, as far as I know," Hanneke said reassuringly. "I think she's been working too hard. And my problems—having Deputy Barlow arrive—well, that caused her anxiety." Her own cheeks flamed. "She's asked me to stay for a while, though."

Adolf ran a hand over his head, leaving hair sticking up and out in a startling variety of directions. "*Danke schön.* For coming back. And for helping. I didn't know what to do."

"You did fine. I'll certainly stay and help as long as I'm needed." Hanneke turned away, reaching for two bowls. She'd filled them both with oatmeal—which looked lumpy and unappetizing, actually, but she was hungry—and set them at the table. "Here. Have some breakfast. We'll both be better for a meal."

They ate in silence. Hanneke studied Adolf surreptitiously. What was the true nature of the relationship between Angela and Adolf? How old was he? No more than sixteen, she guessed, and possibly less. At least a decade younger than Angela. Surely he didn't….

Adolf caught her gaze. "She's been good to me." He seemed a bit defensive, as if worried that Hanneke might chide him. "I had one birth sister, but I lost her."

Hanneke sent uncharitable thoughts to the relatives who had taken in Adolf's sister, but not him.

"I got another sister in Angela," Adolf was saying. "I owe her a lot."

"She couldn't manage this place without you. I've seen it."

"She shouldn't be on her own," Adolf said, a sudden blade of anger in his voice. "Things were fine when Julius was here."

"Her brother."

Adolf nodded. "But he left. He said he was ashamed of her. Because of…." He studied his oatmeal, cheeks once again flaming. "You know."

Hanneke did know. Angela had gotten pregnant, and her brother had abandoned both his sister and his unborn niece or nephew. Hanneke hesitated, then asked, "What of the baby's father? Do you know—"

"*Nein.*" Adolf gripped his spoon so hard that his knuckles turned white. "She's never said. And I would never ask. But if I ever find out who left her this way…."

Hanneke stifled a sigh. Adolf had been kind to her, and he was devoted to Angela. She also suspected that Adolf might, if sufficiently aroused, explode like fireworks.

"Hanneke, I wanted to say that I'm sorry about what happened to you," he said, his flash of anger gone as quickly as it had come. "When you first came here, I didn't know. About Fridolin Bauer, I mean." He shrugged, as if unsure he should be mentioning her personal troubles. "I just thought you were like lots of other immigrants, who ran into money trouble before getting started. Like me. But after you left yesterday, Angela told me you and Fridolin Bauer had married, and—"

"I am trying to look forward now," Hanneke said firmly. "I tried to learn more about Fridolin 's death, but—"

"That's what I'm trying to tell you! I know people who were there."

"*What?*" Hanneke went very still. "Who?"

"Franz and Joe Rademacher. Franz is a bricklayer. Joe—he refuses to answer to Josef anymore—is a builder. They work together—a new smokehouse, chimney repairs, things like that."

"And?"

"Well, they were out at the farm the day Herr Bauer died. Franz and Joe came in here that night, and I heard something about it. I didn't pay any particular attention."

Something inside tightened like hemp twisting into rope. "Where can I find the Rademacher brothers?"

"Right this minute?" Adolf lifted both palms. "I don't know. They could be anywhere in the city. Or on any farm in the area."

"I see." Hanneke got up, wadded her apron to protect her hand, and opened the door to the stove's firebox. The fire was burning well but she added another small log anyway, needing a moment to quiet a surge of restless impatience. She needed to see these Rademacher brothers.

So much for abandoning her search for the truth.

"I'll keep watch out for them," Adolf promised. "I'm sure they won't mind talking to you."

"*Danke*. And...." She hesitated, not wanting to ruin this fragile moment. "There is one more thing you can do for Angela. She cares for you like a brother. And she worries for you. She's afraid that you'll get caught up in some kind of political trouble."

He scowled at the table. "Sometimes things must be done. There are men who brought the spirit of revolution with them from the Old Country. Those men will not let new oppressions beat them down."

Those sentiments were so clearly quotations that Hanneke's eyebrows rose. Adolf had been spending more time with the German activists than either she or Angela had realized. "You've joined, haven't you," she said slowly. "This secret organization of German men."

Adolf became fascinated with the cooked oats congealing in his bowl.

"Did you see Fridolin Bauer at any of the meetings?" Her voice grew sharp. "Was he one of the leaders? You must tell me!"

"I don't know! I didn't *know* him, you see. Just the name."

"*Ja,* of course." Fridolin the bookbinder-turned-farmer likely wouldn't have crossed paths with Adolf the orphan boy-turned-tavern worker.

"Besides…." Adolf looked chagrined. "I've only been invited to one meeting, and there were just a few of us. It was more about recruiting than planning anything."

"I don't think it's a good idea to—" Hanneke began, then swallowed her words when his face hardened into stubborn lines. "Can't you give things time to settle down? I'm afraid this dissension will lead to violence."

"The German men don't want violence," he insisted. "Some of them want to protect their language and laws and customs. A real democracy. They held a convention to talk about that, right here in Watertown, back in fifty-one. That was the year I arrived. Julius…well, Julius thought it was important to stand up to the nativists."

"What else can you tell me about this secret German society?"

"Nothing." Adolf got up and carried his bowl to the dry sink. "I'm not permitted to discuss it with anyone who isn't a member."

So, Hanneke thought, the leaders have opened their ranks to the peasants after all. The upper-class revolutionaries and political leaders had moved beyond plans and rhetoric and were marshaling their troops. She tried to picture the Fridolin she'd known as an agitator. The image didn't form. Had he been a recruit too?

Well, Adolf's situation was most pressing. Hanneke fixed the boy with a stern look. "Promise me two things. First, don't allow yourself to be caught up in something illegal or dangerous. And second, if you ever have reason to hear something about Fridolin from these men…*please,* don't keep it from me. I need to know."

"I won't," Adolf said, and Hanneke had to content herself with that.

Chapter Twelve

Hanneke had just finished cooking Angela's custard pudding when someone knocked on the back door. After wiping her hands on her apron she opened it to find a lean man with red hair. He wore workman's clothing, and had a pack basket slung over one shoulder. He whipped a limp hat from his head and smiled the hopeful smile of peddlers everywhere, Old World and New. "Good day, ma'am. I am Lorenz Kiessling, just *now* from the brewery with *top*-quality fresh liquid yeast, which is *essential* to a good rise. Use it in wheat bread and your customers will *swear* they're eating a cloud. *Just* a penny for half a pint. Can I interest you in—"

"I'm afraid not," Hanneke said, politely but firmly, and closed the door. A penny was more than she could spare. Customers would have to content themselves with the usual sourdough rye bread. The peddler's visit, however, served to remind her that in addition to caring for Angela, responsibility for managing the tavern loomed.

As a young woman, when her mother's health began to fail, Hanneke had taken charge of the household—planning meals, cooking and baking, keeping accounts. Occasionally—when neighbors gathered at their farm to harvest or thresh—she'd cooked meals for twenty or so men. Still, managing a tavern that served twice that many dinners each day, and sold beer as well, was another thing altogether.

When the dishes were dried and put away she took inventory in the pantry. Angela bought produce three times a week from a farmwife, and she ordered meat directly from a nearby butcher. Hanneke planned a dinner of smoked ham, pickled cucumbers, and dried apples stewed with tiny fresh strawberries and a bit of sugar. Adolf knew how much beer was consumed in an evening, and had already promised to handle the day's order.

Only when the kitchen floor was scrubbed, and several loaves of rye bread were set to rise near the stove in round straw baskets, did Hanneke put a coffeepot over the fire. While it heated she washed her face, brushed her teeth, and combed and re-pinned her hair. When the water started to simmer, she pulled the pot from the hottest burner, added a splash of cold water to settle the grounds, and poured herself a mug. The first sip was fortifying, the second almost bliss.

Adolf had hauled her luggage back into the spare room, and Hanneke fetched the blank book Fridolin had made for her. Since she apparently was not meant to flee Watertown after all, it was time to get back to work. And that meant bringing Fridolin into the process. Not the man she thought she'd known, the one she sometimes still turned to for comfort and sometimes berated with silent fury. But the real Fridolin. The man who no one, evidently, had known as well as they'd thought.

She pulled from her pocket the letter and token she'd taken from Fridolin's things and placed them on the table. The letter would have to wait until she had time to try to work through a translation, so she studied the token. It had been stamped with ".25" and the word "Adam's." She had no idea who Adam was, but the newspaper John Barlow had angrily thrown down the morning before was still on the counter. Hanneke retrieved it and pored over the ads and notices. She found only one relevant reference: *Gentlemen are reminded that a good haircut and shave can always be had at Adam's, on the Main Street bridge.*

All right, then. Hanneke opened her book to the list she'd made, and crossed out what she'd already accomplished.

~~Visit farm. Talk to Christine alone.~~
~~Return to Buena Vista, inquire who had opportunity to steal my papers~~
~~Talk with the physician who attended him.~~
~~Find death notice.~~
Talk with Fridolin's friends and neighbors.

112

I will continue to talk with Fridolin's acquaintances as they present themselves, Hanneke thought. She tapped her pencil against her cheek, trying to think of anyone else Fridolin had mentioned, anyone who might be willing to consider the situation more objectively. Perhaps his former employer in Milwaukee? Fridolin had spoken highly of the man, so they might have kept in touch. She didn't know his name, but she did know the name of his business. With luck that would be enough.

Stop at the post office and see if anyone responded to my notice in the newspaper.

She regretted the impulse that led to that notice. It had brought John Barlow to Angela's door, and since the newspaper was read primarily by educated men such as those Fridolin had sometimes socialized with at the Buena Vista—men predisposed to consider her a charlatan—she'd likely squandered money she could not afford to waste. Foolish, foolish. It was more likely that anyone who might actually help had not been counted a close friend by Fridolin or Christine. A hired hand, perhaps. People like the Rademacher brothers. Back in Pomerania, if people wanted to advertise something....

Of *course.* Hanneke carefully tore a blank page from the book and wrote a short note. Then she turned back to her list:

Stop at a blacksmith's shop.
Find Adam's and see if the barber did indeed know Fridolin.

She chewed her lower lip for a moment, then added,

Try to find the Rademacher brothers.
Talk further with Adolf.

She finished her coffee slowly, drawing strength from the simple gifts of the strong drink, the kitchen's quiet, the knowledge that she did indeed have a hot meal waiting at suppertime and a bed to sleep in that night. In those blessed moments of calm, Hanneke vowed that she would not sink into despair again, nor act in any manner that assaulted her dignity.

She slipped the token back into her pocket and stood. Angela was asleep, Adolf busy. She had a good two hours before she needed to be back to finish preparations for the evening meal.

Outside, she headed to the post office. On the next block, she stopped abruptly in front of an impressive brick building bearing a freshly painted sign: The Bank of Watertown. She pictured Fridolin hurrying through that very door to deposit her dowry. What had he held in his heart? Was he excited about having the summer kitchen constructed before her arrival? Was he amused by her gullibility? Had he thought of her at all?

"*Guten Morgen*, Fraulein."

The insolent voice pricked Hanneke from her reverie. She whirled to confront Asa Hawkins.

"Have you business here?" He opened the door and held it wide. "After you."

Hanneke had no intention of cashing the banknote Christine had given her. She couldn't bear the thought of questioning a bank employee about Fridolin's state of mind while Hawkins sneered. And she most *certainly* was not going to ask Hawkins for help.

After an awkward moment, she lifted her chin and walked on. Hawkins' laughter followed her down the street.

When she reached the post office she tried to appear composed. "Nothing for you," the clerk said in German. His accent was poor but after what Hanneke had learned of the Know-Nothings, like Asa Hawkins, she was especially grateful for the man's attempt. She surrendered another precious coin to mail the letter she'd written to Fridolin's former employer in Milwaukee and thanked the clerk effusively.

She walked next to the blacksmith and farrier's shop she'd noticed in the heart of the German settlement in the north-central part of the city. The houses were smaller here than in more wealthy areas, and closer together; the businesses smaller as well, mostly bearing signs printed only in German.

She followed the growing metallic clank of hammer on anvil to the shop. The double doors were open and fastened back against the exterior walls. The acrid smell of coal smoke drifted into the morning with the wheezing pump of the bellows. And while the sweating blacksmith did his work, a knot of men lounged on stools and chairs in one front corner, smoking cigars, talking in a rough *Plattdeutsch*.

Some things are the same everywhere, Hanneke thought.

She walked up the ramp and stopped just inside the shop. "Excuse me," she asked politely. "I'm looking for the Rademacher brothers. They work together doing carpentry and brickwork. Does anyone—"

"Don't know them," one of the men replied. He had the enormous hands of a laborer. A stained bandage around one forearm suggested an injury that had left him idle.

An older, almost toothless man flapped a dismissive hand toward the first speaker. "Everybody knows the Rademachers. Hard workers, those two. Last I knew they were working at the American House. Across the bridge on West Avenue."

"*Danke.*" She turned back to the sunshine and considered the doors. They were, like those on every other blacksmith shop she'd ever seen, plastered with printed broadsides and scribbled notes:

> *New shipment of the finest hardware at Sprechers' Store.*
> *Wanted! Information pertaining to a runaway Negro woman and child.*

Wretched business, Hanneke thought.

> *Karl Klingbeil is seeking any information about his brother, last known to have passed through Watertown in February, possibly on his way to western gold fields—please leave word at the Stag Horn.*

There's a story there, she thought.

> *Missing, one good milch cow, brown and white, last seen at pasture on Ott's farm NE of this town.*
> *Men of The German Star—next meeting at the usual place, at the*

usual time. A star had been inked below the terse message.

That one stopped her. She'd never heard of The German Star. Was that the secret organization Adolf had joined? The one resolved to fight Yankee bigotry and hatred? It seemed likely.

She frowned, perplexed. But if so, why even post a notice, if the information was so oblique that the men it was aimed at surely already knew of the meeting?

Perhaps because the leaders wanted to send a subtle but clear message to any German-speaking lawmen, such as John Barlow, that the society was growing bolder?

No way to know. And I, Hanneke reminded herself, need to complete the afternoon's errands as quickly as possible. She pulled her own notice from her pocket and poked it onto empty nails. *Wanted: Information about the death of Fridolin Bauer. Ask for HB at the Red Cockerel.*

There. The poor German community might not read the newspaper, but Hanneke had no doubt that word of this notice would filter through the neighborhood. If the "responsible" men who congregated at the Buena Vista would not help her perhaps laboring men, who might have chopped firewood or built fences for Fridolin, would.

* * *

Hanneke made her way across the river to the American House, where a sign assured all comers that the boardinghouse was commodious, comfortable, convenient, and agreeable. Behind the imposing structure, Hanneke found two young men building a stone wall. Both were black-haired and stocky, both dressed in coarse wool trousers and stained linen work shirts. When she approached, both removed their felt hats respectfully.

"Pardon me," Hanneke began. "Are you Franz and Joe Rademacher?"

They exchanged perplexed looks. "I'm Franz," one said. He appeared to be the older brother—nineteen or twenty, maybe.

"I understand you were working at Fridolin Bauer's farm on Plum Grove

Road the day he died."

Franz shifted his weight uneasily. "That's right."

Hanneke tried to put him at ease. "I knew Fridolin well, and was distressed to arrive in Wisconsin and be greeted with the news of his death. Can you tell me what happened?"

"We were working on the foundation that day," Franz said. "Herr Bauer had hired us to build a summer kitchen."

My summer kitchen, Hanneke thought. "And he was threshing grain."

"Yes, ma'am. He met us when we arrived. Then he went off to the *Scheune*."

"Did you hear him using a flail?'"

"Sure." Joe shrugged. "You could hear it across the farmyard."

"But we didn't really pay attention," Franz added. "It started and stopped, started and stopped."

Which made sense. Someone threshing alone would need to stop periodically to sweep up the threshed grain, move the spent stalks, and spread new bundles. "When did you realize something was wrong?"

"I saw Fraulein Bauer walking across the yard," Franz said. "I don't know what time, but before noon. We didn't pay her any mind—"

"Until she started screaming." Joe's face twisted at the memory. "I just started running to see what was wrong. Franz too."

"What did you find?"

"Herr Bauer was lying on the floor." Franz cupped his elbows, clearly disturbed by the memory. "His sister was on her knees, crying and shrieking and shaking his shoulder. I asked what had happened, and she just yelled at us to go fetch Dr. Jenkins."

"Did you get a good look at Herr Bauer's injury?" Hanneke asked.

Joe touched the back of his head. "There was blood, here."

"The flail was laying beside him, and there was blood on the beater too," Franz added.

Just as Dr. Jenkins had said, Hanneke thought. "Did you both go for the doctor?"

The boys exchanged another glance. "Probably one of us should have stayed," Franz admitted. "But Fraulein Bauer was beside herself. We didn't know what else to do."

Hanneke could imagine the young men, more terrified of Christine's hysterics than Fridolin's body. "Of course."

"Dr. Jenkins was in his office, and said he'd go right out," Joe added soberly. "But we were pretty sure Herr Bauer was dead. And he was. When we went back the next day Fraulein Bauer gave us a day's wages and said we weren't needed anymore."

Hanneke tried to hide her disappointment. The insight she'd hoped for, the overlooked detail, simply wasn't there.

"I'm sorry we can't tell you anything more," Joe said earnestly. "If you hear that Fraulein Bauer wants to finish the summer kitchen, we'll do the work for a good price. And same to you. Out of respect for your loss."

After thanking Franz and Joe, Hanneke went on her way with little more knowledge than she'd had before. It was discouraging.

But I'm not finished yet, Hanneke thought, and made her way back to the Main Street bridge. A string of wooden shops beckoned customers—some on the bridge itself, some extending out over the river on rickety piers. She had no trouble finding the sign: *Adam's Haircutting and Shaving/Adam's Haarschneiden und Rasiren*. Through the front window, she glimpsed a man sitting in the barber chair, reading a newspaper. Squaring her shoulders, she opened the door and stepped inside.

As she did, the barber turned from a small stove in the back corner of the shop where he had been pouring hot water into a tin basin. The man was tall and thin and black-skinned. Hanneke paused, her polite inquiry driven from her brain by the unexpected sight of a Negro. She had never spoken to a Negro before.

He lifted gray eyebrows in surprise, but his tone was polite as he made an inquiry. Hanneke made out the words 'help' and 'ma'am,' spoken with the inflection of a question.

She forced herself to retrieve the English words. "Are you Mr. Adam?" He nodded.

"I am find—I am *trying* to find if Herr—Mr.—Fridolin Bauer…came here?" The man's eyebrows inched higher still. "*Ja.*"

"Sprechen Zie Deutsch?"

"Ein bissen."

Another entrepreneur who'd learned enough of the language to get by. Was Adam his first name, or his last? Hanneke had no idea how to properly address him.

As she struggled, a door opened and a young woman emerged from a back room. She had very dark skin, high cheekbones, and a white kerchief knotted neatly over her head. She wore a worn but well-tailored blue dress and carried a large basket filled with a tumble of clothes and towels. Hanneke remembered seeing, the day she arrived in town, the laundress pass on the street. Women can find work for themselves, Hanneke reminded herself.

The woman murmured something to Mr. Adam before slipping out the front door. Hanneke collected herself and returned to her task. "Sir, I was an acquaintance of Fridolin Bauer's. I was shocked to learn of his sudden death. I'm visiting people who knew him, asking if they might share any details of his last days or weeks."

The customer waiting for a shave rattled his newspaper impatiently. He was white, well-dressed. A merchant or businessman.

The elderly barber put the tin basin back on the stove and called in English, "Just one moment, sir," before turning back to Hanneke. "Herr Bauer did come in for a haircut and shave now and again," he told her in halting German.

"The last time you saw him, did he seem agitated—" she saw the man's confused frown and tried again. "Unhappy? Angry?"

Mr. Adam looked bewildered. "He just wanted a haircut." He pantomimed scissors, clipping near his own scalp.

"Adam!" the waiting man snapped.

"Danke schön," Hanneke said. She turned away no more illumined. But really, what had she expected a barber to tell her? That Fridolin had indeed unburdened his soul while getting his hair trimmed?

Well, if nothing else, she had learned something about herself, she thought as she left the shop. Her hesitance in speaking to the Negro barber seemed absurd, now. She suddenly wondered if any of the Know-Nothings had ever

119

actually *spoken* to a German or Irish immigrant.

She was forced to pause in the doorway for ten minutes as a farmer and his sons drove an enormous flock of sheep over the bridge, aided by two dogs who ran with bellies low to the boards. The shop floor trembled, but when Hanneke glanced over her shoulder, neither Adam nor his customer showed any sign of alarm. The sheep were fine stock, Merinos, and her fingers twitched with their want to comb the silky fibers, teasing out the matted tips, her fingers growing dirty but soft with lanolin. She liked to spin in the grease, waiting to wash the fibers until they'd been spun into yarn.

The animals moved along, bleating and baaing their indignation. When they'd finally passed, leaving the street studded with droppings, Hanneke stepped from the doorway and followed slowly, trying to gulp away the thick feeling in her throat. She'd imagined raising sheep such as these with Fridolin at the farm, developing breeding stock, selling her yarn and knitted goods....

"Frau Bauer."

The whisper banished Hanneke's sheep dreams. She stopped abruptly, her pulse accelerating. Apprehension seemed ridiculous on this busy street, in the middle of a sunny afternoon, but the fine hairs on the back of her neck prickled a warning.

She searched the faces of passersby—women's beneath kerchiefs or bonnets, men's crowned with silk-covered stovepipes or battered felt hats; faces grinning or contemplative or tired or worried. But none familiar, none looking at her.

Hanneke took one hesitant step back in the direction she'd come, then another. The afternoon suddenly pulsed with the normal cacophony usually unnoticed: snatches of conversation, a bellow of laughter, a factory's steam whistle. High cries of a boy hawking newspapers. Creaking wagon wheels, snapping whips. Distant shouts from a freighter. Two skinny hounds snarling over some scrap.

Hanneke walked slowly, ears straining to hear again what she'd *thought* she heard. Just as she was about to berate herself for a fool, it came again.

"Frau Bauer."

Gooseflesh chilled her arms.

"Frau Bauer!"

The low voice came from a narrow alley between a cigar shop and a tavern. She'd reached the edge of the bridge; the tavern sat on solid ground. The alley was dark with shadows, but Hanneke made out the figure of a man. He raised a hand, beckoned. "Frau Bauer, *please!*"

Hanneke sucked in a ragged breath. Not Fraulein, but Frau. He'd addressed her as a married woman.

The man glanced over his shoulder, then came closer. He wore a hat pulled low over his forehead. In the gloom, he seemed to be of middling height, middling build.

"Who are you?" she demanded.

He beckoned again.

"No. Not until you tell me who you are, and why—why...." Her voice cracked. "Did you know my husband?"

The man looked behind him again, towards the river and whatever alley ran behind the tavern, before stepping closer. Hanneke made out a small splash of something bright yellow—a neckerchief tucked into his sack coat. "Yes. But I must be quick!" he hissed in clumsy German.

Hanneke stepped into the narrow space. "Please, I beg you—what do you *know*? What happened to Fridolin?"

He silenced her with a sharp gesture. "My German is not good. You speak English?" He followed that with an urgent string of words in that language.

It was too much, too fast. *"Nein!"* She stepped closer, as if that might help; close enough to see that his yellow neckerchief was bisected with thin black lines and that his hat brim was nicked; close enough to smell sweat. But she still couldn't see the man's features.

He tried again in German. "It is danger! But I must tell you—"

He whirled just as Hanneke sensed movement behind him. One shadowed figure—no, two—emerged from the gloom. Hanneke stood frozen with shock as they converged on the man who'd whispered her name. A blade flashed. The man in the yellow kerchief gasped, staggered. Then he sagged against the tavern wall. His hat slipped and she saw his eyes, wide with pain or shock or fear, maybe all three. "Go!" he croaked at Hanneke.

She backed numbly into the sunlit afternoon, stumbling into two men emerging from the tavern. "Help!" she cried, grabbing the nearer man's arm. "Please—there's trouble in the alley!"

The man shook her off like a pesky fly. His companion laughed, fogging the air with whiskey fumes.

"*Please!* I need help!" Hanneke's voice rose. Her heart thumped at her ribs. "Is there a constable about?"

Several men paused to stare; several more gave her a wide berth. Finally, an elderly man with a long gray beard and kind eyes put a hand on her arm. "Can I be of assistance?" His other hand was braced against the knob of a carved walking stick.

Hanneke almost wept with relief. "Yes—please—there's been trouble! There, in the alley!" She pointed.

"In the alley?" The old man looked dubious but obligingly turned to investigate.

"Don't go back there! We should fetch a constable or the sheriff—and a doctor…." Her voice faded as the old man hobbled into the shadows.

Hanneke looked around again for a constable. But almost at once, the old man returned. "What did you think you saw?" he asked kindly.

"I don't *think* I saw something! I *did* see something!"

"Very well, what did you see?"

"There was a man, and then two other men—or maybe three—and the first one got hurt!" Hanneke darted around the old man and peered into the alley.

The empty alley.

"There may have been someone there," the elderly gentleman said, in a tone that suggested he might have been talking to a dimwitted child. "But there's no one there now."

Chapter Thirteen

The next morning Hanneke was sitting at the kitchen table, sipping coffee, before the sun crept above the horizon. She'd brought out the lace shawl she'd started knitting, craving the solace of familiar movements and known patterns. But after dropping stitches twice, she abandoned her work.

She and Adolf had handled the tavern alone the evening before. Exhaustion weighted her bones, tugged at her eyelids, but she was also too upset to sleep. Who was the man in the yellow neckerchief? He must have been following her. How else would he have known she would walk by that very alley? Had he been trying to lure her into danger? Or had he truly been trying to tell her something important? *It is danger, but I must tell you—*

Hanneke scrubbed aching temples with her knuckles. She had come so close to learning…something. What had he needed to tell her? The truth about Fridolin's death? The obvious fact that she was meddling where she was unwanted? *What?*

She pressed one hand over her mouth. *Gott in Himmel*, she feared the man was dead. Did his assailants know he had not had time to communicate his message to her? Or might they come after her too?

The afternoon before a constable had, finally, been attracted by the small crowd gathering around Hanneke and the elderly man trying to console her. Someone fetched a foreman from a nearby cigar factory to translate. After hearing Hanneke's tale, the constable strolled down the passageway and back again. "There is nothing to see here," he told the crowd in English, which the foreman had in turn interpreted. "Nothing at all." His expression

123

suggested that Hanneke was one step away from a lunatic asylum.

She had tried again to make her fears understood, but his frown had only deepened. Strangers jostled by, crowding her. Finally Hanneke—sickened, shocked, dazed—had fled.

But she couldn't escape the gnawing fear that her life was in danger too. Perhaps she should try, one more time, to talk with Deputy Barlow. She could tell him what she'd seen…. "And he wouldn't believe a word," she muttered.

She should leave Watertown.

And yet, how could she abandon Angela? The evening before, Hanneke had sounded Adolf out about the possibility of another woman, a friend perhaps, coming in to help until Angela regained her strength. There was no one, Adolf had muttered, brows gathering in a furious scowl. Hanneke could well imagine. Working women would still do business with an unmarried pregnant woman. But set aside their own work or families to move into the Cockerel? Under the circumstances…likely not.

And besides, what about Adolf? He'd worked like a demon the night before, making up for Hanneke's distraction and her unfamiliarity with the customers. He'd met her worried gazes with reassuring smiles: *Don't worry. We can handle things. I'll show you what you need to know.*

Still…Adolf was a sworn member of a secret society—probably The German Star. Fridolin had been involved with men who were dangerous, desperate, or both—and if it all revolved around The German Star, as Hanneke suspected, then Adolf might be about to plunge headlong into terrible trouble.

Her head throbbed again, and she increased the pressure on her temples. Angela and Adolf both deserved to know what she'd witnessed the day before…but more worry might cause additional physical harm to Angela or her unborn child. And Adolf was simply too young and hot-headed to trust with the story.

Fridolin Bauer, if you were standing in front of me, I would slap you. Hard. How did you dare *set these events in motion?*

No response.

Her blank notebook and the German-English dictionary lay on the table. In the lonely dark hours, when every mouse's skitter in the pantry or imagined footfall made her heart race and even knitting had been impossible, she'd tried to distract herself by translating the letter she'd taken from Fridolin's things in the farmhouse.

Dear Fridolin,

The shipment you requested is on its way. I expect it to arrive in Watertown by mid-month. You'll find paper, and also a small pot of paint, all I could send for the time being. I will also take advantage of transport to send a parcel to Mr. Rutherford. I hope you will be so kind as to deliver it at the ironworks.

I regret that things have been so difficult for you of late, and wish that I could offer some assistance.

Yours in Christ,

M.

Hanneke regarded her laborious translation with gritty eyes. The last paragraph of the translated letter was both the most interesting—and the most infuriating. M. must have been a good friend, for he'd confirmed what no one in Watertown admitted to knowing: that life had been 'so difficult' for Fridolin. But Hanneke had no way to identify or find M. The return address on the envelope said simply 'Milwaukee.'

The reference to the ironworks seemed to be of no particular importance. M. sounded as if he was merely asking Fridolin to do him the favor of passing along the extra parcel to this Mr. Rutherford. It didn't seem likely that Rutherford would be able to help. Nonetheless, she had to follow every strand that might lead back to Fridolin's death. Perhaps I can find him, Hanneke thought. Perhaps he'll talk with me.

The rest of the short letter held no promise. Fridolin had ordered paper and paint from a friend in Milwaukee. She had assumed that the two gorgeously bound books he'd given her had been made earlier, while he was still working in Milwaukee, but perhaps not. She'd seen his bookbinding tools still packed carefully in the farmhouse attic. Fridolin had clearly not been a comfortable farmer. Maybe turning his old trade into a hobby had brought him some satisfaction. If that had been the case, some part of her still cared enough to be glad for him.

And at least Fridolin had evidently had one friend to turn to. She didn't recall anything to suggest that Fridolin had been a particularly religious man—certainly not as overt a Christian as his friend M. appeared to be. But if faith, or this mysterious friend, had given Fridolin some comfort in his last troubled days…well, for those things too, Hanneke was glad. Even if anger still quivered inside her heart like a plucked violin string.

She turned a page in the blank book. Focusing on her feelings would accomplish nothing. She needed to consider the facts that she'd learned since arriving in Watertown. She picked up her pencil again and started an inventory.

> *Fridolin arrived in Wisconsin in 1850; worked as a bookbinder in Milwaukee until 1853; came to Watertown and bought an established farm on Plum Grove Road.*
>
> *His sister Christine emigrated with him and kept house for him in Milwaukee, and later at the farm.*
>
> *He had a good friend in Milwaukee, "M," with whom he was still in contact.*
>
> *He still engaged in at least occasional bookbinding, perhaps as a hobby, since his farming skills were limited.*
>
> *He spent leisure time at the Buena Vista, favored tavern of Germantown's Forty-Eighters and Latin farmers.*
>
> *By all accounts he was liked and respected in Watertown.*

What did that collection of facts reveal? Exactly nothing.

So, keep going, she ordered herself. And yes—there was one odd detail she'd noticed the day before.

All of the letters Fridolin sent me over the winter were written in weak, brown ink, but the only ink I found at Fridolin's farm was high-quality black. Christine had used black ink even when writing rough drafts of the two business notices.

The letters to me, Hanneke concluded, were not written at the farm. So… where had Fridolin gone to write to his wife?

- *Fridolin hired Franz and Joe Rademacher to build a summer kitchen. The work was started, but not completed, before he died.*
- *He banked at the Bank of Watertown.*
- *According to Christine, there was very little money in Fridolin's account when he died.*
- *He got his hair cut at Adam's barbershop on the Main Street bridge.*
- *Dr. Jenkins was his doctor (and Christine's).*

Hanneke leaned back in her chair, struck by something she should have noticed before. Fridolin was a member of the German Singing Society, and spent time at the Buena Vista. Nonetheless, in a city with a large German community—where it was possible to live and conduct all business in the native tongue—Fridolin had chosen not to exclusively patronize German establishments. He'd spoken fluent English, so perhaps he'd been trying to break down walls between German and Yankee factions in Watertown in a peaceful and practical way.

Or perhaps…perhaps, in an effort to gain information The German Star might find useful, Fridolin had deliberately made choices that allowed him closer access to Yankee men of substance in Watertown.

Hanneke shuddered and slapped the book closed. Enough. She shoved to her feet and prowled the kitchen, elbows clasped, forearms crossed protectively over her chest. The true morning was dawning now. Soft sunlight slanted through the window. And if she didn't take some kind of action, she'd surely go mad.

She tiptoed upstairs and peeked in on Angela. Fast asleep. Good. Adolf was, presumably, asleep in the stable.

Back downstairs, she put away the lace project and tucked needles and a half-knit stocking, which required less attention, into her pocket. Then she wrapped her warm wool shawl around her shoulders and tied on her bonnet. She left the coffee and some rye bread on the table for Adolf. After tucking a few things into a market basket, she left the tavern.

She walked briskly, head down. At this hour most pedestrians were men in heavy trousers and stained smocks trudging toward one of the foundries or mills. She was grateful that Watertown was still so young; most of the buildings weren't crammed together as they had been in the Old Country, and the open spaces were reassuring. Still, the flat space between her shoulder blades prickled as if remembering the hand that had shoved her into traffic the night the Know-Nothings paraded. The skin on her upper arm tingled, as if afraid that someone might grab her and drag her into some shadowed alley.

On the Main Street bridge, she stopped by the narrow passage where she'd seen the man who'd addressed her as 'Frau Bauer.' Her stomach muscles knotted as she stared into the dim alley. Empty.

Several moments passed before she stepped from the sunlit morning into the alley's cool shadows. She hurried to the end and looked around. The building on her right stood firmly on the riverbank. The attackers could have easily slipped behind the tavern before stealing into the narrow space between the two buildings.

She walked back into the shrouded passageway. It had been...about here. Crouching, she pulled a candle and a lucifer match from beneath the cloth in her market basket. With her back to the street, trying to avoid any curious stares from pedestrians, she lit the candle....

And immediately saw what the policeman would have seen yesterday if he'd only bothered to look. A dark smear of blood stained the tavern wall. More had crusted in the dirt.

She glanced over her shoulder, then raised the candle. There...the ground was scuffed. Beyond it, two long lines showed in the dust. She berated herself for a fool; she should have studied the alley *before* walking through. As it was, her own footsteps had tracked right through the marks. Still, she was almost certain what had caused those two parallel tracks—the man in the yellow neckerchief's heels as his attackers dragged him from the alley.

Hanneke blew out the candle and hurried back to Main Street. She wanted to feel sunshine on her shoulders. She also wanted to lock herself back inside the Cockerel.

Then she heard a shout.

There was a wide gap between buildings across the bridge. Several men were leaning over the railing. A boy who looked about twelve ran by and wriggled through the watchers, disappearing toward the front. Someone shrilled a high whistle.

Hanneke sucked in her lower lip, feeling a sense of dread. After checking for traffic, she walked slowly across the bridge. She couldn't see anything but the backsides of the growing group leaning over the rail: linen and cotton shirts, a few vests, leather braces, patched trousers.

"Excuse me," she said.

One of the men turned. The excitement in his pockmarked face faded. "Oh, *nein*. You must go back."

"What is it?"

"It is nothing for a lady—"

"I need to see!"

They might have argued for an hour if a Yankee man in a trim black hat, with a gold watch chain looping from his pocket, hadn't appeared behind them and bellowed something. Most of the men leaning over the railing jerked around and hurried back to whatever jobs were waiting for them.

Hanneke stepped to the rail. The Rock River rippled below, sunlight glazing a swath of water with new gold. A short distance downriver, near one of the mills, several men were wading hip-deep, close to shore. "What is it?" she asked.

"They said somebody *drowned*," the boy at her elbow said breathlessly.

Hanneke turned, snatched up her skirt, and began to run.

She turned on First Street and passed a few buildings before cutting through a yard to the river bank. A growing crowd ringed half a dozen men hauling something—no, some*one*—from the river. A man. He was hatless, his dark hair plastered against his skull. Wet trousers clung to his legs. A corduroy sack coat sagged heavily about his chest. Even dulled by water, the knot of neckerchief visible at his throat was a vivid yellow. Yellow, cross-hatched by black lines.

Hanneke felt as if *her* lungs had filled with water. The morning seemed to kaleidoscope in on itself. Nothing seemed real—not the smell of mud and fish, not the hot sourness coating her tongue, not the babel of shouts and mutters.

A fat man was chattering in English. He held a fishing pole over one shoulder and pointed toward the mill's huge paddlewheel, now still and dripping. Hanneke could easily imagine the scene: an early morning fisherman spotted a body in the water, bobbing against the wheel.

Two of the men who'd pulled the body to shore crouched over the dead man. The gawkers parted silently as Dr. Jenkins, who had evidently been summoned, elbowed his way through. He knelt and quickly examined the victim before ripping the shirt open with a sound that slashed the morning.

"He didn't drown!" a man standing near Hanneke muttered. "He was knifed!"

Hanneke blinked, breaking the paralysis that had seized her. Someone straining for a better look jostled her. She swallowed hard, fighting the urge to retch. Too many people, too close. The killers had been no more than shadows and rustles of movement. She had no way to identify them. One of them might be standing right next to her. With his knife.

As she began backing away, Deputy Sherriff John Barlow pushed through the crowd. "Deputy!" she gasped. "I—"

"Not now!" He shoved past.

Hanneke clenched her teeth. For the briefest moment, she had seen Barlow only as a lawman who spoke German. Someone who would listen to her. Someone who would understand—not just her words, but her fears.

She turned abruptly, swimming upstream against new onlookers straggling toward the riverbank. She took one more wary glance around—and confronted Asa Hawkins. He'd been striding toward the knot of people but stopped short, his gaze locked with hers. His expression had been tight but when he looked at Hanneke, something else passed swiftly over his features, something she couldn't identify. Hawkins' eyes glittered like the ice coating Hanneke's bones.

Then he tipped his hat and smiled. It was a calculated smile, feral and wolf-like.

Chapter Fourteen

Hanneke plunged into the kitchen, slammed the door behind her, shot the latch, and leaned against it. Her heart thumped against her ribs.

Adolf was filling the wood box. "Where have you been?" he complained, dropping a log into the box with a clatter. "Angela was asking for you."

"I'll—I was out. It's smoky in here. Didn't you open the damper?" Hanneke turned away and busied herself unnecessarily at the stove. "I'll take care of Angela. She needs breakfast. No, not breakfast. Tea. I wish I had beef tea. Beef tea would be best. But red raspberry leaf tea will help also." Hanneke reached for a little crockery jar. It slipped and crashed to the floor with a clatter that made her jump. She gazed at her hand. Her fingers were trembling.

Adolf stared at her. "What is *wrong* with—"

"Nothing." Hanneke stooped over the mess. The crock had cracked but was still usable. The tea leaves it held had spilled onto the floor, though, and would have to be discarded. She brushed them into a pile. "Would you please take care of the day's beer order?"

"I've got plenty of time to—"

"*Now*, please!" Hanneke hissed. She had no authority to give Adolf orders. But after a moment of sulky silence, he began hauling empty casks out to the handcart he used for transport.

Hanneke brewed ginger and chamomile tea and warmed some bread over the stove. Then she carried the breakfast tray upstairs. Angela was dozing, but she stretched and blinked as Hanneke came into the room. "Is everything well?" she mumbled.

"Yes, of course." Another straight-out lie. I am becoming much too practiced at deception, Hanneke thought. "I'll just leave this."

"No, please—wait." Angela put her hands on the mattress and gingerly pushed herself upright. "What's been happening? Is Adolf behaving?"

"Adolf has been an enormous help," Hanneke said carefully. She didn't want to give Angela anything new to worry about. "Now, you really must rest."

"I will," Angela said, although she didn't lie back down. "Hanneke, I hate to ask for anything more, but…could you keep an eye on Adolf?"

Hanneke wasn't sure what she was being asked to do. "Keep an eye on Adolf?"

"These are such troubled times…." The younger woman spread her hands helplessly. " I don't want him to get into trouble."

"I don't either," Hanneke assured her, choosing not to confess that she was already worried about the boy. "Of course. I will do my best to look out for him."

"*Danke schön.*" Angela sank back on her pillow.

Back downstairs Hanneke circled the kitchen, arms hugged across her chest. The morning felt too still, too quiet. Somehow, very quickly, she had become somewhat responsible for both Angela and Adolf. It was too much, more than she could manage….

And it is a blessing as well, she scolded herself. Other than worrying about their welfare, the responsibility didn't feel burdensome. Two people had gifted her with their friendship and hospitality. Those friendships could bolster, not drain, her spirits while she addressed true problems.

And those were abundant. She thought of Fridolin Bauer smiling as they strolled through the garden at Theodor and Minnie's home in Treptow, and the smudge of blood staining the flail in his grain barn. She thought of the murdered man's white, wet face. She thought of Asa Hawkins' malevolent leer. Her efforts to resolve the truth behind Fridolin's lies had led to even uglier events. And she didn't know what to do next.

Finally, she filled a wooden bucket with water from the pump, grabbed a boar-bristle scrub brush and a sliver of lye soap, hauled it all into the tavern proper, and got to her knees. She scrubbed violently, trying to let the rhythmic motion calm her body, the scratch of bristles on wood fill the silence, the focus on dirt and stains fill her mind.

She was halfway across the room when someone knocked on the back door. She scrambled to her feet. The knocking came again, louder.

Hanneke hurried into the kitchen, wiping her hands on her skirt. When she peeked out the window she saw Deputy Sheriff John Barlow, glowering.

She unlocked the door and jerked it open. "What do you want?"

His mouth tightened at her tone. "I want to talk with you."

Oh, so *now* he wanted to talk? She debated a moment before allowing him entry. "Fraulein Zeidler is not well, so please keep your voice down. Let's go into the taproom."

"I'm sorry to hear that Fraulein Zeidler is unwell," he said as he followed her from the kitchen, but his tone was perfunctory. In the taproom, he gestured toward her scrub pail and brush. "You're having a full morning. From viewing a murder victim to scrubbing the floor."

I am so *weary* of this, she thought. "Tell me your business here, Deputy Barlow, or leave. I have no energy for riddles."

He stared at her for another long moment. Then he took two of the chairs that had been up-ended on a table and planted them back on the floor. He made a gesture toward one, and she sat.

He dropped onto the other. "I still don't know who you are," he said. "But all week, every time I turn around—every time there's some kind of trouble—there you are. Why is that?"

"I don't know. I wish I did."

He pulled his hat from his head and placed it on the table in front of him. It was a farmer's hat made of tan felt, with a dark sweat stain circling the edge of the crown. "What happened yesterday afternoon?"

"…What do you mean?" Hanneke narrowed her eyes. What did this man know? And how did he know it?

Barlow sighed. "Ernst Off came to see me last night. Seems one of the city constables had encountered a German woman who looks like you, claiming she'd seen someone attacked by the Main Street bridge. She left the area before providing her name. Then this morning, when a body turns up, who do I see but *you*."

Hanneke stood and began to prowl the room, trying to think. She was tempted to evade Barlow's questions. What had he ever done but dismiss her concerns and accuse her of wrongdoing?

But he was a deputy. And she was frightened.

She faced him. "Yes, it was me yesterday afternoon. A man—that man from this morning—was attacked in the alley between two buildings, right at the edge of the bridge—"

"You just happened to be walking by, and happened to glance down that passageway, and happened to see this attack?"

His sarcasm grated nerves already raw. "I was walking by and heard him call my name." She told Deputy Barlow what had happened.

Barlow looked skeptical. "He called you Frau Bauer."

"He did."

"And you have no idea who this man was?"

"As I *told* you, I do not. I remember his eyes after he was stabbed...." They would haunt her—so wide, so surprised, so full of pain. "I might not have known that poor man pulled from the river today was him if it wasn't for his neckerchief."

"That's not proof positive that the dead man is the man you spoke with."

"You asked me what happened. I've told you. Make of it what you will."

"Hmm." John Barlow got up and walked to the bar, placing his palms flat upon it as if in thought. After a moment he turned to face her again. "Why didn't you give the constable your name?"

"He never asked for my name. He acted as if I belonged in an asylum. He hardly glanced in the alley. If he had, he would have seen blood."

"The constable doesn't speak German. Perhaps you should have tried harder to—"

Hanneke stamped one foot. "I *did* try! At first, no one stopped to help at all. By the time an old man finally did, the alley was empty. When that constable eventually came and someone interpreted for me, he was indifferent. He seemed to think that I was hysterical." Hanneke's cheeks warmed with anger. "I thought of trying to find you, but frankly, I assumed you would disbelieve me. Do you? Or are you willing to tell the others what I saw?"

Deputy Barlow crossed his arms and leaned back against the bar. His mouth had gone tight again, chin jutting forward, but he was staring out the window. On the street, oxen bellowed as a drayman tried to navigate the ruts.

Hanneke shook her head slowly with disbelief. "You won't. A man is dead! A man is dead, and you won't—"

Barlow slammed one fist down on the bar so hard that glasses rattled. "I can't, you foolish woman!"

Hanneke stared at him.

In a lower voice, he said, "I can't. Not until I know who the leaders of the local Know-Nothing Lodge are. That's why I didn't talk to you by the river this morning."

It took Hanneke a moment to understand. "...You think that some of the constables are involved."

"I didn't say that," he hissed. But he didn't meet her gaze.

She dropped into a chair. For a long moment, no one spoke. Then she asked, "Who is—was—the dead man?"

"I don't know. No one has recognized him or reported someone missing. We didn't find any identification on his person."

"The kerchief he wore was distinctive. I'd certainly recognize the fabric again if I saw it. Perhaps you could check with shopkeepers."

Barlow snorted. "We don't have any reason to believe that the man was local, so why would you think we could track that cloth? The dead man was most likely traveling through Watertown. Or perhaps newly arrived. In any case, that cloth might have come from anywhere."

Hanneke pinched her lips together. And what would the harm be in checking?

"As far as I know, you were the last person to speak to him," Barlow added. "If what you say is true—"

"Deputy Barlow!" Hanneke stamped her foot again. "If we are to continue this conversation, I insist that you refrain from questioning my veracity. Don't you have better things to do than harangue me?"

His jaw tightened again. "I assure you, I would far rather be home tending my sick wife and cutting my ripe hay."

Hanneke held his gaze. Little creases fanned from the corner of his eyes. They were dark, brooding. She could see that he felt conflicted, that he was worried, that he was tired. But she was unwilling to listen to any more accusations, veiled or otherwise.

Finally, he blew out a long breath and crossed one muddy work boot over the other. "Is there anything else you want to tell me?" The words were civil, even if they seemed to come from between clenched teeth.

"No," Hanneke said, "but I have more questions. What can you tell me about Asa Hawkins? All I know is that he hates German people."

"Hawkins." Barlow muttered the name like an oath. "He runs a freight-hauling business. He orders goods and livestock and brings everything in to sell." The deputy's mouth curled with contempt. "Mean as a slave-catcher, that one. It was bad enough when such men only hated Negroes, but now their bile spills onto the foreign-born as well. Not just Germans. The Irish too, certainly. And whatever Norwegians or Swedes cross their path."

That brought little comfort. "Hawkins seems to take a special pleasure in—in trying to intimidate me."

"I suspect that Hawkins is one of the Know-Nothing leaders, but he is a coward—the kind of man who stays in the shadows while inciting others to violence." Barlow muttered something in English. "But I have no proof that he's broken any law. Certainly no reason to arrest him. And he is a prosperous man who moves in powerful circles. His brother is a prominent businessman with a much more pleasant demeanor, much admired in town."

Hanneke remembered the store she'd passed the other day: *J. Hawkins, Wholesale Drug Ware House.*

"I'd like to say that such things make no difference," Barlow was saying. "But they do."

As they all too often did in the Old Country, Hanneke thought. How many hungry immigrants had sacrificed everything known and dear in order to make a new home in a place where, they'd been told, such hatreds did not exist? How shattering it was to say goodbye to family and homeland, make the journey, only to meet hatred and contempt. If Fridolin *had* been working against such nativists…well…that would excuse a lot. Certainly not everything! But a lot.

"Deputy Barlow," she said, "yesterday morning you refused to tell me anything about the German men—some of them, anyway—forming a secret society of their own. I've heard of The German Star—"

His eyes widened. "You know about that?"

"Just that it exists," she said impatiently. Really, the man was exasperating. "I know that some German men have formed a secret society of their own to stand against the Know-Nothings."

Barlow growled. "The Know-Nothings present a real menace, and anyone foreign-born is right to be alarmed. But only a few extremists advocate violence. And from what I can tell, most of those are driven as much by frustration in their own failures as anything else. They were revolutionaries in the Old Country, but their revolution did not succeed. Now they are here, many incapable of running a business or managing a farm, searching for a new path to glory. Those are the men who formed The German Star."

"Fridolin wasn't a revolutionary," Hanneke said slowly, and had to add, "as far as I know. But he did once say that 'good German men won't allow themselves to be treated as something less than those who happened to be born on American soil,' so he did have some interest in the matter. If Fridolin—"

"I have no reason to believe that Fridolin Bauer was a member of any such society."

"But you don't know for sure."

John Barlow abruptly dug a couple of coins from his pocket and dropped them onto the counter. "Can I have a beer?"

Hanneke went behind the bar and filled a mug from one of the kegs. Barlow drained a third of it and wiped his mouth on his sleeve. "No, I don't know for sure whether Fridolin was or was not a member of The German Star. The man I knew—thought I knew—wouldn't have joined such a group."

138

"The man I thought I knew wouldn't have done a lot of things," Hanneke observed. "Which leads to my current situation."

Barlow took another gulp of beer.

"Deputy Barlow, someone doesn't want me in Watertown, doesn't want me asking questions about Fridolin. Someone pushed me in front of a cantering horse. A man I don't know called me 'Frau Bauer' and then seconds later, was knifed right before my eyes. I believe he was the same man pulled from the river this morning."

"And I'll say again: You should leave Watertown."

Hanneke picked up the rag she'd used to wipe the bar down the night before and refolded it into a neat rectangle. "Fraulein Zeidler has been kind, and I am in her debt. I need to stay here, at least for the time being." She looked up from the rag. "And I want to know the truth about Fridolin."

"You told me what you knew of The German Star, but you didn't tell me how you'd gathered that information."

The abrupt observation made Hanneke's nerves prickle back to alert. "Well, I saw a notice nailed to a blacksmith shop door."

"I've seen that notice as well, and others like it. But they say nothing of resisting Know-Nothings. Who told you the two were linked?"

Hanneke rubbed at a smudge on the bar. She would not lie outright to Deputy Barlow, but she was not willing to implicate Adolf, either. "I heard it here, in the tavern. I've been helping Fraulein Zeidler. Many men come in and out. I hear fragments of conversation." She shrugged and found another smudge to rub clean. More lies of omission. It was becoming a habit.

John Barlow stared blindly out the window long enough for Hanneke to finish the visible smears, and start on the invisible ones. Eventually, he said, "Then I ask for your cooperation in this matter. Watertown has become a powder keg. I don't know who can be trusted. Every week the newspapers report attacks against the foreign-born, all over the country. A few months ago a German mob exchanged gunfire with police in Chicago. Mobs in several Wisconsin towns have already gotten violent in recent months. I am *not* willing to allow that to happen here."

"But surely—"

"I have embraced my wife's people," he interrupted gruffly. "I've kept easy company with Germans for years. Now, some of my oldest friends won't greet me on the street. I don't even know if they look away because they are members of The German Star, and planning some violence, or if they think I might somehow—despite my marriage—be associated with the damn Know-Nothings."

Morning light streaming through the window illumined the fatigue in Barlow's eyes. He must feel something like I do, Hanneke thought. Not knowing who he can trust. She had a sudden impulse to inquire after his wife's health, to see if she could help.

He spoke first. "If you hear any other such 'fragments of conversation'"—his tone was sardonic—"you will inform me."

Hanneke didn't want to be drawn any further into the conflict between nativists and immigrants, but it wouldn't do to further antagonize the deputy. "*Ja*," she agreed.

"I'll try to stop by here from time to time," Barlow said. "Not in the evenings when you're open, though."

Hanneke nodded. That was wise.

"There is something you don't know," Barlow said. "But it will appear in the next newspaper, so I might as well tell you now. There's a gunmaker and locksmith who has a shop on Second Street. He sells firearms and locks, grinds razors and scissors, makes repairs, that sort of thing."

Hanneke refrained from informing Barlow that she had a reasonable idea of what a gunmaker and locksmith did.

"Two nights ago, someone broke into the shop. The owner lives upstairs, and when he heard the noise and came to investigate, he was knocked on the head. He's all right, but by the time he came around, the shop had been cleaned out. Rifles, pistols, even blades...all gone."

Hanneke stared at him open-mouthed with dawning horror. "You think the Know-Nothings are gathering arms?"

"It could be the Know-Nothings. It could be The German Star. The thing is, if the guns are found in time, we might be able to avoid tragedy. If not...." Barlow spread his hands, palms up. "So. You will stay close to the tavern, and keep your ears open."

A thought shot through Hanneke's mind. "Deputy Barlow—"

"No arguments." He picked up his hat and started toward the door.

"But I think—"

"And that is part of the problem," he said. "You think too much." He let himself out, shutting the door firmly behind him.

Hanneke glared at the door. Arrogant man!

But something quivered beneath her indignation—a memory flickering through her mind. A memory she didn't want to revisit, but once touched refused to go quietly back to the part of her mind where she walled away unpleasantness.

The night after Fridolin had proposed to Hanneke, he had again joined the family for dinner. Talk turned to politics, and Fridolin told them that German immigrants in America watched with anxiety the political unrest in Europe. "The German-language papers are full of it. Everyone fears that the Russians will provoke a war."

"It seems to me," Hanneke said, "that our greatest enemy is not the Russian or the Turk, but the ever-increasing poverty stalking us. Too many people have no bread to eat, no meat, only salted beets. I think—"

"And that is the problem," Minnie murmured. Then she raised her voice. "Hanneke, dear, will you help me in the kitchen?"

When the two women were alone, Minnie's smile disappeared. "You must not enter the men's conversation in such fashion!" she scolded. "At least not before the wedding has taken place. You will scare Herr Bauer off."

"I hardly think I was too forthright," Hanneke had objected. "I think Herr Bauer is looking for a partner, not a porcelain doll."

Minnie had scoffed that notion aside, but Hanneke had clung to it, through the wedding, through the last months of her mother's illness, through the long winter months of preparing for her own trip to Wisconsin. She liked the notion of being a partner. For the most part, that idea had been framed by the farm: a partner in planning, a partner in labor, a partner in harvest. And she had believed that Fridolin had wanted a partner.

Since learning of Fridolin's deception, though, she'd felt a nibbling fear that he'd simply changed his mind about wanting to make a life with her. Had her letters been too full of advice, too heavy with opinions? Had he concluded—like everyone else—that she spent too much time thinking?

"*Nein*," she muttered. Two things she'd found in the house—the book she'd given him and the advertisement for Merino sheep marked with her initial—suggested that he had indeed wanted a partner. It was pleasant to think that Fridolin had truly respected Hanneke's mind, even if Minnie and Deputy Sheriff John Barlow did not.

I will never know, Hanneke thought. And perhaps it was just as well that Barlow hadn't permitted her to speak her mind. She'd been thinking about the German society's decision to recruit boys, and whether that signaled an escalation in their activities. But if she'd expressed her concern, Barlow would have pressed for details. She didn't want to say anything that might cause trouble for Adolf.

You are not helpless, she reminded herself, and there is still much to do. She wanted to talk with Rutherford, the man at the ironworks M. had mentioned in his letter. Also, it might be possible to find the origin of that distinctive, bright yellow-and-black cloth that the dead man had worn about his throat. If she could find a shopkeeper who remembered selling that cloth, perhaps the dead man could be identified.

That was certainly the poor soul's due. And identifying the dead man might also lead her closer to understanding Fridolin's secrets.

Chapter Fifteen

The Vulcan Iron Works was an industrial complex of wood-frame buildings on the banks of the Rock River. Hanneke smelled the blast furnace's hot metallic breath from a block away, reminding her that in Roman mythology, Vulcan was the god of fire. As she came closer, she heard a turning mill wheel's rumble, the wheezy rhythmic blow of an enormous bellows, the discordant clang of hammers on anvils.

Broadsides on the exterior wall of the closest buildings advertised plows, road scrapers, harrow teeth, and fanning mill parts. A notice assured visitors that "All kinds of produce—pumpkins excepted—will be taken in exchange for castings." Several potential customers were examining a two-horse treadmill in the yard. Hanneke felt a lurch beneath her ribcage when she noticed a threshing machine among the other implements on display. If Fridolin had owned one of those, instead of using a flail....

Well. There was nothing to be gained by thinking about *that*.

Hanneke straightened her shoulders before approaching what she thought might be the office. She stepped into a noisy space where a dozen or more mechanics worked. As she blinked against the sudden gloom, a shower of crimson sparks flared sizzle-bright somewhere toward the back.

A man hurried from the shadows, grasped her arm, and firmly towed her back outside. He delivered a tirade in firm English. Hanneke caught the words "no" and "lady."

"*Sprechen zie Deutsch?*" she tried.

"*Nein.*" The man shook his head. He wore no jacket or even a vest, and his shirt was dark with sweat.

"Please…Mr. Rutherford?" Hanneke said in English.

The man crossed his arms implacably, backing into the door as if afraid she might bolt past him. "*Nein,*" he said again. He pointed toward the street, then made a shooing motion with his hands.

"*Ich bin kein streunendes Huhn,*" Hanneke told the man tartly. I am not a stray chicken. But she had no choice but to leave.

After retreating a safe distance, she regarded the ironworks. What now? Wait, and try to catch Mr. Rutherford as he left? She had no idea what he looked like, or if he was even here. She didn't even know if the man was a laborer, a skilled craftsman, or a supervisor. She suspected the latter, given the tone of M.'s letter, but still—there could be many of those in a works this size. Besides, in such cruel conditions, supervisors might dress as their workers did.

She tapped one foot impatiently, debating the value of persisting here. M. had asked Fridolin to deliver a package, nothing more. That didn't prove that Mr. Rutherford had ever even met Fridolin. Perhaps their only nebulous link had been acquaintance with M. Nonetheless…she was loathe to walk away without looking Mr. Rutherford in the eye.

While debating, she heard a creak and rattle behind her. She turned to see two barefoot boys, clearly brothers, trudging toward the ironworks. They pulled a handcart, not unlike the one Adolf used for heavy loads, but neither of these boys looked older than ten. Both thin as fence rails, they strained forward with the weight of the two large barrels in the cart. A row of small pails hung from poles attached to each side of the cart; clearly empty, they bounced against the wood panels with each step.

When they neared the door, the brothers dropped the cart shafts to the ground. The smaller of the two rubbed his hands on his backside before helping remove the pail-laden poles from the cart. "Fetch the dipper," the older boy said in German

Hanneke eyed them speculatively. Perhaps they would help. She waited to approach until they had filled all of the pails with beer from one of their barrels.

"Excuse me," she said, with a friendly smile. "I'm trying to get a message to Mr. Rutherford, inside. Do you know him?"

The boys exchanged a glance, as if trying to decide if anything was amiss. Finally, the taller boy shrugged. "Sure. Mr. Rutherford was the one gave us permission to come in."

Ah. So Mr. Rutherford *was* a supervisor...perhaps even the owner. "I'm not permitted inside," Hanneke told the boys. "I'm sure the gentlemen are concerned for my safety." She didn't want to think about these children's safety in such a place. "Would you be willing to give Mr. Rutherford a message? There's a penny in it for you."

"All right," the older boy said promptly. "Peter will take the message. But you pay first." He held out one grubby and calloused hand.

Hanneke fished the penny from her reticule, trying not to wince. She had only a few pennies left, and this would likely be more money spent in vain. Still, she dropped the coin into the boy's palm. "Please tell Mr. Rutherford that Frau Fridolin Bauer is waiting outside, and wishes to speak with him. Peter, is your English good enough for that?"

"Oh, sure," Peter scoffed. Then, when his brother jerked his head impatiently, he carefully picked up both poles. Eight full beer pails hung from each pole, four in front of a hand, four behind. Hanneke's heart clenched, and it was difficult to refrain from objecting as the child paused to balance the weight, his thin shoulders hunching Then Peter walked to the factory and disappeared inside.

"That's a heavy load for him," Hanneke observed. "Wouldn't it be better if you carried the pails inside, and he waited with the cart?"

"No." Peter's older brother leaned against the cart and folded his arms, looking as weary as John Barlow had earlier that morning. "Nobody will bother him inside, and the beer gets sold real quick. It's better I stay out here. I can fight better than him if somebody tries to steal our setup."

Hanneke couldn't argue with that.

They waited in silence. When Peter finally emerged, sixteen empty pails dangled from his poles, and his step was lighter. But he was alone. "Did you speak with Mr. Rutherford?" Hanneke asked.

"Of course!" Peter looked wounded. "I told him what you said."

"And?"

The boy shrugged. "He said he didn't know you. And that he didn't have time to leave the work anyway. But he gave me something for you." He snaked one hand into a pocket and pulled free a crumpled card.

Hanneke snatched it eagerly. It was a small tract, published in English on one side and German on the other. Her surging spirits deflated as she read the German words: *A MESSAGE FOR THE AGES. Repent all ye who sin, and turn your heart toward your God.* Below that, someone had hand-written two Bible verses: *Job 38:31-32* and *Isaiah 40:26*. A line of print at the bottom noted *A gift from the Wisconsin Bible Society*.

"He gave me one too," Peter announced, holding it up so proudly that Hanneke suspected it was the first gift he'd ever received.

The older boy jerked his head again, this time toward the cart. "Come on. We're wasting time."

"*Danke schön.*" Hanneke slipped the booklet into her apron pocket with her knitting. The boys lashed the poles and buckets to the cart and plodded toward the next factory.

Hanneke watched them go, trying to decide what had just happened. She had hoped that identifying herself as Frau Bauer might trigger Mr. Rutherford's interest. Perhaps the Yankee had never heard of her or Fridolin, and handed cards noted with Bible verses to everyone he met. The German community might be buzzing about the strange woman who had appeared with claims of marriage to Fridolin Bauer, but that didn't mean that the Yankees knew anything about it.

Or perhaps Mr. Rutherford had heard of the scandal and selected verses intended to condemn or shame her. Clearly, he was as religious as the mysterious M. who had written to Fridolin. Had Fridolin held such deep religious convictions? She hadn't been aware of any during their days together. But then…there were many things about Fridolin she hadn't been aware of.

* * *

146

A handful of Watertown stores carried cloth, and Hanneke visited them all. She examined bolts of cotton and fingered ready-made cravats and neckerchiefs. She found bright yellow cotton with black checks, and pale yellow cotton with black dots, and golden-yellow cotton with feather-shaped paisley designs. No bright yellow with black stripes.

John Barlow was right, Hanneke admitted reluctantly as she stepped from the last store. Searching for the fabric used to make the dead man's neckerchief had been a fool's errand. She was no closer to learning anything about the man who'd been attacked and killed in the alley.

She squinted at the sun. She needed to get back to the tavern soon, but she should have time for one more quick errand.

At the German blacksmith shop, the smith was re-tiring a wagon wheel in a round fire pit beside the building, so the idlers had shifted outside as well. Hanneke ignored them and pulled down the note she'd left on the shop door—the one asking for information about Fridolin's death. Seeing the dead man pulled from the river had convinced her that advertising her quest in this public manner, even among the German working class, was too dangerous.

She was about to turn away when something else caught her eye—another note, written on the back of an envelope and speared on a nail: *Eggs, which may be relied on as pure and fresh, for sale. See Frau Muehlhauser on Muehlhauser Lane.* The message was innocuous, but it was written in pale brown ink—exactly like the ink Fridolin had used in his letters.

Had it merely been hanging here for so long that the sun had faded it? No, surely not. It was hanging very close to where she'd posted her own notices. If it had been there on her first visit, she would have seen it.

Hanneke cast about for someone to question. The old man who'd talked to her on her first visit was on the fringes, leaning on his cane. "Pardon me," Hanneke began. "I'm trying to learn where Muehlhauser Lane is. Is it nearby?"

He waved a gnarled hand. "Oh, no. It's across the bridge, out of town. Northeast of here."

Northeast of here. "Near Plum Grove Road?"

"Well, yes!" The man gummed some tobacco and managed a feeble squirt over his shoulder. "Off the main road. Pass the turnout for Plum Grove, then take the next left." He frowned suddenly, squinting at her. "But what do you want to go out there for? Are you one of those Bible Society women?"

Hanneke's skin tingled. Plum Grove Road. The Bible Society. Stray threads of information seemed to converge. "Well, I—yes. I am." Hanneke looked away as she spoke, her cheeks hot as the iron rim glowing orange in the fire pit. That was no lie of omission. She had spoken falsely. And about a Bible Society, of all things.

"Well, I hope your Society *can* help the family. They need it."

Hanneke leaned forward. "Things have gotten so bad for the Muehlhausers?"

Behind them, the blacksmith poured a bucket of water on the rim, shrinking it around the wheel. The old man waited until the hiss of steam died before answering. "Muehlhauser is a drunkard."

Hanneke blinked. This was a serious charge within German communities. Most men knew their limits. "I see."

"The minister has tried to get him to stop, but without success. Maybe the Bible Society will fare better." He shook his head. "And his wife deserves more than she's got."

"I'll do my best," she said briskly. "Good afternoon."

"You can't miss the place," the old man called after her. "Muehlhauser has a habit of dumping bad beer in the pigsty. Look for the farm with drunken pigs."

Hanneke's mind was tumbling. The matching ink...the Muehlhauser farm's proximity to the Bauer farm...could Frau Muehlhauser be the woman Clara Steckelberg believed Fridolin had been visiting clandestinely? Hanneke was practically twitching with the urge to march straight out of Watertown on the northeast road. She wanted to look Frau Muehlhauser in the eye. She wanted to learn the truth, tawdry as it might be, about Fridolin's life and character.

However, she was needed at the tavern. Taking care of Angela, keeping an eye on Adolf, making sure the weary laborers who visited the Cockerel received a decent meal—despite her personal sense of urgency, those things came first.

But tomorrow, she promised herself as she turned toward the tavern, I will visit the Muehlhauser farm.

* * *

Angela was asleep and Adolf absent when Hanneke arrived back at the Red Cockerel. She barely had time to put the chairs down before the first patrons arrived. And how am I to handle the taproom, the cooking, and the serving alone? she wondered. Angela clearly needed the rest. As for Adolf…she didn't know if she should be angry or worried.

There was nothing to do but set to it. She built up the fire in the cookstove to reheat the pea soup she'd prepared that morning. When she opened the front door she found half a dozen men waiting patiently.

She'd never tended bar before. It was easy enough, for almost everyone ordered only beer. Still, keeping customers happy and money counted amid the growing chatter required concentration. She'd been at it for some time before belatedly remembering that this type of activity was exactly why Deputy Barlow had ordered her to listen for any "fragments of conversation" about Know-Nothing activity or plans being made by men of The German Star. Since she wanted information as much as John Barlow did, she tried to eavesdrop on the workers crowding the bar and slumping at the tables.

"…a man that harsh has no business supervising others…"

"…and I told him, there isn't an Irishman alive who can be trusted to…"

"…letter just about broke his heart…"

"…make more money claiming bounty for a runaway than I do in six months of wages…"

"…had hoped to get the contract for the new building the German Evangelical Lutheran Society is planning, but…"

"…said it was just a mild fever, but three days later she was dead, and…"

Dipping in and out of the conversations as she poured beer and delivered bowls was not uplifting, but it did put her own problems into perspective.

There was a great deal of misery in the world. So far, though, none of the lamentations were attributed to the Know-Nothings or a secret German society. I'll have to disappoint Deputy Barlow once again, she thought.

Adolf appeared sometime later, slipping in the kitchen door just as Hanneke plunged into the room with a stack of dirty dishes. He looked guilty.

She set the tinware down with a clatter. "Where have you—"

"Sorry," he mumbled, avoiding her gaze. "I'll go take care of the bar."

Hanneke grabbed his arm as he tried to sidle past. "Adolf. You know Angela's not well. You know I can't cook and serve and pour beer at the same time. Where have you been?"

"There was a meeting. I had to go."

This was exactly what she did *not* want to hear. "Oh, Adolf...."

"I know I left you alone at a bad time, and I'm sorry!" He wrenched free of her grasp. "But I have to go when and where I'm told. The Know-Nothings will not prevail. Events are in motion."

That parroted declaration did nothing to ease Hanneke's concern. "What events?"

"Don't worry." He lifted his chin.

"*Please*, Adolf. You're frightening me. Just tell me what—"

A heart-wrenching mix of excitement and fear and bravado flashed in his eyes. "I can't say anything more!" Then he bolted for the taproom.

Fighting despair, Hanneke hung her head. She'd promised Angela to watch out for Adolf, keep him from trouble. But clearly, trouble had already found him.

Chapter Sixteen

Adolf swept the taproom after the last customer left, then disappeared without a word. Hanneke washed stacks of dishes, scoured the kettles, picked over beans and put them on to soak for the next night's meal. When all was tidy she settled at the table. Exhausted, she wanted nothing more than to go to bed. But Deputy Barlow might yet knock on the door.

When she reached into her pocket for her knitting, she discovered the tract Mr. Rutherford had asked the young beer bucket boy to pass on to her. *My faith is strong, thank you,* Hanneke thought. She had little patience with those who tried to impose their religious beliefs on others.

She was about to toss the tract into the stove's firebox when she saw again the references to Bible verses that someone, presumably Mr. Rutherford, had written on the printed card. *Job 38:31-32, Isaiah 40:26.*

She didn't know either of those verses. And...as she thought back, picturing the young beer boy proudly displaying his own gift, she was certain that no handwritten notes had been added to his tract.

Curiosity piqued, Hanneke fetched the Bible Fridolin had given her and found the first text: *Can you bind the beautiful Pleiades? Can you loose the cords of Orion? Can you bring forth the constellations in their seasons or lead out the Bear with its cubs? Do you know the laws of the heavens?*

The verses made Hanneke misty-eyed, remembering Fridolin's joyful awe when considering the night sky. Had Mr. Rutherford scribbled this particular verse with Fridolin in mind? With a perplexed frown, Hanneke thumbed through the pages until she found the second verse: *Lift your eyes and look to the heavens: Who created all these? He who brings out the starry host one by one, and calls them each by name. Because of His great power and mighty strength, not one of them is missing.*

Hanneke sank back in her chair. Two verses about astronomy, Fridolin's favorite pastime. This was no coincidence. When the boy told Mr. Rutherford that Hanneke Bauer wanted to speak to him, he'd written these verses before sending the child back to deliver the tract.

This has to mean something, she thought. But what? *What?*

She slipped the tract back into her pocket in exchange for her knitting, and completed several rows of the cabled stocking. Finally, with no sign of Deputy John Barlow, she dragged herself to bed.

The next morning, when she took Angela a breakfast tray, she was heartened to see a bit more color in her friend's cheeks. "You are looking better," she observed.

"I'm feeling better too," Angela said. "If all goes well today I hope to come downstairs for the evening rush. If nothing else I can sit and wash dishes. I feel guilty for letting you and Adolf carry all the weight."

Hanneke felt torn. Should she tell Angela what Adolf had said about "things happening?" For now, Hanneke decided, I will carry that alone. "Let's wait and see how you feel, all right?" she asked. "Is there anything else you need? I'm going out."

* * *

As predicted, the Muehlhauser hogs were indeed drunk.

Hanneke stopped by their pen, which fronted the lane. One lop-eared hog lay on its side; the other on its back, four legs pointed toward the clouds. They were large Saddlebacks, black with a white belt. When she leaned over the fence, she smelled tinges of yeast and hops among the thick black scent of the animals' mucky wallow. Disgraceful, really. She wondered if a diet of bad beer would taint the meat.

Then she lifted her gaze to the house—just a rough little cabin, actually. In the absence of a barn or stable, the cabin walls were hung with tools: a sickle, a scythe, corn knives, tin basin, wooden bucket, butcher knife. A butter churn, a washstand with two tubs, and two heavy grub hoes stood against the walls beneath the feeble protection offered by the overhanging eaves. A garden stretched listlessly off to one side; hops twined around a row of tall poles beyond. Aside from a few desultory red chickens scratching for insects in the shade, the farm itself seemed unnaturally still.

And unbearably sad. Hanneke's suspicion that Fridolin had come to the Muehlhauser home to write letters to his new bride faltered. What kind of haven could this wretched place provide? Surely Herr Muehlhauser, known drunkard, had not served as a confidant.

Fridolin Bauer wasn't heading toward any political meeting. He was headed toward a woman. Hanneke remembered the distaste that had curdled Clara Steckelberg's voice as she confided that she'd seen Fridolin sneaking about at night. The Muehlhauser property lay just north of the Steckelberg land and touched corners with the Bauer farm. But even now, after so many revelations, Hanneke wasn't ready to believe *that*....

Lost in thought, Hanneke didn't notice the woman who stepped outside until she emerged from the shadows. Her dress had once been blue, but was badly faded—sun bleached almost white on the shoulders. Her face was so thin that the cheekbones seemed sculpted of clay. She might have been a decade older than Hanneke, perhaps two. She looked more worn out than aged, so it was impossible to tell.

"Are you Frau Muehlhauser?"

The woman nodded.

"My name is Hanneke Bauer. Fridolin Bauer was my husband."

Frau Muehlhauser studied Hanneke expressionlessly. A small brown bird landed on a branch, twittered an encouraging song, then flitted away. Finally, the older woman nodded. "So. You've come."

Hanneke clenched the fence rail, welcoming its splintery bite. "Do you... you know who I am?"

The woman turned away. "Come inside."

"Please tell me!"

"You must come inside. We don't get much traffic, but I don't want anyone passing by to see us together."

"Why not?" Hanneke demanded, but received no answer. She reluctantly followed the older woman inside.

The gloomy room was cluttered and smelled stale. A cast-iron spider stood over dying coals in the fireplace, still holding evidence of the morning's meal. Three tin pails on the table brimmed with tiny strawberries; another held hulled fruit. Frau Muehlhauser sat down at the table and gestured at the chair on the other side. Hanneke sat and removed her bonnet, unspoken questions buzzing inside like a swarm of bees.

"I hope you will call me Gerda." Frau Muehlhauser sounded almost shy. She picked up a knife and deftly sliced the stem from a berry. "I almost feel as if I know you."

Hanneke's heart skittered in her chest. "I beg you. Tell me…"

"I will," Gerda said. "But first, you need to understand something. Once I've told you what little I know, I won't ever speak of it again. If you tell anyone else what I've said, I will call you a liar."

Hanneke leaned back. This is not what she wanted. She wanted someone to publicly identify her as Fridolin's wife!

And yet…what she wanted *most* was to hear the truth. At least whatever part of the truth this woman guarded. "I understand."

Gerda reached for another tiny berry. "How did you find me?"

"Your note on the blacksmith shop's door. I recognized the ink that Fridolin used to write me letters. At least it looked just the same. Did he write those letters here?"

"Yes. He didn't want Christine to know."

"Why?"

"I don't know."

Hanneke let a long breath escape and clenched her hands in her lap, steeling herself for the next question. "Why did Fridolin come here? Was he looking for…company?"

A smile twitched at the other woman's mouth. "Yes. But not what you're thinking. We were friends. Nothing more than that, I assure you."

Hanneke searched Gerda's eyes. They were so calm, so guileless, that

Hanneke believed she was hearing the truth. Relief escaped in a long breath. "But...how did your friendship come to be? How did you two become so familiar? No one else in Watertown even knew I existed! Yet obviously he told you about our marriage."

"He came here because he was a kind man." Gerda flicked a bit of green leaf from a berry with her thumbnail. "I met him soon after he and Christine moved into the old Jaeger place. He came by wanting to meet his neighbors. My husband was drunk." Her hands stilled, and she looked away.

"I see."

"Well. There's no need to go into detail. But Fridolin...well, I think he pitied me. He took to stopping by. At first, he always had some excuse. 'We picked more cucumbers today than Christine can handle,' or, 'These gooseberries will spoil if you don't make use of them.' Later, he'd come and ask if I had enough wood chopped, or needed anything taken to town. Things like that. Sometimes, after he left, I found a few coins tucked under a crock, or left on the mantle." She met Hanneke's eyes directly for the first time since they'd come inside. "Fridolin Bauer was a good, kind man."

"I want so much to believe that... but if that's true, why did he not tell people about me?"

"I don't know, and that's the truth," Gerda told her. "I never asked questions. I think that was why he came to feel so comfortable here. Sometimes I'd make him a cup of tea. Sometimes we talked a little. But I always let him decide how it was going to be. I like to think that after a while, he came not just from kindness, or pity, but because he appreciated having a place to sit and be still. Someplace peaceful."

"And no one ever noticed these visits?" Other than Clara Steckelberg, who had evidently kept her suspicions to herself.

"I don't think so. He came the back way, and took care to visit when Christine wasn't about, I think."

"Forgive me, but...where was your husband during these visits?"

Gerda shrugged. "My husband Oscar's main occupation is making beer in the brew shed out back. Sometimes he was working while Fridolin was here. If Oscar was sober, he and Fridolin might chat a bit, although they had

155

little in common. Most often Oscar wasn't home, though. Or if he was, he was dead drunk and snoring in the shed." She met Hanneke's gaze. "It isn't his fault, you know. On his own, a German man knows when to stop. But in America Yankees buy rounds and expect everyone else to do the same."

Gerda might have been talking about the weather, for all the emotion her voice contained. Hanneke wanted to reach across the table and squeeze the other woman's hand. She wasn't sure the gesture would be welcome.

"Anyway, Fridolin had been visiting for…oh, I don't know, maybe a year before he ever asked for anything," Gerda continued. "Then one afternoon late last fall, after he got back from Pomerania, he sat right there in that chair you're in and watched me write a grocery list. Then he asked me if I'd be willing to let him use some of my ink. I said I didn't have any spare paper, and he said that didn't matter, he could bring some from his bookbinding supplies the next time he came. 'But not ink,' he said. ' Christine would know if I used our ink.'"

Hanneke pressed her fingertips to her temples. Fridolin earned their living, yet he didn't feel able to use ink? Christine must have guarded the household accounts like a falcon. "Couldn't he have simply purchased ink in town?"

The older woman shrugged. "Christine evidently watched every penny. Anyway, once the idea of writing letters here came to Fridolin, it just seemed to suit. He could take his time instead of trying to find someplace in town, or at the farm, where someone might see him. He'd spend a good long time writing those letters. After he'd finished one, he'd give me money for postage and ask me to mail it."

Hanneke leaned forward again. "And he told you he was writing to me?"

"I don't think he'd planned to. But the first time he wrote a letter here I said something about how he'd taken such care with it, and he said, 'It's important that I get the words just right. This is a special letter.'"

A special letter, Hanneke thought. Special. She had *not* imagined his respectful affection.

"I said that it was a shame that an important letter would be written in such poor ink. I make my own ink from tea and pokeberries, you see. He

156

stared at the paper for a moment—I remember this so clearly—and then he looked at me and said, 'Gerda, I'm writing to my wife.' I'm sure a bee could have flown right into my mouth, I was that surprised. He smiled a little and told me that he'd gotten married while traveling back in the Old Country. And he said, 'I don't believe Hanneke is the kind of woman who would worry about something so inconsequential as brown ink.'"

Hanneke swiped at a tear. Her heart felt both heavy and light at once.

Gerda dropped another stemmed berry into the small bowl. "And he said that I mustn't tell anyone. Made me promise. It's a promise I've kept."

"But he didn't say why?"

"No.

"And to the best of your knowledge, he never did tell Christine about me?"

"No. I don't think he did."

So. Christine had been telling the truth, and Deputy John Barlow too.

"And I won't tell now. I'm sorry." Gerda gave Hanneke a sympathetic gaze. "She wouldn't believe me anyway, though. No one would."

Gerda was probably right about that, Hanneke thought, reaching into her pocket for the comfort of her knitting needles. Hadn't she initially found it hard to believe that Fridolin had spent time at so rude a place? She was ashamed of her earlier assumption.

But there was more she needed to know. "Gerda...did Fridolin ever mention anything to suggest that he might be involved in politics?"

She shrugged. "He didn't like the Know-Nothings. None of us do."

"Did he seem worried about anything before he died?"

For the first time, Gerda hesitated. Don't stop now, Hanneke begged her silently.

Gerda hulled three more strawberries before responding. "I think he *was* worried. I don't know why. But toward the end he'd sometimes come and just sit, smoking his pipe and staring at the wall. Not contented, but like something weighed on his mind."

Or his conscience? Hanneke wondered. "I've come to believe that my husband was involved in a secret society called The German Star, which formed to fight the Know-Nothings. He never mentioned it? Please, think hard. Anything you can remember might be helpful."

Gerda shook her head, but her hands had stilled. "There was one time he said something strange. When he was leaving one afternoon, he apologized for being a bad companion. I told him I was grateful for his company in any case, but sorry that he had some burden on his shoulders. And he said...." Gerda closed her eyes, as if wanting to make sure she remembered correctly. "Fridolin said, 'I *am* worried. And frankly, it would be a relief to talk with someone about it. But I've made my choice and forged it in iron. I wouldn't do things differently even if given the opportunity.'"

Hanneke put her knitting down and crossed her arms over her chest. Fridolin's choices had left her alone and destitute in a strange new country. Was fighting the Know-Nothing influence truly worth that cost?

He had evidently thought so.

"He cared about you," Gerda said, as if reading her thoughts. "I could see it in his eyes when he told me he'd married. I could see it in the way he lingered over those letters. When he was writing to you he seemed...I don't know. Peaceful, somehow."

That was all very well. Reassuring, even. But knowing he cared won't keep a roof over my head, Hanneke thought. She didn't speak aloud, though. Gerda Muehlhauser carried her own burdens.

Instead, Hanneke asked, "Were you shocked to hear how Fridolin died? It seems...well, such a clumsy thing. Was he so poor a farmer?"

"I don't think he cared for farming. He never spoke of building up his place the way most men do."

"I was surprised to learn he was still threshing last year's grain." Hanneke didn't mention that she'd actually seen the surprising amount of unthreshed wheat still piled in the barn. "I know Fridolin was traveling for much of the autumn, but still."

Gerda nodded. "Yes, that's true too. I remember on my father's place...." She spread her hands. Then she added, "I do think Fridolin took some pride in his harvest. Wheat, you know. That's the big cash crop. We had a terrible storm about two weeks before Fridolin died. Fierce winds and torrential rain. I asked Fridolin if his roof had held. A bad wind can just peel open a thatched roof, you know. Anyway, he said 'Yes, and a good thing it was. After the sacrifices I've made to get my crop in the barn, I've got to protect it.'"

"Farming's hard work for those born to it," Hanneke said quietly. "Harder still for those used to a trade."

"Yes."

Silence stretched between them. Outside a dove cooed. Hanneke felt drained, and she tucked her knitting away. "Gerda, thank you for speaking with me. I'm most grateful." She gestured toward the pail of berries. "Would you like me to help you take these things outside? It's a pleasant day."

"*Nein, danke.*" Gerda reached for another berry. "I'm more comfortable inside."

Hanneke hated leaving Gerda alone in this grim cabin. "Do you have children?"

"I've not been so blessed."

Hanneke felt a fierce stab of hot anger—anger at God, anger at men who didn't care for their wives—and sisters—as they should. "Do you...well, do you attend one of the churches? Watertown's not a far walk in fair weather, and there are surely other people who might offer some help...."

Gerda regarded Hanneke before saying, "Some of the good women of Watertown look at me with contempt. And I can not forgive them for it. Yes, my husband is a drunkard. But my only crime is accepting a man in marriage that I did not know well. I had no way to predict what my life would become."

Nor did I, Hanneke thought. This time she did reach over and take Gerda's hand. "It was good of you to talk with me," she said again. "And—and I'm glad to know that Fridolin had a friend like you." Strange as it seemed, Gerda Muehlhauser had perhaps known Fridolin better than anyone else.

With her free hand, Hanneke scrabbled into her reticule, beneath the table, and scooped up the last of her coins. She left them on the chair, to be discovered later.

Outside, Hanneke put on her bonnet and started to walk back up the drive. Then she paused, turning to look back toward Fridolin's land. After the last hour, she understood him only slightly better than she had before, and she hadn't forgiven him his secrets and lies. But Fridolin had found some measure of peace at Gerda's house, and a part of her was glad for that.

Now, unexpectedly, she felt an urge to retrace the path where Fridolin had so often walked. She didn't think Gerda would mind, so she skirted the brew shed and a small field behind the cabin.

Woods bordered the south edge of the Muehlhauser property. It was peaceful here, shady and cool. White trillium bloomed in the shade of oaks and other hardwood trees she didn't recognize. She found a faint path, marked with a few crushed ferns and other signs of recent use. She liked knowing she was walking where Fridolin once had, even if any mark left by his shoes was long gone. Unlike the marks left on me and Christine and Gerda, Hanneke thought. At least Fridolin had brightened Gerda's life a bit. His kindness to a woman in unfortunate circumstances was perhaps his best legacy.

After a few minutes, Hanneke emerged from the trees and looked around, wanting to understand the landscape. Ahead of her was a narrow field behind Fridolin's *Scheune*. She knew that John Barlow's land was just to the west. His fields had been well prepared, and already neat rows of green showed in the soil, but there was no sign of him. If Christine was home it was unlikely that she would see Hanneke either, for the big grain barn's main doors remained closed, shielding her from view.

Hanneke picked her way through the rutted field behind the barn. Stone supports lifted the structure, encouraging air circulation that helped preserve the grain. She had imagined herself helping stack wheat and rye in there on sticky-hot days, winnowing on breezy ones, perhaps cleaning fleeces on the threshing floor on cool ones.

But it was May, and this back field had not yet been worked. There were no lambs gamboling in the pasture, no dye plants seeded in the garden. The farm was for sale. There was nothing for her here. She braced for the bitter stab that usually came with thinking about everything that she'd lost…but although money from the sale was both needed and her due, the reminder wasn't as cruel as it had been.

Perhaps, she thought slowly, it was time to start turning her back on her dreams, on her marriage, and on this particular farm.

Besides, this beautiful barn had a dark side. Fridolin had died inside—possibly by his own clumsy hand, possibly by another man's evil intent. If it *had* been a deliberate act, had the murderer fled north over this very ground? Perhaps it had been a Know-Nothing Yankee, or perhaps even another German who had quarreled with Fridolin. Hanneke glanced around, as if some clue might be lying on the ground awaiting discovery. But she saw nothing—no dropped work glove or footprint in the mud or anything else a fleeing killer might leave behind.

Well, Hanneke thought briskly, that's quite enough of *that*. She needed to get back to town.

As she started to turn away, though, something caught her eye—a small mark on one of the boards near the barn's northwest corner. She walked closer…and felt a sudden chill, as if a cloud had passed over the sun. Someone had carved a perfect star into the board with a few sure knife strokes.

"The German Star," Hanneke whispered. This had nothing to do with astronomy. Did the mark indicate membership in the secret society? More likely it signaled a meeting place. Clara Steckelberg had seen men traveling by without lanterns on moonless nights. The big barn would be an ideal place for a clandestine gathering.

Deputy Barlow's voice echoed in her memory: *There's a gunmaker and locksmith who has a shop on Second Street…. The shop was cleaned out. Rifles, pistols, even blades…all gone.* The big barn would also be an ideal place to hide stolen weapons.

Hanneke pressed a hand over her mouth, turning that idea over. Evidence suggested that since Fridolin's death, Christine hadn't set foot in the barn. One of the huge storage bays was still filled knee-deep with unthreshed wheat. It would have been easy for the thieves to hide their plunder here. And the carving suggested that the thieves were not Know-Nothings, but members of The German Star.

Had Fridolin been part of this scheme? Despite his duplicity, Hanneke still had a hard time associating the man she'd known with violence. Perhaps he had joined the Star with good intentions and had been horrified to watch the group develop a strategy that involved bloodshed. And perhaps he'd dared object, even threatened to expose the society's leaders…and been killed for it.

Hanneke glanced about, half-expecting armed men to burst from the trees, but the countryside remained serene. She forced herself to breathe slowly, deliberately, until her nerves had steadied. If the stolen weapons *were* in the barn, the men responsible surely wouldn't retrieve them in broad daylight.

She folded her arms. She was loathe to creep into the barn again. The only entry was from the front, facing the house and farmyard, and for all she knew Christine was working in the garden. I did something shameful and foolish once at this place, she reminded herself, and vowed not to do so again. She was more composed now, and unwilling to risk being seen skulking about. All she could do was share her suspicion with Deputy Barlow.

Who would, based on past experience, ignore her concerns. If he even let her voice them in the first place.

This is not my problem! she thought. She had a hunch, nothing more. It was too late to help Fridolin.

But…it might not be too late to help Adolf, and any other earnest young men that leaders of The German Star had recruited, sworn to secrecy, and made promise to obey any commands. Hanneke pictured Adolf brandishing a pistol, Adolf getting arrested, Adolf getting shot. And she pictured Angela's face when she heard the news.

Hanneke also imagined how *she* would feel if, after promising to keep an eye on Adolf, he came to harm because she hadn't done everything possible to protect him.

Very well. She would take one quick look inside the barn. If she found nothing, she could hurry back to tend Angela and prepare for the evening rush with an easier mind. If she did find the stolen weapons, she'd tell Barlow. This time, he would have to listen.

Chapter Seventeen

Hanneke flattened against the barn's side wall and inched closer to the farmyard. The yard and back of the house looked deserted—even the geese were nowhere to be seen. Perhaps they'd already been sold. The only sound was the breeze riffling through the trees by the stable. There was no laundry on the line or hoe propped against the wall to suggest that Christine was in the middle of outside chores.

That doesn't mean Christine wasn't looking out a window right that minute, but Hanneke wasn't turning back now. She lifted her skirt with one hand and walked swiftly to the small barn door. It was still unlocked. She quickly slipped inside and eased the door closed behind her.

The barn interior was hazy-dim and musty. When she walked onto the threshing floor everything looked exactly as it had—tarp, wheat, and flail on the floor; one empty storage bay and one filled with bundled grain. Hanneke eyed that bay grimly. Her simple idea—that this would make a good hiding place—became daunting when faced with the actual task of searching. It would take a very long time to go through the entire bay. And it would be impossible to do so without leaving clear signs of disruption.

Surely the thieves would have faced the same problem, though. If the weapons *were* here, chances were good they were buried in the straw close to the threshing floor. That would provide the quickest hiding place, and the disturbed bundles along the edge could most easily be tidied.

She stepped to the front wall, knelt in front of the bay, slid both hands into the piled wheat bundles, and rummaged. Her heart skittered a little too fast. I will not linger any longer than necessary, she promised herself. One

163

quick pass along the edge, and—

A faint sound broke the stillness. Hanneke snatched her hands from the straw, wide-eyed with unease, straining to hear. A moment later the sound came again—a cry of some sort. What *was* that? The plaintive lament of an orphaned kitten? Hanneke's nerves stretched tighter. Her heart was pounding like a flax break now. She looked over both shoulders. No one.

She plunged her hands back among the grain bundles, scrabbling back and forth, up and down. No…nothing here…no. Every few minutes she crawled sideways to explore more terrain. The brittle straw scratched her hands, rustling too loudly for comfort, but she couldn't bring herself to stop now.

She was almost to the back wall, about to give up, when one hand hit something cool and hard and metallic. A pistol, she realized with a harsh intake of breath. She pulled it free, incredulous that she'd actually found a weapon. The gun was heavier than expected, with a warm wooden grip and long barrel—

A board creaked behind her. As she whirled, Asa Hawkins loomed over her.

"What—" she gasped, but couldn't speak further as he roughly jerked her up. In an instant he'd crushed her against his chest, pinioning her arms with one of his. She kicked frantically, legs tangling in her long skirt and petticoats.

He hissed something in angry English.

Hanneke fought harder. As she sucked in breath to scream, Hawkins clamped one large hand over her mouth and nose. She felt damp cloth, smelled something sweet, tasted grit on her tongue. *"Nein!"* she screamed, but the protest echoed only in her head as her limbs grew leaden. Then everything faded to black.

* * *

Emerging from the depths wasn't pleasant. Hanneke became aware of a fuzzy head, a queasy stomach, a mouth dry as parchment. The light was dim.

The sour air stank of chickens. She felt bruised. She had no idea where she was and for a few moments, no memory of how she got there.

Then it came back: Asa Hawkins appearing behind her in the barn, his face twisted with fury. He'd grabbed her, and...what? She remembered the damp, sweet-smelling cloth he'd pressed over her mouth and nose. Had he *drugged* her? The notion terrified her. It also angered her, though, and she tried harder to clear the woolly feeling from her brain. Might Hawkins have used chloroform? There were probably many possibilities, but she'd read about chloroform's growing use as an anesthetic.

She also remembered the sign she'd seen on J. Hawkins' Wholesale Drug Ware House: *Dealer in Drugs & Medicines....* If J. was a relative, Asa Hawkins had access to such substances.

She pressed her hands at her sides and felt packed earth. Hawkins had taken her from Fridolin's barn. Where was the Yankee now? She went still, every nerve straining to sense him in the gloom, to hear him breathing. Finally, she quavered, "Hello?"

No response.

With great effort, she pushed herself upright. She seemed to be in a shed of some sort. There were no windows, but in the murkiness, she discerned threads of light marking the thin spaces between the sides and top of a door and its frame.

Out, Hanneke thought. The urge to be gone from this place was overwhelming.

Not trusting herself to stand, she hitched up her skirts with one hand and began a scrabble-crawl across the floor. It quickly became apparent that her cell had indeed been used to keep chickens. Fairly recently.

Well, nothing for it, she thought, and kept going. When she reached the door she raised a hand, groping for a knob or latch, but her fingers found only rough boards. She put her shoulder against the door and shoved with all her strength. Nothing happened.

She was trapped.

Why? Hanneke moaned silently, sinking back to the floor. Was Hawkins's hatred of German people so strong that when he'd found her alone, he'd chosen to kidnap her and lock her inside this dreadful place?

No. There had to be another reason why he'd done this.

And…what had Hawkins been doing in Fridolin's barn anyway?

The *guns*.

She rubbed her forehead, fighting the lingering haze, trying to think. Asa Hawkins was a Know-Nothing. Those nativists might have stolen the weapons from the gunsmith's shop. If so, that meant they were planning a violent attack against Watertown's foreign-born residents. Perhaps it had been a Know-Nothing, not a member of The German Star, who'd decided that a threshing barn, disused since the owner's death, would be an ideal place to stash the guns.

If so, maybe Hawkins had come to check on them. Or…maybe he'd seen Christine's notice about selling the farm, and realized the weapons needed to be moved before prospective buyers arrived.

In any event, Hawkins had seen her uncover a pistol, and that had enraged him. Remembering the fury contorting his face, and the venom in his voice, provoked a convulsive shudder.

What did he intend to do with her? Was he keeping her out of the way long enough for the Know-Nothings to wreak whatever evil they were planning? Or had he simply abandoned her to die in here?

Panic bubbled up inside. She placed her cheek against the door frame. *"Help!"* she screamed.

Instead of an affirming shout from outside, she heard a whimper. From *inside* the shed.

Hanneke's heart crawled into her throat. "Hello?"

The silence was ominous.

I did not imagine that sound, she thought. Her head was still fuzzy, but that whimper had been real.

She began a slow crawl around the shed, one hand groping ahead of her. She'd turned two corners before her fingers touched something rough and scratchy. She snatched her hand back even as her brain identified it: *burlap*. A bag that had once held corn for the chickens, perhaps.

When Hanneke patted the sack her fingers brushed something soft and smooth and warm.

She flinched away even faster. This time her brain struggled with the sensory information. It can't be, she thought dumbly.

Wishing she could claw away the shadows, Hanneke inched closer, gently exploring with both hands. Tears welled in her eyes. Unbelievably, unimaginably, she'd found a baby.

The whimper she'd heard had come from this child. And—she'd heard something in Fridolin's barn too, right before Hawkins attacked her. Had that mewling noise come from this child as well? Hanneke traced one small foot, found a paper-thin gown, discovered a wet diaper, discerned that the baby was a girl.

But a new fear constricted her heart. The baby wasn't moving, hadn't made another sound. "Oh please," Hanneke whispered as she eased the girl up from the sack and into her arms. She lay a hand on the baby's chest and sagged with relief when she felt an almost imperceptible rise and fall.

The child must have roused briefly when I screamed for help, Hanneke thought. Had Hawkins drugged this child? The very idea sent a scorching flame of anger through her. She'd felt a grainy residue on the cloth he'd used on her, so perhaps he'd masked the taste of his poison with sugar for the little girl. But *why*? Why under all the heavens would he do such a thing?

Well, no time to contemplate that now. "I've got to get you out of here," she whispered. She impulsively leaned close to kiss the top of the child's head. Her lips met something more textured than she'd expected. This was a colored child.

Hanneke blinked, trying to take that in—and to discern what that discovery meant. Deputy Barlow's observation echoed in her mind: *Hawkins is mean as a slaver.*

"Mein Gott," Hanneke whispered. Maybe Asa Hawkins actually *was* a slaver.

She remembered the notice posted on the blacksmith's shop door: *Wanted – information pertaining to a runaway Negro woman and child.*

And John Barlow had also said, *I spent three hours yesterday riding all over the county trying to track down a man's stolen property.* Maybe that "property" was a mother and child. But if so, how had this baby gotten separated from her mother? The question brought a twist of nausea to Hanneke's gut.

Then a new sense of urgency heightened her focus, and she eased the baby back onto the burlap sack. Questions could be considered later. Right now she *had* to get them both away safely before Hawkins returned. The door was barred from the outside, but perhaps there was a tool in here that she could use to pry it open.

Her frenzied search of the room, however, turned up nothing at all. The walls were made of hewn logs, with no shovels or spades or anything else hanging from or leaning against them. I've got nothing, Hanneke thought, fighting despair. No tool. No weapon. No way to get this precious child to safety.

Tears of frustration burned her eyes as she reached the door again, empty-handed. Pressing one cheek against the crack she imagined sunshine warm on her skin, the friendly wave of some passerby. Freedom was so close she could almost taste it. She instinctively slid one hand into her apron pocket, seeking the comfort of yarn in her hands....

And hiccupped a dazed laugh. She did indeed have one tool: her set of four very thin steel knitting needles.

Just feeling the cool metal beneath her fingers was reassuring. I am a capable woman, she reminded herself. There had to be *something* she could do.

The line of sunshine framing the door was broken on one side in one spot about three-quarters of the way up. A latch? She closed one eye, squinting with the other. The obstruction was about four inches high—too tall for a standard metal latch. Something simple would suffice for a chicken shed. Farmers often pounded a narrow bracket near the edge of a door, and another at the same height on the wall, and barred the door by dropping a board in place. That's what she was seeing, a board nestled on two brackets. The gap between door and frame was too narrow for even her fingertips. But she'd be able to get one or more of her steel knitting needles in there.

After ripping the half-knit sock from the needles she gathered all four in one fist. She tried sliding them through the gap, hoping she might actually be able to lift the board. It proved too heavy, though. After losing her grip several times, she gave up.

Gnawing her lip, she reconsidered. After a moment she slid one of the needles into the gap as far to the right as the narrow space permitted, at an angle, with the tip coming up beneath the board that held the door closed. She carefully clenched the other end of the needle in both hands, getting the best grip she could. Then, holding her breath, she hitched the needle up and to the left.

The board *barely* moved. But it did move.

Getting the bar edged over sufficiently to clear one bracket took a *very* long time. Hanneke didn't realize she was close until one end of the board finally slipped free, the door swung open, and she fell forward from the shed. "Ow!" Her hands hurt so badly she could scarcely flex her throbbing fingers. But she was *free*.

She took a frantic look around, half expecting to see Asa Hawkins pounding furiously across the yard to incarcerate her again, but saw no one. The shed she'd just escaped was one of a handful of wooden buildings clustered near the Rock River. The yard was piled with barrels, crates, lumber. A few cattle milled in a pen. This must be Hawkins's property, the place where goods and livestock could be stored and housed before he sold them to the highest bidder.

Be *quick*, she ordered herself as she stuffed her knitting needles back into her pocket. She scrambled into the shed and got her first real look at the sleeping baby: sweet face, black skin, a gown of faded blue cotton. The girl was perhaps a year old. She was much too thin and desperately in need of a clean diaper, but still breathing. Hanneke scooped up the baby and the burlap sack, and fled.

She scurried across the yard without any sign of pursuit. A sign by the front drive confirmed her suspicion:

Asa Hawkins, Auctioneer
Dealer in merchandise of all kinds.
Freight hauling, livestock sales, etc.

Auctioneer…merchandise of all kinds…those seemingly innocuous phrases were now heavy with malice. Hanneke was acutely aware of the baby's warm weight in her arms. She arranged the burlap to cover the sleeping child.

The road in front of Hawkins' property was deserted. She saw a mill beyond, but no workers. Hanneke darted across the lane, where a grove of trees gave at least the illusion of shelter. It seemed as if an eternity had passed since she left Gerda's farm, but the sun was still overhead. Perhaps… five o'clock? She decided she was south of town—not too far out, she hoped. She craved people, crowds. After a quick glance around she began walking toward Watertown.

But…where should she go? Apprehension trembled her knees, parched her mouth. Where could this precious little one be truly safe? Who could be trusted with the knowledge of the child's existence? Certainly, none of the Know-Nothings, and John Barlow suspected some of the city's small force of constables to be secretly involved.

The only person in Watertown that Hanneke truly trusted was Angela. Perhaps Angela could tend the baby, Hanneke thought, while I try to find Deputy Barlow. But Fridolin had told her about the 1850 Fugitive Slave Act, which demanded that Wisconsin residents help return any runaway to their owners, or aid slave catchers in their vicious hunt. The penalties for aiding escaping slaves—even babies—were harsh. Assuming that this child had indeed been born into slavery, taking her to the tavern meant asking Angela to break the law.

Angela, who was terrified of the police. Angela, who was struggling financially and already in danger of losing her tavern.

Angela, my only friend, Hanneke thought. Just that morning she'd reflected that having Angela—and Adolf too—as friends was giving her the strength to start facing the rest of her life. Taking this baby to the Red Cockerel might bring the law down on them all.

Hanneke didn't know what else to do, so she blinked hard and kept walking.

She strode through the outskirts of town, praying she didn't meet Hawkins or another slave-catcher. When a wagon rumbled closer from behind she lowered her head, holding her breath. The farmer on the seat nodded laconically, flicked his whip at the oxen, and passed by without another glance. Still, her anxiety grew. Were the two men lounging by that cabin over there slave-catchers? Were the elderly man and woman in the passing buggy people she could ask for help, or Know-Nothings who'd contemptuously turn their backs on a German-speaking woman in filthy clothes?

Do not give in to fear, she ordered herself. Just keep going. She couldn't knit with the baby in her arms, but there was something she *could* do to help keep herself calm. She could think.

She thought about the extraordinary circumstances that had led to this moment.

She remembered how quickly, among their spirited debates back in Treptow, she and Fridolin agreed that slavery was abhorrent.

She remembered Herr Wettstein, the hotel owner in Milwaukee, saying that Fridolin often came to the city. Why, Hanneke wondered for the first time, would an incompetent farmer make frequent trips to that city? Fridolin could have sold any excess produce, grain, or livestock at Watertown's market. Why go to Milwaukee?

She remembered that the cryptic letter she'd found among Fridolin's things had come from Milwaukee. *The shipment you requested is on its way. I expect it to arrive in Watertown by mid-month. You'll find one large and one small pot of paint, all I could send for the time being.* Innocuous enough, but could that have been a veiled reference to mother and child?

She remembered what Fridolin had told Gerda Muehlhauser: *After the sacrifices I've made to get my crop in the barn, I've got to protect it. I am worried. And frankly, it would be a relief to talk with someone about it. But I've made my choice and forged it in iron.* Had "crop" been a code word? Had that last odd phrase been an oblique reference to shackles? Had he been worried about slavers catching some terrified man or woman or child?

And she remembered the star carved on Fridolin's barn—low on the back, where it was unlikely to be noticed unless a traveler was looking for it.

That simple design didn't reflect Fridolin's interest in astronomy or mark him as a member of the secret society of German men determined to fight the Know-Nothing movement. But it might represent the North Star, a signal of safety to those in need.

Hanneke desperately wanted to believe that her husband had been helping runaway slaves. Even after all the lies and revelations, she wanted to maintain at least some of the respect she'd once felt for the man she'd married. If Fridolin, a bookbinder-turned-farmer of apparently mild temperament, had scoured up the courage to risk his own safety to help those in such fearful need...she could only applaud him for it.

Even if his marriage to *her* had been one of the sacrifices he'd worried about. Even if everything had somehow gone terribly, fatally wrong.

Chapter Eighteen

Hanneke's gnawing anxiety eased a bit when she turned into the alley behind the Red Cockerel. The baby was stirring with twitchy movements that Hanneke found reassuring. As far as she knew, all she'd attracted while walking through Watertown were a few disdainful looks and quick sidesteps. *Good thing I stink of chickenshit,* she thought. No one looked twice at the burlap-wrapped bundle in her arms.

When she opened the kitchen door Angela whirled from what appeared to be an agitated pace across the room. "Hanneke, I've been frantic! Adolf has—" She abruptly swallowed her words and she stopped, eyes going wide. "What have you done?" Her nose wrinkled. "And—what do you have there?"

Hanneke's anxiety roared back like a locomotive. Something here at the Red Cockerel was dreadfully wrong. Angela was pale. The kitchen stove was cold, its burners empty. Conversation and laughter should have been drifting from the taproom, but the building was oddly silent. "Why isn't the tavern open?"

"Because trouble is coming, and I didn't dare...." Angela spread her hands in a helpless gesture.

"What kind of trouble? Where's Adolf?"

"I don't *know*! He told me he couldn't work tonight." Angela began pacing again, one palm pressed against her belly. "When I asked why, he said 'Things are going to explode this evening.' Those were his exact words. Then he left." She reached one wall, turned, and started back. "With him gone... and I didn't know where *you* were...." Her eyes grew glassy. "Hanneke, I'm terrified that something terrible is going to happen. Adolf could get killed!

Or hurt. Or end up in jail." She twisted her fingers together as if wringing an invisible cloth. "I'd go look for him myself, but—"

"*Nein.*" Hanneke was loathe to leave the tavern—and the child!—but the thought of Angela going out was intolerable.

Hanneke turned away, struggling to construct the best plan. This child needed her, Angela needed her, Adolf needed her. She was terrified of failing all three.

Well, that simply wouldn't do. There was no time for panic. She drew in a deep breath and turned back to Angela. "I will go out and look for Adolf. In a few minutes. First…." She eased back the burlap covering the baby. The little girl's eyes were closed but her mouth pursed and unpursed as if she had something to say.

Angela's mouth formed a perfect O. "Under *Heaven*…where did that Negro baby come from?"

"I'll tell you everything, but may we please go upstairs?" Without waiting for an answer, Hanneke led the way.

In Angela's room, Hanneke knelt on the wool carpet by the bed. When she eased the girl from the sack the baby's eyes remained closed, but her thin arms moved. Hanneke hoped that whatever drug Hawkins had used to silence the child was losing its grip.

"*Hanneke,*" Angela said with some annoyance, "where did—"

"You know Asa Hawkins?"

Angela sucked in a harsh breath. Her shoulders stiffened. "I do."

Hanneke wondered again how Angela had tangled with Hawkins, but right this moment, that wasn't important. Words tumbled over themselves as Hanneke described the star she'd seen on Fridolin's barn, her aborted search for stolen weapons, being attacked by Asa Hawkins, waking up to find herself—and the baby—incarcerated in a chicken shed on Hawkins' property.

Angela sank onto the bed and listened with an expression of growing horror. "*Mein Gott.*"

"Do you have any diapers set aside?" Hanneke asked. "This poor girl…."

"Of course. In that drawer." Angela pointed to her dresser. "And take one

174

of the gowns. There's water in the ewer."

Hanneke found a stack of neatly folded diapers. She used one to gently wipe the child clean, then pinned a second in place. The dirty diapers went into Angela's nightjar. Finally, Hanneke replaced the baby's ragged gown with one that Angela had obviously sewn in preparation for her own child. It was a start.

"I don't know for sure," Hanneke said, "but I think this child was born into slavery. A few days ago I saw a broadside at a blacksmith shop. Someone was looking for information about a runaway Negro woman and child."

"But...how could a mother get separated from her child?"

"I'm sure it's possible. I've heard stories...." Hanneke swallowed something bitter as images of snarling dogs and relentless slave catchers flashed through her mind.

Angela shook her head. "I don't understand why Hawkins was out at Fridolin's barn in the first place."

"I have a theory." Hanneke scooped up the baby and sat down beside Angela. "At first I thought the star carved on the barn was a symbol of The German Star. But maybe it was carved to represent the North Star. Isn't that what runaways use to help guide them north?"

"I...I've heard that's so," Angela whispered. Perhaps she was imagining a desperate mother risking all for the sake of giving her baby a chance at freedom.

Hanneke snuggled the baby against her chest, hoping the girl might be calmed by a heartbeat. It felt as natural as if she'd had a dozen children of her own. Then she looked at Angela. "So—may I leave her with you while I look for Adolf? I considered telling Deputy Barlow what happened, but I'm afraid he'll take this innocent child and return her to...." She shuddered.

"You're not suggesting that we keep her here?"

"Just until I can figure out how to get her back to her mother, or at least among her own people."

Angela sucked in her lower lip. "If she is a slave child, we're breaking the law to even have her here."

"I know. I do know I'm putting you in a terrible position to ask." Hanneke

175

fought to keep her voice steady. "But I am asking, Angela. Please."

Angela stood and walked to the door, her back straight and uncompromising.

Hanneke's stomach knotted as the seconds ticked by. Blinking back tears, she stroked the baby's cheek. If Angela turns us out, Hanneke thought, where will we go?

Angela turned back. Her expression was implacable, and her fingers were twisting her apron. For a heart-wrenching second Hanneke thought that she was about to be ordered from the tavern with the baby.

Then Angela reached for the child. "Of course I'll watch her." Her voice was low but held a fierce note. "May God forgive me for hesitating."

* * *

Angela lined a potato crate with a quilt and eased the baby inside. When Hanneke went back downstairs she drew the kitchen curtains, built up the fire in the cookstove to heat water, and helped herself to a thick slice of rye bread and a piece of cheese.

"I'm going to tidy up before I go back out," Hanneke called up the stairs. "And may I borrow your bonnet? I want to make it difficult for Asa Hawkins to spot me in a crowd."

"Of course."

In her own bedroom, Hanneke quickly stripped down to her petticoat and chemise, washed, and pulled on the green and brown plaid work dress. After re-pinning her hair she felt respectable again.

As she tied on her knitting pocket she reached inside to remove the tangle of yarn remaining after she'd pulled the needles free back in Hawkins's shed. Something fell to the floor—the religious tract Mr. Rutherford had sent to her the day before via the young beer boy. The tract had landed face-down, and when Hanneke picked it up, she realized that someone had ghosted a faint penciled note in German on the margin: *Turn to the Bible in your darkest hours. Begin with Genesis 2:7, and take comfort.*

Hanneke was no Bible scholar, but if she wanted to offer someone comfort in their darkest hours, she wouldn't start with Genesis. Still, she quickly checked that verse in the Bible Fridolin had given her. She frowned, considering, then—*"Oh."*

She slid the tract back into her pocket. Then she broke off the mess of yarn from the ruined stocking and returned the tidy ball and needles as well. Time to go.

She hurried upstairs and checked the baby. The girl was still sleeping, her breathing even. "Come back as soon as you can," Angela said.

"I will. Don't open the door for anyone except me or Adolf. And..." Hanneke hesitated. They had to be realistic. "Even if I find Adolf, I doubt I'll be able to separate him from his comrades. Trying would only humiliate him, strengthen his resolve. But I'll do what I can." Even if all that meant was watching whatever happened. If the boy was injured or taken into custody, she and Angela needed to know.

Angela's eyes were troubled, her voice low. "Be careful."

Moments later, as Hanneke hurried down the alley, she struggled to come up with a strategy. Short of spotting a growing crowd to suggest that the Know-Nothings and The German Star men were about to clash, she had no idea where Adolf might be. That being the case, she might as well start looking on the Main Street bridge over the Rock River. After all, her hunch about the Genesis verse might be wrong. This would likely be a quick stop.

The early evening was soft and warm. She kept a sharp eye out for Asa Hawkins but saw only courting couples out for a stroll, a woman pushing a pram, several giggling schoolgirls, mechanics heading home with toolboxes in their hands. She heard the purr of turning mill wheels along the river, and the quavering calls of an old woman selling morels from a tray. Soft thumping sounds drifted from a back lot where a red-haired man, crouched on his hanging ladder, evened the straw ends of a newly-thatched stable with his beater. A soot-streaked chimney sweep sauntered past with brushes held over one shoulder.

It all seemed normal, and that was disturbing. There's trouble coming! Hanneke wanted to tell them all. Go home and stay there! But no one would believe her. When a constable passed, idly swinging a pocket watch on a chain, she nodded politely and kept walking. He probably wouldn't believe her either…and possibly, if the man was a Know-Nothing, he knew far more about whatever storm was approaching than she did.

Traffic on the Main Street bridge was light. She hurried toward the sign she remembered: *Adam's Haircutting and Shaving/Adam's Haarschneiden und Rasiren.* Curtains were drawn over the shop window. When she tried the door, she found it locked.

Hanneke rapped firmly. No one responded. "Mr. Adam?" she called and knocked again. "Please, sir, I only—"

The door opened just far enough for Adam to peek through the crack. "I'm closed. You must go."

She rammed the toe of one shoe into the gap before he could shut the door again. *"Please.* Just a moment of your time."

He eyed her for a moment, his gaze inscrutable, before stepping back to allow her entry. Once she was inside, he locked the door behind them. The shop was dim, the barber chair empty, scissors and combs neatly laid out on a towel for the morning.

"Thank you," Hanneke said. Suddenly she wasn't sure where to begin. "When I was here a few days ago, I told you that Fridolin Bauer was an acquaintance of mine. Actually, he was my husband."

Something flared in the tall man's eyes, then disappeared. "Ma'am," he said politely in his soft, halting German, "I barely knew Herr Bauer. He came for haircuts. That's all. I don't understand why you are here."

"This is why I'm here." Hanneke pulled the religious tract from her pocket. "I received this, indirectly, from Mr. Rutherford at the Vulcan Iron Works. There is a note on the back that says *Turn to the Bible in your darkest hours. Begin with Genesis 2:7, and take comfort.*"

Adam didn't react.

"Genesis chapter two, verse seven, says this: 'And the Lord God formed man of the dust of the ground, and breathed into his nostrils the breath of life; and man became a living soul.'" Hanneke moistened her lips with her tongue. "That man, of course, was Adam. I think I was sent here to learn something, to find something…"

"I can't help you. Herr Bauer is dead."

"But I believe my husband was helping runaway slaves get to Canada."

Adam stepped back to the door, put his hand on the knob. "There is nothing for you here."

"I'm not asking only for myself!" Hanneke said urgently. "This afternoon a man named Asa Hawkins assaulted me in Fridolin's barn. Hawkins drugged me and abducted me. When I awoke I found myself locked in a shed. And a baby Negro girl, who was also drugged, was in there with me."

Adam remained very still, but Hanneke sensed a change within him—a shift, almost imperceptible, but real. She waited. The plaintive sounds of a lament drifted from the bridge as several singing Irishmen passed.

Finally, Adam spoke. "Where is this child?"

"When I was able to escape the shed, I took the baby with me. She's safe. For the moment." Hanneke stepped closer. "But I don't know what to do! I want Hawkins punished, but I'm afraid to turn the baby over to a deputy sheriff or—"

"Don't." The word was sharp as a razor.

"Then what should I do? What happened to her mother?"

"The mother left that baby behind because she heard slave catchers approaching. With dogs. She was willing to sacrifice herself so that the child might escape."

Something sour rose from Hanneke's stomach, coating the back of her throat. "Was she captured?" she whispered.

"No. The men searching for her are still here. Still looking."

Danke Gott, Hanneke thought. Mother and child could be reunited. "Where is she?"

"I do not know. There are only a few of us who do...what we do. We are never given more information than necessary. It is safer for everyone."

"Yes, of course, but she must be frantic!" Since arriving in Watertown Hanneke had been grieving only the lost promise of motherhood. She couldn't imagine the grief of a young mother who'd been forced to leave her child behind. "We've got to let her know that her baby is safe. What about Mr. Rutherford? He is an abolitionist, yes?"

Adam closed his eyes and dropped his chin. Hanneke couldn't tell if he was thinking, or wrestling with emotion, or both. Finally, he looked up again. "I should *not* discuss this with you."

Instinct compelled her to simply meet the man's gaze. Adam's eyes were anguished and uncertain. You can trust me, she vowed silently.

After a long moment, he seemed to come to a conclusion. "Yes. Mr. Rutherford is an abolitionist. Most of us can only hide one or two people at a time, but Mr. Rutherford has a hidden room at the ironworks that can hide half a dozen. It's in the smallest building, near the river. The hiding place is above a joiner's shop on the second floor."

"Can you find out if the baby's mother is there?"

"Once the sun starts to set it's best that I stay behind my own doors. Not just for my own sake." Adam's gaze bore into hers, trying to make her understand something he wasn't willing to articulate.

Not just for his sake, Hanneke thought, but for the sake of other runaways. It suddenly occurred to her that there might be, right this minute, another terrified black-skinned person huddled somewhere nearby—even beneath this roof—with nothing to do but trust Adam and pray.

Adam glanced toward the door as the sound of running feet approached, passed, faded again. After what seemed a very long time he said, "I'll learn what I can. Come back to see me early tomorrow morning."

Hanneke nodded. Could she and Angela keep the baby safe that long? They had to.

Adam stepped to the window and inched the curtain aside to show a small white china vase on the sill, filled with decorative grasses. "You see this? If this is gone in the morning, knock. If the vase is still there, keep walking. You understand?"

"Yes."

"Do not come back when I'm doing business. Might be a slaver sitting in my chair."

The thought of Adam shaving a slave-catcher, trimming his hair, made her feel queasy.

"Or a Know-Nothing," he added. "They're almost as bad."

"I understand."

Adam's eyes narrowed. "I believe a slaver killed that man they pulled out of the river."

Hanneke caught her breath. "I saw the man get attacked! Who was he?"

"The thing to remember," Adam said as he unlocked the door, "is that it could have been *you*."

Chapter Nineteen

Hanneke walked quickly back in the direction she'd come, trying to outpace her apprehension. Adam's terse reminder—*It could have been you*—had iced her marrow. What had she gotten herself and Angela into? If Asa Hawkins hadn't already discovered that she'd escaped from the shed with the baby, he could any time. She remembered the fury in his eyes when he'd surprised her in the barn. Once he realized that she'd fled, he would want to silence her before she could report his assault.

Fridolin Bauer, she snapped silently, *do you know what you have done?*

No response.

Hanneke rubbed her temples. As if hiding from slavers wasn't enough, she still had no idea what trouble Adolf was in.

At the edge of the bridge, she paused. Dusk was descending, and buzzing chimney swifts circled overhead. None of the nearby pedestrians looked threatening. Just down First Street, the clustered buildings of the Vulcan Iron Works appeared quiet and still.

Hanneke bit her lip. Was the baby girl's mother huddled so close by? Were other runaways hiding there? Hanneke remembered another line in the letter written to Fridolin by M. in Milwaukee. *I will also take advantage of transport to send a parcel to Mr. Rutherford. I hope you will be so kind as to deliver it at the ironworks.* Was that code telling Fridolin that his help was needed to pass some desperate soul on to Mr. Rutherford? She imagined frightened parents trying to comfort children. She pictured old people with aching bones and bleeding feet, women in threadbare dresses shivering in the cold, hungry men praying to escape the hounds.

It was maddening not to know. But members of The German Star might be gathering in Watertown right this minute, ready to burst onto the street. She'd promised to search for Adolf.

Hanneke decided to start with taverns German men might frequent, especially those with meeting rooms, so she headed away from the Rock River. German immigrants had made homes throughout Watertown, but the neighborhood surrounding Angela's tavern, in the north central part of the city, was particularly Germanic. The lots in this part of town were small; the houses built close together. She stopped at boarding houses and drinking establishments to ask about Adolf. "He said he had a club meeting, but I'm not sure where the group was gathering," she explained over and over with a polite smile, "and he's needed at work." No one offered any clear information. Some people merely shrugged. A few seemed evasive.

That may be nothing but my imagination, Hanneke thought wearily sometime later as she emerged from an establishment advertising *Wurst und Bier*. She sighed, dabbing at beads of sweat on her forehead. She had skipped the Buena Vista Hotel on Fourth Street, the most obvious possible gathering place. Some of the Latin farmers and philosophy professors and divinity scholars who regularly gathered there might be leaders of The German Star. It was easy to imagine them lecturing and proclaiming and postulating, all the while recruiting idealistic, uneducated young men like Adolf.

Setting her shoulders, she turned toward the hotel. Before trudging half a block, however, she heard distant shouting—and then a drum's militant rattle. She felt a sinking sensation in her stomach. It has begun, she thought. The trouble Adolf had predicted had begun.

Two young boys raced by with a shaggy dog eagerly keeping pace. Hanneke followed them back to First Street. A crowd was already gathering. Her heart tightened when she saw the procession marching from the north. Once more, men wearing top hats and frock coats led the column. Some carried torches that flickered wildly against the evening's gray-blue sky.

The Know-Nothings were parading once more.

Hanneke wanted to see what was happening, but not again would she stand near the street where someone could shove her into traffic. She stepped onto a low porch so she could watch with her back pressed safely against the solid brick wall.

Perhaps fifty men marched behind the leaders. Some of them carried signs. Hanneke remembered Angela's bleak translations: *We will not yield to a foreign hand. Beware the foreign influence. America, our native land.* One sign portrayed a crudely drawn German immigrant with an oversized beer stein in each hand. That one was labeled for all to read: *Deutscher Säufer*—German Drunkard.

Then she saw that some of the men carried guns.

Abruptly, a fit of welcome anger boiled away her fatigue and fear. She'd seen too much hatred and cruelty today. All any of us want, she fumed, is a hearth of our own. An opportunity to work hard and contribute to this country. That was not too much to ask!

Tempted as she was to march into the street and confront their hatred, she forced herself to think calmly. Watching these nativists applaud themselves for their supposed superiority would accomplish nothing helpful. Instead, she rose on tiptoes, considering the men marching, the onlookers. She heard mutters and grumbles around her but so far, no sign of anything worse. *If* The German Star had somehow known about this parade, and *if* those German men truly planned to confront the Know-Nothings, then Adolf and his comrades had most likely gathered somewhere south of here.

Hanneke stepped from the porch and slipped through the crowd. "*Entschuldigung,*" she murmured over and over as she jostled people aside. She managed to reach Main Street and trotted a block away from the river before turning south again. If she could get ahead of the Know-Nothings, she *might* be able to find the German men before a brawl erupted.

She'd trotted several more blocks before turning again toward the Rock River. Back on First Street, she paused, chest heaving, looking again at the Vulcan Iron Works. The spacious factory yard might actually be a safer place to observe whatever was about to happen. Hanneke scurried across the street and found a secure spot backed against the big two-horse treadmill on display.

The Know-Nothings were just a block away now. She looked south just as another parade appeared from around a bend. In the shadows, she estimated a group of two dozen men, maybe more. This group had no drummer. They carried no signs. But some carried their own blazing torches and as they drew closer, Hanneke saw firelight glinting on metal. Some of these men also carried pistols or rifles. Others walked with pitchforks or spades over their shoulders.

I have found The German Star, she thought grimly, and they are ready for a fight.

Things are going to explode this evening.

Hanneke hugged her arms over her chest as the German men came closer, ever closer. Where was Adolf? In the twilight, it was impossible to identify any of the marchers. The drumbeats winched Hanneke's nerves tighter and tighter. The space between the two groups had dwindled to half a block.

Men and some women crowded the walkway across the street. A few joined Hanneke in the factory yard too. The people were quiet, though. Expectant. When several tin whistles suddenly shrilled in the hush, Hanneke almost jumped from her skin.

Four—no, five—mounted men trotted from a side street and turned onto First in the gap between Know-Nothings and The German Star. Lawmen, she thought, but they were so sorely outnumbered she felt no relief. Their horses pranced skittishly as if sensing the tension. Two of the riders eased north to face the Know-Nothings, and two turned toward the Germans. Hanneke held her breath, terrified that one group or the other would shove past. But the first line of German men stopped, and the Know-Nothings halted as well.

The mounted man alone in the center stood in his stirrups. "I am Sheriff Giles!" He pulled his mount in a tight circle so he could address both groups. "I order you to disperse!" The nearest horsemen repeated Giles's command in fluent but accented German. It was John Barlow, Hanneke was sure of it.

"We have grievances!" one of the Germans yelled. Some of his comrades hollered their agreement. Others shifted their weight uneasily, adjusted their grips on their hoes or pickaxes or rifles.

"This is not the way to address them!" Barlow insisted.

Listen to him! Hanneke silently urged Adolf and his comrades. *Go home before someone gets hurt!*

Know-Nothing voices rose as well. Hanneke didn't know if they were taunting the Germans, admonishing the lawmen, or repeating their political views, but a palpable anger almost crackled in the air.

"Disperse at once!" the sheriff bellowed.

For a long moment, no one moved, as if each side was daring the other to stand their ground. Then Deputy Barlow's horse abruptly reared with a high-pitched whinny. As Barlow struggled to control his mount Hanneke saw several of the German men throwing stones toward the lawmen. A flying glass bottle shattered against a mounting block. Some of the marchers brought rifles to their shoulders.

"Adolf!" Hanneke cried, although she knew it was useless. Growling Know-Nothing men surged toward the police. Barlow's horse reared again, throwing the deputy from the saddle. He landed in the street but Hanneke lost sight of him as the German men shoved forward, flowing around the closest mounted man. That deputy raised a truncheon, brought it down in a brutal blow.

The middle ground gave way to chaos. *"Adolf!"* Hanneke was trying desperately to pick him out of the crowd. Men were grappling, throwing punches, grunting, and cursing. One German man swung a heavy grub hoe and a Know-Nothing crumpled, clutching one arm as his top hat fell into the street. Somewhere a woman screamed.

In the factory yard, a man ran past Hanneke, toward the street. "Fire!" he roared in German. *"Fire!"* She whirled, ready to scold him for encouraging the armed rioters.

The rebuke died. Flames were shooting through the roof of the closest building. The Vulcan Iron Works was burning.

Adam's voice echoed in her mind: *Mr. Rutherford has a hidden room at the ironworks that can hide half a dozen. It's in the smallest building, near the river. The hiding place is above a joiner's shop on the second floor.*

Horrified, Hanneke imagined humans locked in a windowless room as the first tendrils of smoke crept through the cracks. All of the buildings in the compound were made of wood, all dry as tinder after a week with no rain. The blaze was likely to spread fast.

A few men were sprinting toward the burning building. Hanneke ran around it, swerving to avoid falling sparks and aiming for the last shop. Sounds from the street brawl faded beneath the fire's growing roar and crackle.

The shop's door was secured with a padlock. She jerked on it frantically, then banged on the door. "Fire! You have to get out!" A glance over her shoulder confirmed that flames had already leapt from the first building to the second, snaking across the shingles.

This building, the smallest, was still unscathed. Perhaps there was another door around back, deepest in the shadows, closest to the Rock River. Perhaps Mr. Rutherford had left that door unlocked so a "package" might slip in or out.

She ran along the front of the shop, down the side, around the corner—and jolted to a stop. Asa Hawkins was trotting toward the back door from the building's far side. Even in the twilight, she recognized the bulk of him, the silhouette of his hat with its ridiculous plume. He's come for the slaves, she thought. He didn't want 'valuable property' to burn.

A new flare of fury and contempt swept her forward again. *"No!"* she screamed. No to the evil of slavery, no to the xenophobia, no to this man's casual contempt and cruelty.

Hawkins had reached the door, but he whirled as she approached. The first flames appeared on the roof above. In the wavering light, his eyes went wide.

He raised a hand and pain exploded in Hanneke's cheek and jaw. In the next instant, the back of her head cracked against the wall.

Then—for the second time that day—everything went black.

* * *

Sounds penetrated the dark stillness first. Something soft and fluid, something monstrously harsh, the faint clang of church bells. Hanneke became aware of pain in her face, her head, her hip. Smoke stung her nostrils...

Smoke. Memories returned in a rush: The street brawl between Know-Nothings and immigrant Germans, the ironworks fire, her futile attempt to help anyone who might be trapped in the smallest factory building, an enraged Asa Hawkins.

With a groan, Hanneke opened her eyes. In her desperate desire to free any runaways trapped inside the factory building, she'd acted like a madwoman. What had she expected Hawkins to do? At least he hadn't drugged her this time, hadn't locked her away. Instead, he'd apparently dragged her to the riverbank and left her among the weeds. Nearby, flames raged against the night sky. All of the ironworks buildings were burning now. Vulcan, god of fire, had won the night.

She lurched to her feet and stumbled unsteadily toward the street. The yard was full of men with buckets and brooms now, dark shadows against the glare. But it is too late, she thought. Too late to extinguish the fire. Too late to help anyone who might have been trapped inside. Waves of heat shimmered through the yard. The fire crackled and roared like an angry beast. Flames were consuming the roof and walls of the smallest building. The roof of the building closest to the road had already collapsed.

Hanneke skirted the conflagration. A bucket brigade had formed near the road. Silhouetted in the wavering light, men in work shirts labored with men in top hats, splashing neighboring shops in hopes of keeping the fire from spreading. Evidently, Watertown had no fire department, leaving immigrants and nativists with a common goal.

The street itself was almost empty. Hanneke had no idea if anyone had been hurt or arrested. Perhaps the fire had forestalled the brewing riot.

It felt irresponsible to simply walk away. But there's nothing I can do here, she thought. She had not glimpsed Adolf. And Asa Hawkins might be watching her, waiting for a chance to finish what he'd begun.

No one accosted her as she walked the few blocks back to the tavern. She approached the Red Cockerel from the back alley. The curtain was drawn but a soft light glowed a welcome from within.

Hanneke tapped on the kitchen door. "Angela? It's me." Almost immediately the door opened. Hanneke slipped inside.

"Did you find Adolf?" Angela demanded as she quickly locked the door behind them.

"I did not." Hanneke sank into a chair. "The Know-Nothings paraded again tonight, down First Street this time, and a group of German men marched to meet them. Both sides were armed, and there *was* a brawl, but… it was twilight. I couldn't see Adolf." She met Angela's worried gaze with a helpless gesture. "I'm sorry."

"But what happened to *you*?" Angela was considering her with dismay.

Hanneke realized she must look as bedraggled as she felt. She untied the ribbons beneath her chin and removed the borrowed bonnet. The satin was dirty and torn beyond repair. "Oh, *Angela*. I'm so sorry. I'll…" Her voice trailed away. What could she do? She had no money to replace the bonnet.

"I don't care about the hat!" Angela sat across from her and leaned over the table. "Tell me what happened."

Hanneke told Angela everything that had transpired since she left the tavern earlier that evening. "So there's no way to know," she concluded, "but I'm terribly afraid that the baby's mother might have been hiding in one of the buildings." She looked around. "Where is the baby?"

"Leah is upstairs, sound asleep." Angela met Hanneke's startled look with a defensive little shrug. "I needed to call her something. She did have a crying spell after you left. I managed to feed her a little milk and she settled down."

That was a sliver of good news, at least.

"But…" Angela leaned back in her chair. "It terrifies me to know that Asa Hawkins attacked you again. That man *must* be arrested."

"How can I report his behavior without endangering Leah?" Hanneke couldn't bear the thought of watching that innocent little girl returned to the people who, according to the law, owned her.

Angela pressed a hand against the bulge beneath her apron, perhaps trying to reassure her own unborn child.

Hanneke struggled to find some reassurance to offer her friend. But there was none, really. If Asa Hawkins didn't already know that Hanneke was staying at the Red Cockerel, a few simple questions would reveal that quickly enough. And since Leah had disappeared from his chicken shed with *her*, surely he'd make an appearance at the tavern soon.

Hanneke planted her elbows on the table and buried her face in her palms. As long as the baby is here, she thought, we are all in danger.

For a long moment neither spoke. Then Angela said, "I'm going to make some hot tea."

Hanneke straightened, trying to rouse herself. "Hot tea would be delightful, but please, stay where you are. I'll—"

Thump-thump-thump!

"Oh!" Angela gasped as the kitchen door rattled beneath the force of a pounding fist. Hanneke's skin prickled.

Their unseen visitor banged again.

"What should we do?" Angela whispered. "What if that's Hawkins?"

Hanneke swallowed hard, considering the kitchen. She stepped to the dry sink and grabbed a carving knife, clenching her fingers around the handle. Then she crept closer to the door. "Who's there?"

"Deputy Sheriff Barlow! Open the damn door!"

The women exchanged glances. Angela hitched her shoulders up and down.

Hanneke opened the door and had to step back as the deputy shoved into the room. He looked dreadful—exhausted, dusty, his face drawn with tension and fatigue. The right sleeve of his coat was torn and he walked with a slight limp.

"Please, sit," she urged. "I was about to make tea—"

"I do not want tea," Barlow growled. "I came to make sure you are all right."

Bewildered, Hanneke exchanged another wary glance with Angela. "I am."

"And put that down." He glared at the knife until she complied. "Is anyone else here with you two?"

Hanneke held his gaze. "No."

Barlow rubbed one hand over his face.

"Please," Angela dared, "have you seen Adolf, the boy who works here?

Did you arrest anyone at the fight? Did anyone get hurt?"

"I have not seen Adolf," Barlow told her. "But—"

A baby's cry, thin but unmistakable, drifted from the second story. Oh, *liebchen*, Hanneke moaned silently, not now.

Barlow's eyes narrowed and he turned toward the stairs. "There is a child up there." It was not a question.

Neither woman answered. Hanneke's heart thumped wildly. What would she do if John Barlow tried to take the little girl?

"Is it a Negro baby?"

She couldn't find words. The baby wailed again.

Deputy Barlow's shoulders slumped. After a pause, he looked at Hanneke. "I want to speak to you in the stable. Bring a lantern."

Hanneke felt a new stab of unease. "Angela can hear anything you have to say."

"In the stable!" Barlow barked. "Now!" He opened the door and stood waiting to usher her outside.

Whatever is coming, Hanneke thought, it is best to keep Angela out of it. She picked up the lantern hanging near the door, opened one of its glass panels, and lit the candle inside. When the flame was steady she gave her friend a tiny nod, trying to look reassuring. Then she followed the deputy outside.

He strode across the alley, tapped twice on the door, and eased it open. "It's Barlow," he muttered. "With the woman." He looked at Hanneke and cocked his head: *Go ahead.*

Hanneke's apprehension grew as she slipped inside. Barlow followed and shut the door behind them. The space smelled familiar—the faint lingering odor of long-gone animals, musty straw. There was one box stall where Adolf slept, and two stalls with stanchions on the opposite wall.

A man was sitting on an overturned water tub in the far corner. He was in shadows with head hung low, but he was too broad-shouldered to be Adolf. Hanneke raised the lantern and stepped closer to the seated man. He slowly raised his head.

Hanneke recoiled. The walls seemed to press in. The man waiting was

Asa Hawkins.

Chapter Twenty

Hanneke whirled. "Let me pass," she hissed at Barlow, who was blocking her exit. "This man assaulted me!"

Asa Hawkins muttered something in English. Barlow snapped back in the same language.

"He drugged me and locked me in a shed on his property!" Hanneke insisted. "He belongs in jail!"

Barlow rounded on her. "For the love of God, woman! I beg you, for once in your life, just *listen*." He jerked off his hat and ran a hand over his hair. "Hawkins was worried about you. Somehow, amidst the bedlam in the street and in the ironworks yard tonight, he managed to find me."

Hanneke stared from one glowering man to the other. This was absolutely nonsensical.

"He asked me to find *you*." Barlow held up one palm to forestall further interruptions. "And the child. He wanted to make sure you were both all right."

"That's ludicrous." Hanneke clenched the lantern handle so hard it hurt. "He attacked me! He locked me up with the baby, and he—"

Hawkins said something else in English. In the shadows, his face was as tight and sour as ever.

German words squeezed between Barlow's gritted teeth. "I don't like him any more than you do. But Hawkins says he's been involved with the Underground Railroad—"

"The what?"

Barlow waved an impatient hand. "It's what people call the routes and

193

hiding places runaways use when trying to get north. Hawkins says he's been helping the local leader for several years."

"That's—that's preposterous." The notion of Asa Hawkins helping *anyone* was beyond belief.

"He was the one trying to get a mother and her baby from one safe place to the next. When they realized that the slavers were almost upon them, the mother insisted that they leave the baby girl behind and try to draw the slavers away. They left the baby in Fridolin's barn."

Hanneke felt dazed. That matched what Adam had told her.

"Hawkins decided to talk to the men, pretending to be in sympathy, all the while sending them in the wrong direction. The plan was for Hawkins and the woman to meet back at Fridolin's barn. But she never came. Instead, *you* did."

"But...if that's so, why didn't he just hide from me? Or explain the situation?"

Deputy Barlow repeated the questions in English. Hawkins snarled a response.

"He says he had no reason to trust you and that the best place to hide you and the baby was his own property," Barlow translated. He asked another question of Hawkins, then turned back to her. "He'd given the child some chloroform on a lump of sugar, but she was making some noise and he didn't want you to discover her. He had a wagon parked nearby with a false floor."

"But why incarcerate me?" Hanneke demanded.

Hawkins interrupted with another angry torrent of English words.

Barlow waved a hand, damming the flow. "He went looking for the baby's mother. He hadn't expected you to wake before he returned, much less escape."

Hanneke wasn't convinced. "What about this evening? I was terrified that the mother or other runaways were trapped inside one of the ironworks buildings—"

"Why did you think that?" Barlow asked sharply.

She had no intention of betraying Adam's confidence. "The point *is*, I was running to check the building near the river when Hawkins struck me so hard I hit my head and lost my senses."

"Well, Hawkins had the same idea. Evidently one of the supervisors at the ironworks sometimes hides runaways."

Rutherford, Hanneke thought. Hawkins must have revealed that dangerous information to Deputy Barlow.

"When you appeared," Barlow continued, "Hawkins was afraid that you'd scream for help and draw attention just when he might be helping runaways escape."

Which might have been disastrous, Hanneke admitted grudgingly. "Was the mother there?"

Asa Hawkins seemed to understand her question. He unleashed another low, angry torrent of words, jabbing one finger toward her.

"He says you slowed him down," Barlow said. "After dragging you a safe distance away, he ran back to the shop building and kicked the door in, but the fire was already so bad that he didn't get far. He saw no one. We don't know if the mother—or anyone else—was inside."

That was not what Hanneke had wanted to hear. "How do we know this isn't some story he concocted to save himself from my accusation?"

Deputy Barlow rubbed his chin wearily. "You are, of course, free to make a formal charge against him. Just be aware that doing so would bring *everything* out in the open."

Hanneke crossed her arms, thinking that through, trying to find a way to get Hawkins his due without endangering baby Leah.

"He took an enormous risk when he confided in me," Barlow added.

She snorted. "He wouldn't have done so out of concern for *me*. He must have some other motive."

"Perhaps. But it looks like he did try to get inside the building. He's got a bad burn on his hand."

Hanneke noticed for the first time that Hawkins's right hand was wrapped in a cloth and dangling at his side. And he'd never gotten to his feet—odd for a man who routinely used his bulk to intimidate others. "Oh, for heaven's sake. Why did you bring him here instead of taking him to a doctor?"

"He insisted that—"

"Get him inside at once. I'll tend to the burn in the kitchen." Hanneke marched from the stable. The men followed more slowly.

In the kitchen, Angela was waiting anxiously. Hanneke said, "You need to know that Deputy Barlow brought Asa Hawkins here."

"Hawkins?" Angela pressed one hand against her throat.

"He claims he's been helping runaway slaves, not catching them." Hanneke put another log into the firebox and poured water into a kettle. "I'm not convinced. But—he's injured, and I need to tend him. I suggest you wait upstairs with Leah."

Angela nodded silently and disappeared just as Deputy Barlow helped Asa Hawkins into the room.

"Sit." Hanneke pointed Hawkins toward a chair.

Hawkins clearly wanted to do no such thing. But when Barlow snapped a command, Hawkins grudgingly acquiesced. "Tell him to put his hand on the table," Hanneke added. When Hawkins did, she moved a lamp closer—and caught her breath. The kerchief Hawkins had wrapped around his hand was bright yellow with thin black stripes. The man killed on the Main Street bridge had been wearing an identical kerchief.

For the first time she allowed herself to admit that Asa Hawkins might be telling the truth. "Deputy Barlow, did you see…?"

Barlow leaned close. His eyebrows rose.

"Yah," Hawkins said savagely, and continued in English.

Barlow listened, then translated. "He says this particular kerchief pattern is a sign to runaways. The man killed on the bridge—his name was Loomis—was also helping runaway slaves escape. Loomis and Hawkins were friends. Hawkins believes Loomis was killed by the slavers."

"But how did Mr. Loomis know my name?" Hanneke demanded. "He called me 'Frau Bauer!' Why was he trying to talk to me the day he was knifed?"

The two men had a brief conversation. John Barlow finally nodded, but he stared at the floor for a moment before addressing Hanneke again. "Because Loomis was also a friend of Fridolin's," he said slowly. "They worked together on the Underground Railroad. And Fridolin asked Loomis to look out for you in the event that something happened to him. To Fridolin, I mean." The deputy looked away, sucked in a long breath, exhaled slowly. Still, he was man enough to meet her gaze before finishing the tale. "According to Hawkins, Fridolin told Loomis that he had married you."

* * *

Hanneke didn't know whether to hug Asa Hawkins or strike him. She settled for providing what aid she could to his blistered hand. The fact that he submitted to her care suggested that he was in pain. She settled his hand in a basin of cool water before searching Angela's pantry for medicinals. Angela didn't have an aloe plant, but Hanneke did find a pot of honey. That would do.

Back in the kitchen she patted Hawkins's hand dry and applied a thin coat of honey to minimize swelling and fight infection. Then she ripped a clean dish towel into a bandage and tied it in place. "Deputy Barlow? Tell him that he must leave the blisters alone or risk complications."

The deputy complied. Hawkins jerked his hand away, but nodded.

For the first time since Hawkins had entered the kitchen, Hanneke looked into the man's eyes. Conflicting emotions flickered across his face—a sullen gratitude for her ministrations, embarrassment for the need…and the deep, abiding contempt he'd *always* shown her. She thought he might manage to thank her, but instead, Hawkins gave a noncommittal grunt and headed for the door.

"Wait!" Hanneke commanded. There was something she still didn't understand. "Helping runaway slaves is a noble thing…I have to ask, are you truly a Know-Nothing?" It seemed impossible that a man like Hawkins would risk his life to help runaway slaves reach freedom, but march with men who loathed immigrants.

Barlow repeated the question in English. Hawkins stared at Hanneke as he responded.

"He said," Barlow began, "'of course I am. I despise the institution of slavery. That doesn't mean I want hordes of filthy foreigners telling the rest of us how to live our lives.'"

"And were *your* ancestors 'filthy foreigners' when they came to this country?" Hanneke demanded. "Your parents? Your grandparents?"

Hawkins left without waiting for the translation. He slammed the door behind him.

The kitchen was quiet for a long moment as Hanneke and Deputy Barlow wrestled with their thoughts. She felt her anger seep away, replaced by a bone-deep weariness of body and soul. I will never understand this country, she thought. *Never.*

The deputy finally broke the awkward silence. "It seems, Frau Bauer, that I owe you an apology."

Frau Bauer. The title was an admission, a gift. "You do," Hanneke agreed. How she had ached to hear that acknowledgment! But she was too tired for malice.

Deputy Barlow removed his hat and shuffled it in his hands. "Might I ask...is your offer of tea still good?"

"Of course." She waved him to the chair Hawkins had vacated. Soon she had two cups and saucers on the table and tea steeping in the pot.

Deputy Barlow stared out the window for a moment, then turned to meet her gaze. "This has been an evening of revelations. I never guessed that Fridolin was involved with the Underground Railroad. Never suspected."

"I did." She poured them each a cup of tea.

Barlow actually smiled. "I'm not surprised." Then he sobered again. "But sharing the news of your marriage when he returned from Pomerania wouldn't have compromised his anti-slavery work in any way. I still cannot *begin* to understand why Fridolin kept that a secret."

"I can't either." Hanneke sighed. Asa Hawkins had accomplished what she had not—convince John Barlow that his friend and neighbor had indeed married *her* while traveling in Pomerania the year before. And...had he solved one of the mysteries as well? "According to Hawkins, Mr. Loomis was killed by slave-catchers." Just as Adam had said.

"Hawkins *thinks* so," Barlow said carefully. "It takes a hard man to do that kind of work. If slavers somehow figured out that Loomis was helping runaways, they might have killed him in spite. But we have no proof."

"No," Hanneke conceded reluctantly. "Still, if Hawkins is right, then perhaps the slavers also killed Fridolin."

Although Barlow must have asked himself the same question, he chewed that over for a long moment. "It's certainly possible, but—again, we have no proof."

Hanneke closed her eyes. Finding that proof seemed desperately important. As furious as she was with Fridolin Bauer, she wanted his death to have been the result of a high ideal, not a foolish accident.

But there was something more urgent to discuss. "Deputy, about the baby... *Please* don't take her with you tonight. I know someone, someone who might be able to help."

"Rutherford?"

"No. Someone else." She raised one palm, forestalling his question. "I won't tell you who. That person hopes to learn something about the mother's whereabouts. Although," she conceded unhappily, "that was before the fire."

Barlow regarded her, one eyebrow cocked.

"That individual asked me to visit tomorrow morning. If the mother is alive, she can be reunited with the child and, I trust, spirited on to Canada. I promised to keep the baby safe at least that long."

"You do realize that by law, that baby is—"

"Do not tell me that innocent child is 'property!'" Hanneke felt tears scald her eyes. "I won't stand for it."

"Nor will I," John Barlow said quietly. He rubbed both palms over his face. "I have sworn an oath to uphold the law, but I also do my best to honor God's law. When the two are in conflict, well...God is the higher power. For the time being, I will say nothing, and do nothing, about the baby."

Hanneke's shoulders slumped with relief. *"Danke schön."*

"I trust that you will say nothing more about Hawkins."

"Yes." She drained her cup and poured more tea, relishing the warmth. "Deputy Barlow, did you know that the Underground Railroad operated in this area?"

"I suspected as much, but I didn't go looking for evidence." He rolled his shoulders as if easing an ache. "It doesn't surprise me that someone created a hiding place at one of the factories along the Rock. Runaways often travel along rivers when they can. Water confuses the dogs."

"Hawkins's property is on the riverbank as well," Hanneke mused. She rubbed her temples. Despite his story, despite even the yellow and black kerchief, it was still difficult to reconcile the ill-tempered Know-Nothing with heroism of any kind. "Do you truly believe Hawkins helps runaways?"

"I do. He described how his work as an auctioneer and freighter makes it possible. No one questions seeing wagons coming every day, loaded with crates and barrels. It's probably been easier for him to help transport runaways than almost anyone else in the area. His tales ring true." Barlow leaned back in his chair and sighed. "I've been looking for cause to arrest him for some time. Now he *tells* me he's been breaking the law, and I will do nothing."

"Why did he confess all this to you? Why not talk to one of the Yankee lawmen?"

"Since he wanted my help with *you*, he may have decided that a deputy who speaks German was essential."

"But I've seen you two snarling at each other like angry dogs! Surely he would have been more comfortable confiding in someone else."

"You must understand, many abolitionists believe the *only* way to destroy the institution is to change the law. They don't condone assisting runaways. That may be why Hawkins didn't trust another lawman with his secret. And if the Watertown constables are Know-Nothings, he wouldn't have wanted to complicate those relationships. Ironic, isn't it?" He snorted without humor.

"Indeed," Hanneke said slowly as she turned the tangle over in her mind.

"Or..." Barlow lifted one palm and let it drop. "Hawkins may have known that I have no confidants, and therefore am the man most likely to hold my tongue."

His voice was even, but Hanneke sensed the buried pain. By virtue of John Barlow's marriage to a foreign-born woman, he was obviously a moderating influence—a go-between among Germans and Yankees. But that double connection could also be a liability, giving both groups cause for mistrust.

She turned the conversation back to safer ground. "Might Hawkins's public face all be a sham? The anger, the scorn, the nativism? Is it all calculated to keep people from suspecting that he's involved in something brave and kind?"

"I have no idea." The weariness was back in Barlow's voice, reminding Hanneke that his day had been as long and difficult as hers. "My God, what a night. The Vulcan Iron Works fire was a tragedy. Still, it probably prevented a different tragedy. God knows what violence the men marching tonight—on both sides—would have unleashed."

"Did you discover who stole the weapons?"

"It appears the Know-Nothings did. That group was much better armed than most of the German men." He drained his tea, stood, and carried the cup and saucer to the counter.

Hanneke stood as well. "So," she said briskly. "What are you going to do now?"

He misunderstood her question. "I will talk with Christine Bauer—"

"No, you mustn't!" Realizing what she'd said, Hanneke swallowed a shaky laugh. "It's not that I don't want the truth known, I assure you. But we must keep Fridolin's role in this Underground Railroad a secret." She remembered the haunting fear in Adam's eyes—not just his own fear of slavers, but fear that the burgeoning catastrophes might endanger more mothers and children and fathers who'd risked all to reach freedom.

"But..." Deputy Barlow frowned as he thought that through. "All right, I see your point. Still, I cannot in good conscience stay silent altogether. I will tell Christine that although for legal reasons I can not reveal all the details, I have learned that your marriage is legitimate. I think she'll believe me. Where that leaves issues of inheritance, and the farm..." He spread his hands. "I don't know."

There is no good solution there, Hanneke thought. And she must have been more tired than she even knew, for new tears welled. She groped for a handkerchief and wiped her eyes. "I'm sorry."

Barlow regarded her with a look she couldn't decipher. "You," he said, "have nothing to apologize for." With that, he settled his hat on his head and left her alone.

Chapter Twenty-One

"The men are gone," Hanneke called up the stairs. Angela crept back down, scanning the room as if to ascertain for herself that the two had departed. Hanneke brewed more hot tea and told her friend everything she'd learned from Asa Hawkins and the deputy.

Angela looked stunned. "Of all people...Asa Hawkins has corroborated your marriage to Fridolin Bauer?"

"Hardly what I expected," Hanneke agreed dryly. "But Deputy Barlow believed him."

"Hawkins is a horrid man." Angela clutched her elbows, shoulders hunched. "After my brother left he came here several times, claiming Julius owed him money. Hawkins showed me no proof, just threatened to have me arrested."

"Could you be held responsible for your brother's debt?" Hanneke demanded. Honestly, Asa Hawkins was—in most regards—a despicable man. "What did you do?"

"I gave him nothing. He persisted for a while, then gave up."

"Good," Hanneke muttered. She hated to imagine Angela pregnant, abandoned by her brother, and worried about bills, having to contend with Hawkins's threats.

The oil lamp on the table started to sputter. Angela adjusted the wick and eased her shoulders. "I'm sorry about Fridolin, Hanneke. Have I ever said so? I'm truly sorry that he died."

"Fridolin's death was a sore loss, but in truth...he was a complicated man." She hesitated, trying to sort through feelings that had become as tangled as a ball of yarn attacked by kittens. "Fridolin did something unforgivable, but...I played some small role in my own disappointment."

"Surely not!"

"I only had a short time to get to know him. I had much longer to wait and wonder and imagine our life together." Hanneke inhaled slowly, released the breath. "In those months I created in my mind a perfect marriage. A perfect partnership at a perfect farm. In hindsight, I think it was inevitable that to some extent, I would have been disillusioned."

After a moment Angela asked, "What are you going to do?"

"I don't know," Hanneke admitted. "I can't predict how Christine will react when Deputy Barlow tells her that my marriage to her brother was legitimate. My stolen papers haven't been recovered, and it will take a long time to get documentation from my family and Fridolin's lawyer in Germany. Christine could sell the farm any day, if she chooses, and disappear with whatever she gets for it."

"You and Christine are both in need," Angela observed hesitantly. "Perhaps, if you offered to help, she might change her mind about selling."

"You mean...*both* of us live at the farm?" It was a new idea, and strange. Hanneke tried to imagine Christine and her becoming the friends they should have been, making dye baths for Christine's plumes and Hanneke's wool, sharing heavy chores like tamping sauerkraut and molding candles, and grinding sausage. Each would have their own little business—knitting and bonnet making. Perhaps they could rent the fields.

For a moment it sounded idyllic. But would it be possible to look at Christine, Hanneke wondered, or for Christine to look at me, without the specter of Fridolin's betrayal rising between them? Hanneke knew she was not the same woman who spent the winter in Pomerania dreaming of a new and satisfying life in Wisconsin, and she wasn't sure yet who had taken that woman's place.

The hour was too late to confront such complicated questions. "I need some time to think. The one thing I *know* I'd like to do is help you here, at least until the baby comes." And maybe longer. With an infant to tend, Angela would need more assistance than ever. And Adolf would still need looking after.

"That would be a comfort." Angela reached across the table for Hanneke's hand and gave a grateful squeeze. "I—"

The door rattled as someone tried the latch. "It's me! Adolf!"

"Danke Gott." Hanneke hurried to the door, wrenched it open, and pulled the boy inside.

Angela lumbered to her feet. "Where have you been? We were frantic!"

"Let me look at you." Hanneke raised the lamp and studied him with growing dismay. A gash on his forehead oozed blood. His shirt was torn at one shoulder. He looked so shaken that she feared he might break down in tears.

He wouldn't want that. "Sit," she ordered. "Let me tend to that wound."

Adolf obeyed. "I'm sorry, Angela. I didn't mean to frighten you."

"But you did." Angela's voice trembled. "How could you be so selfish?"

"I—I didn't think…" The boy shifted his weight, looking anxiously from one woman to the other.

"Tell us what happened," Hanneke murmured. "And sit still."

He told them the tale—haltingly at first, then faster and faster. He had indeed been among the men marching to meet the Know-Nothings. "I was nervous," he allowed, "but proud too. We must stand up against the insults we've received—*ow.*" He grimaced as Hanneke dabbed at the gash with a wet cloth.

"You're lucky your head wasn't split open," Angela snapped.

Adolf swallowed hard. "Once the fight started, though…I couldn't make sense of anything. Then someone hit me. I don't even know if it was a nativist or a deputy. I…well, I ran." He looked ashamed.

Hanneke pressed a clean cloth against the wound and tied it in place. "There. You'll have a scar, but it should heal well enough. Be sure to keep it clean."

"Danke." Adolf turned to Angela. "I'm truly sorry."

Angela wasn't ready to forgive. "Who did this? What men decided that attacking the nativists was a wise plan? Who compelled boys like you to participate?"

Adolf shook his head. "I can't say. I took a vow." He held up one hand to avert the expected protest. "But I am done with their business."

"For good?" Hanneke asked. "Or until the next time they demand your help?"

"For good." Adolf studied his knuckles, scraping at a bit of dried blood with his thumbnail. "During the meetings, when the leaders were talking, their plans sounded…I don't know, noble. But when the fight started, all those noble ideas turned into something ugly."

"We can't fight violence with violence, Adolf." Angela's voice was like ice, hard and cold. "Or hatred with hatred."

His chin dropped lower. "I know."

"Promise me you won't march with those men again."

"I promise," he mumbled. "Truly, Angela. I swear it." With that, Angela thawed enough to fold him into her arms.

It eased Hanneke's bruised heart to see them, but she still had other worries. "Now, what you need most is rest," she said. "Off you go. And sleep in tomorrow morning. Breakfast in bed is what you need, so one of us will bring a tray."

Angela didn't speak until Adolf had gone out to his pallet in the stable. "You don't want to tell him about Leah."

"Not unless we have to," Hanneke agreed. "That knowledge would be a heavy burden. I'm praying that when I visit Adam tomorrow, he'll have found the girl's mother."

* * *

Hanneke insisted that Angela also get some sleep. "I'll keep watch over Leah," she promised. "You need to preserve your strength."

With Leah in her arms, Hanneke drowsed on her bed. Sometimes she roused long enough to coax the child to sip milk or swallow morsels of boiled chicken. The baby seemed unharmed from the drug-induced sleep Hawkins had inflicted, fretting when hungry or in need of a clean diaper. On the whole, though, she was quieter than other babies Hanneke had tended.

Perhaps she'd been born with the bone-deep understanding that silence was the safest course. Perhaps Leah's mother had whispered to her the urgent need for stealth. Her dark eyes seemed grave, as if she understood the danger stalking her. In the hours before dawn, when the tavern was silent and the darkness, broken only by a candle's glow, Hanneke held the baby close, singing to her, murmuring reassurances.

Just as the sky began to lighten, Hanneke passed Leah back to Angela's care and walked to Adam's barbershop on the Main Street bridge. She desperately wanted to hear that the baby's mother had been found, safe and eager to be reunited with her child.

Adam was waiting, dressed as any middle-class businessman might, hair neatly combed and parted on one side. Still, Hanneke sensed his fatigue. She wondered where he'd gone during the night. Who he'd talked to. What risks he'd taken.

He wasted no time on idle chatter. "There's been no sign of the mother."

Hanneke's heart sank with the leaden weight of her disappointment. "I'm sorry to hear that." They stood just inside his shop, as they'd done the evening before. Through the door came the sounds of a city coming to life: an occasional carriage passing, a rooster crowing, a shouted greeting as two friends met on the street. "What should we do now?"

"Bring the baby here tonight, after sundown."

Hanneke hesitated. Would the child truly be safer here with Adam than at the inn? "But..."

"The baby will be taken on to Canada."

She felt an unexpected wrench of loss. I was eager to pass the child on to her mother, she thought, but I had not anticipated *this*. "Who..." she began, but swallowed the question. It was not her place to ask who would travel north with the child.

She realized that Adam was watching her, waiting. "Of course," she said instead. "I'll bring her." She nodded politely and left the barbershop.

But as she began walking back to the tavern, a new idea took root in her heart.

* * *

Back at the Red Cockerel, Hanneke reported the exchange to Angela. "Of course we'll keep her here until tonight," Angela assured her. "I don't think we can keep her hidden from Adolf, though." She put one hand on Hanneke's arm. "I do trust him. He's young, but he has a good heart. And he did keep his vow of secrecy regarding The German Star.

There was no help for it, Hanneke decided reluctantly. "If he gives an equal vow of secrecy about Leah, I will be content."

The sound of a tolling bell drifted through the morning. Hanneke stiffened, remembering the bells ringing the alarm as the Vulcan Iron Works burned. Then she realized that it was Sunday morning. These bells were calling the faithful to service.

I arrived in Wisconsin on a Sunday, she thought. Was that truly just a week ago? It seemed impossible. Suddenly she felt as if the bells were ringing for her. "Angela, would you mind if I go to church?"

Her friend looked surprised, but shook her head. "Of course not. I don't attend anymore, so we'll be fine here."

Hanneke quickly changed into her burgundy silk dress. Asa Hawkins's brutal strike had left her cheek sore, and mottled a vivid purple and green. I'm already the subject of gossip, she thought, so the bruise will change nothing. She lifted her chin and reached for her straw bonnet. The morning was already sticky-hot.

The service had started by the time she reached St. John's Lutheran Church, an impressive red brick structure on North 5th and Cady Streets. She slipped into a back pew, bowed her head, and closed her eyes. The familiar order of service helped soothe some of her emotional bruises.

After the final prayer, she left quickly and hurried down the steps. She'd turned onto the street when she heard hasty footsteps behind her. "Please," someone called. "Please—wait!"

Hanneke turned to see a small woman wearing mourning attire hurrying toward her. Christine Bauer, Hanneke thought with astonishment, even before Fridolin's sister lifted the veil covering her face. Her eyes were bloodshot and puffy. Beads of sweat dotted her forehead, and the humidity had caused her veil to bleed dark smudges near her forehead.

"I'm glad I saw you," Christine began. Then her brow furrowed, and she gestured toward Hanneke's cheek. "What happened?"

"Nothing I care to dwell upon."

"Of course." Looking chagrined, Christine glanced away for a moment before plunging ahead. "John Barlow came to see me last night."

He wasted no time, Hanneke thought. Barlow was a man of his word.

"He told me that he has reason to believe that you and Fridolin were legally married in Germany." Tears glistened in Christine's eyes. "He couldn't tell me more than that, but...that was enough."

Hanneke chose her words carefully. "I am truly sorry that Deputy Barlow's news adds to your burdens, but it is best to know the truth. And the truth is, Fridolin kept secrets from both of us."

"I am still struggling to understand how he...well." Christine pulled a black-edged handkerchief from her reticule and wiped her eyes. "I have decided to leave Watertown."

Hanneke blinked. She had not anticipated such a sudden capitulation. "What about the farm?"

"That property has brought nothing but misery, and I don't want it!" Christine's voice rose, and a few people nearby turned their heads. She made a visible effort to speak more quietly. "And apparently I have no claim to it."

Hanneke had an absurd impulse to hug her sister-in-law, to try to assure her that somehow, all would be well. She thought about Angela's suggestion that she and Christine share the farm.

"You can do what you wish with the property. John Barlow agreed to handle the legalities for me. I moved into the Buena Vista this morning."

It was already too late for some sort of partnership. Too late to offer Christine even sympathy. "Where will you go?" Hanneke asked. "Are you able to travel?"

Christine understood the oblique question. "I have enough money to reach Milwaukee. Friends there will help me. I plan to open a bonnet shop."

209

The words were brave, but Christine looked anything but confident. She dabbed her forehead, then glanced at the now-stained handkerchief. "Oh!" She hiccupped a sob. "This wretched crape…"

Without thinking, Hanneke said, "Scrub the stains with oxalic acid and cream of tartar."

What little color Christine had left faded from her skin. She crumpled the handkerchief into a ball.

Hanneke knew she'd made a mistake. *Christine can't possibly know that I saw those very items while prowling through her house,* she told herself, and tried to recover. "That is, if you have some handy."

"Yes, I…I will."

Hanneke didn't like Christine's pallor. "Christine…are you well?"

"It's just the heat."

And the literal weight of mourning attire, Hanneke thought. "You must take care of yourself as well as honor your brother's memory," she said gently, then pressed her lips together to prevent any more unwanted advice from popping out.

"Even now," Christine whispered. "Even now, you're being kind. I think we might have been friends, if…"

Hanneke felt that loss as well. "If Fridolin had given us a chance."

"Yes." Christine lowered her veil again. "I must go." She started to turn away, then stopped. Quickly, silently, she unpinned the mourning brooch from her bodice and pressed it into Hanneke's palm. Then she scurried back to the churchyard, where Josephine Wiggenhorn, proprietress of the Buena Vista Hotel, put a protective arm around Christine's shoulders.

Stunned, Hanneke stared at the brooch; at the single yellow lock of Fridolin's hair preserved beneath glass. It was a precious talisman of her husband; a tangible sign of her widowhood. Her fingers trembled as she pinned it to her own bodice.

Then she walked numbly back to the tavern, struggling to grasp her rapid turn of fortune. *I am not penniless after all,* she thought. *I suddenly have some huge decisions to make.*

"Frau Bauer?"

Hanneke froze, her heart suddenly racing like a runaway mare. She hadn't noticed the gentleman standing in front of the Red Cockerel. The last unknown man to call her by that name, Mr. Loomis, had been murdered moments later.

"It is you, isn't it?" The man spoke German with an English accent. His smile was kind and brought crinkles to the corners of his eyes. He had gray hair and a beard, and wore a black suit with fancy waistcoat and soft silk cravat—a man of some means, but not ostentatious wealth. "I didn't mean to startle you. I'm Micah Ainsley." He paused, as if waiting for some reaction.

The name meant nothing. "I don't believe we've met."

"We have not, but I thought that perhaps...well." Mr. Ainsley nodded. "I thought that Fridolin might have mentioned me."

Hanneke's heart fluttered even faster.

"You see, I knew him quite well," Mr. Ainsley added. "Is there somewhere we can talk in private?"

* * *

Five minutes later they were settled at a table in the taproom. Angela had assured Hanneke that all was well before closing the kitchen door and leaving them alone.

"Please, sir," Hanneke said hoarsely. "How did you know my husband?"

"I own a bookbinding business, and I hired Fridolin when he first arrived in Milwaukee," Mr. Ainsley explained. "We got on quite well. In time, some of our conversations turned to political matters. Matters of conscience. You see, I have long been an abolitionist."

This is **M**, Hanneke realized. Micah Ainsley was the man who had sent Fridolin the cryptic letter she'd found among his things.

"As I came to trust Fridolin, and heard him speak of his abhorrence of slavery, I shared with him my own efforts to assist desperate souls trying to flee their bondage. He asked how he could help." Micah Ainsley waved one hand. "I won't share the details, but in time we came to agree that he could do more good from outside the city. He left Milwaukee and bought

211

the Watertown farm for that reason."

Hanneke took that in. She'd been proud of Fridolin when she realized he'd helped runaway slaves. She'd had no idea he'd been so deeply involved.

"Fridolin was a courageous man, and deeply committed to the cause," Mr. Ainsley continued. "I will admit that when he returned from Germany and told me he'd married, I was shocked. And concerned, especially when he confessed that he'd not had time to discuss with you his secret work." He tapped one finger on the tabletop. "However, he assured me that you were an intelligent, spirited, and compassionate woman—those were his words—who would support his efforts."

An intelligent, spirited, and compassionate woman. Hanneke tucked that description away like a sugared fig to savor later when she was alone.

"For obvious reasons, Fridolin and I kept our communications to a minimum. I didn't know that Fridolin had died until I received your letter. I felt compelled to meet you. To try to explain. I didn't dare write to you, so…here I am."

Hanneke cleared her throat. "I'm very grateful."

"I was horrified to learn that my friend had died. A farm accident, you said?"

"No, I don't believe so." Hanneke glanced over her shoulders but the room remained empty. "I've been told that a man who was murdered in Watertown this week, a Mr. Loomis, was likely killed by slave catchers. I suspect that Fridolin suffered the same fate, even though his death was made to look like an accident."

Mr. Ainsley bowed his head for a moment. "We all know the risks, but I'm sick at heart. Fridolin was a wonderful man, and now…now here you are."

"A friend of Fridolin's told me about a conversation they had shortly before his death." Hanneke paused, trying to remember Gerda Muehlhauser's exact words. "He said, 'I wouldn't do things differently even if given the choice.' His friend didn't know what he meant, but *I* think Fridolin remained resolved about his choice to help runaway Negroes, even if that choice had a heavy price."

They sat in pensive silence for a few minutes. Then Micah Ainsley pulled a watch from its pocket and checked the time.

"Just one more moment, please," Hanneke said. "Do you know why Fridolin didn't tell his sister and his friends about me?"

"Why...what?" He blinked, obviously startled. "I didn't realize he hadn't done so."

"Ah." Hanneke nodded. There was nothing more to say about that.

"I need to catch the returning stage to Milwaukee, but I have two more things to discuss." He extracted an envelope from his frock coat and handed it to her. "There is some money inside. I can't help feeling somewhat responsible for your current situation."

"You're not." She tried to push the envelope back across the table.

"I absolutely insist. My friend left you in a terrible position. If the circumstances were reversed, I know he'd have done the same for my widow."

Hanneke wasn't comfortable taking money from Mr. Ainsley, but she could tell that it would hurt him to refuse. After a moment she tucked the envelope away.

"Second." Mr. Ainsley leaned closer. "Fridolin once told me that he'd left something for you. Something he wanted you to have if...well, if *this* happened."

Hanneke sat up very straight. "He did? What is it?"

"I don't know," Micah Ainsley said, "but I can tell you where to look."

Chapter Twenty-Two

After Mr. Ainsley left, Hanneke found Angela in the kitchen rocking chair. Leah sat with her, eyes open and alert. Watchful.

"Adolf promised to keep our little visitor a secret," Angela said. "The back door is locked and all the curtains are drawn."

"Where is Adolf now?"

"He and some friends left to go swimming in the river."

The image brought a quick smile to Hanneke's face. That was exactly what a young man should be doing on such a sultry day.

Angela tipped her head. "May I ask…who was your visitor?"

Hanneke pulled a chair close and repeated what Micah Ainsley had shared. "I feel as if I'm finally starting to understand what led me here, to this moment." She rubbed her palms on her knees.

"Fridolin did much good, and that's to be admired," Angela said quietly. "Still, it's hard to forgive the hurt he brought to you and his sister."

Hanneke felt the same way. "I also had an astonishing conversation with Christine this morning." She told Angela the tale, and pulled her shawl aside to reveal the brooch. "At least I do own the farm. It may take some time to sort things out and find a buyer, but I am no longer without means. It's Christine who's been left with nothing." She thought about that, fingered the unopened envelope in her pocket, and came to a quick decision. "I'll be back shortly."

* * *

At the Buena Vista, Hanneke asked for proprietress Josephine Wiggenhorn. "Please pass this on to Christine," Hanneke said, placing Micah Ainsley's envelope of money on the counter. She left before Josephine could ask any questions.

After that errand, Hanneke returned to the tavern, changed into a day dress, and settled in the kitchen with Angela and the baby. Two big kettles of chicken stew were already simmering on the stove in preparation for the evening meal.

Hanneke fed Leah some mashed carrots and changed her diaper before settling into the rocking chair. It was a comfort to rest like this, the child a warm weight on her lap. "You make me feel closer to Fridolin," Hanneke murmured. By helping protect this little girl she was, in her own small way, continuing the work her husband had begun. The work that almost certainly had led to his death.

Angela watched for a long moment before saying, "You are thinking about keeping this child."

Hanneke found it shocking to hear her barely-formed idea laid bare, and she avoided her friend's gaze. "If Leah's mother is dead—"

"We don't know that her mother is dead. The woman may have died in the fire, but she also may have gotten away. She might be hiding out there somewhere even now, terrified that she's lost her baby."

Hanneke's heart ached. "But until we know for sure…"

"You would not be admired for taking in a Negro child."

Hanneke almost laughed. "That makes no difference to me."

"As long as she is in Wisconsin, she is in danger. By law, that child is a—"

"The law is wrong!" Hanneke flared. Her arms tightened around Leah, who wriggled in silent protest.

"I agree," Angela said steadily, "but a child can not be kept secret forever. Let your friend take the child to Canada. If her mother *is* alive, they may yet be reunited."

For a long moment, there was no sound but the gentle creak of the rocker. Then Hanneke said, "I thought that…well, I thought that perhaps this baby was the good that was meant to come from heartache." Hanneke laid her cheek against Leah's head.

"But surely what's most important is giving this child the best chance for a good life. And that is not here. Not with us."

Hanneke gently stroked one of Leah's little hands, each perfect finger. She'd had a proper bath, and the sour smell of neglect had been replaced with something clean and fresh. Hanneke felt a flare of resentment and wished that her friend had kept her observation to herself.

The worst of it was...Angela was right.

With an effort, Hanneke cleared her throat. "I know."

Angela stood and squeezed Hanneke's shoulder. "I'm going up to rest." Her footsteps faded on the stairs.

Hanneke was dozing when someone tapped on the back door. She jerked upright, mouth suddenly dry as cotton. Angela had left a quilt on the floor by the chair and Hanneke settled Leah there. Then she eased aside the curtain and peeked out the window. John Barlow was waiting.

She let him in and locked the door behind him. "After church this morning, Christine told me you paid her a visit last night."

"There was no point in delaying." He looked at Leah, who had managed to roll from her back onto her stomach. "That's the baby," he said unnecessarily.

"It is. Please, sit down."

He removed his hat and pulled out in a chair. "Have you learned anything about her mother?"

"I'm afraid not." Hanneke returned to the rocker. "There is no news, good or bad. I was instructed to deliver the baby to—to someone after dark tonight. She'll be taken on to Canada and hopefully reunited with her mother. Although I don't think that's likely." Abruptly she leaned over and scooped up Leah.

Barlow studied them for a long moment. Finally, he said, "I do hope you are not becoming attached to that child."

Was it so obvious? "It's just that..." Hanneke regarded the baby, avoiding Barlow's gaze. "It's just that...I have nothing left."

"That's not true. You have the farm."

She sighed. "Yes. I have the farm."

"It doesn't have to be a millstone around your neck. Sell it and start fresh somewhere else."

And where would I go? she wondered. Not to Milwaukee, where Christine was trying to start her own new life. Most definitely not back to Pomerania.

Well, thanks to Angela, she had a few months to sort that out. And her predicament was certainly not John Barlow's problem.

He pulled some papers from his vest pocket and handed one to her. "I brought you the deed to the farm. As you can see, Christine signed it over to you. I don't see any reason why you can't put the property up for sale immediately."

Hanneke stared at the signature, clear and bold in black ink. "Yes. *Danke schön.*"

"There is just one other thing." For the first time he hesitated, considering the paper in his hand. "Christine was behind on taxes. Let me translate for you."

Hanneke listened to the brief note with a growing sense of disbelief. *Owed on your eighty acres: one dollar for recording the deed, four dollars for land tax, and two days of road work.*

"All male landowners are required to contribute road work," Barlow explained. "Don't worry. We'll get that provision struck."

She didn't know whether to laugh or to cry. "Roadwork is likely all the payment I *can* make. I don't have five dollars." Only because she had *just* given Micah Ainsley's gift to Christine.

Barlow looked uncomfortable. "I wish..." He lifted his palms in a helpless gesture.

"Don't concern yourself." She starched her spine and met his gaze. "I do have a bit of news as well." She told the deputy about her visit from Micah Ainsley, sharing everything but his name and profession. She wanted John Barlow to understand the good that Fridolin had done since buying the farm on Plum Grove Road.

"I'm glad to know that," Barlow admitted gruffly. "If Fraulein Zeidler is here to watch the baby, I'll drive you out to the farm. You can fetch whatever Fridolin left behind."

Deputy Barlow had driven a small wagon into town, pulled by a black Morgan horse whose coat shone like obsidian in the sun. He helped Hanneke step up to the seat before settling himself and gripping the lines. "Gettup, Belle."

Watertown was quiet this Sunday afternoon. Clouds were gathering overhead. They paused to let a mother duck lead a string of fuzzy ducklings across the road. Two giggling girls played with a puppy in a shady yard.

Deputy Barlow turned to Hanneke. "Do you mind a short stop? It's not out of the way. Dr. Rausch has a tonic prepared for my wife. I planned to fetch it yesterday, but…"

But things got out of hand, Hanneke thought. "Of course I don't mind. You're doing me a kindness."

The doctor's office was only a block or two northwest of the tavern. As she waited on the wagon seat, Hanneke wondered what illness had been plaguing Frau Barlow. Back in Pomerania Hanneke had grown exasperated with physicians who provided medicinals that either plunged the patient into a stupor or had no effect whatsoever. Watching her own mother struggle had provoked her to learn what she could about herbal remedies. But, she reminded herself, the deputy's wife is none of your concern.

A few moments later Deputy Barlow returned with his parcel, and they drove out of town. Dark storm clouds were lowering as they reached Fridolin's farm on Plum Bottom Road. The weather seemed appropriate, for already the farm felt abandoned. Hanneke looked away from the *fachwerk* house and abandoned garden as Barlow turned into the drive. Those things don't matter, she thought. Hidden in the *Scheune* at the back of the courtyard was some final gift from Fridolin.

Micah Ainsley's directions had been clear: *Go behind the grain barn. Crawl around the stone pillar supporting the northwest corner. Look for a trap door above your head that leads to one of the grain storage bays.*

The barn floor was about three feet off the ground. As they approached the building Barlow said, "There's no need for you to wriggle about." He dropped to his knees and crawled beneath the structure. "I see the trap door."

Hanneke crouched so she could watch his progress. Raising both arms, he put his palms against the trap door above him. When he managed to shove it aside he was met with a shower of grain and chaff and dust. Coughing, he rose to his feet, disappearing partway through the hatch. He maneuvered his elbows onto the barn floor on either side of the hatch and scrambled from sight.

Hanneke wanted to follow, but reluctantly decided that even a successful scrabble through the hatch might damage her clothes as much as her dignity. "Do you see anything?" she called. "The tin box is supposed to be right in the corner."

"There are still a lot of grain bundles here." Amid dry rustles, more chaff and broken straw sifted through the hatch. Then, "I've got it!"

Barlow's boots reappeared, then the rest of him as he dropped to the ground. He held out a rectangular tin box. Fridolin was the last person to touch this, Hanneke thought, accepting it with care. The box was simple enough, about eight inches by twelve, heavy as a good loaf of hearty rye.

"It's an ingenious hideaway," Barlow added as he wrestled the trap door back into place. "Runaways could approach from the woods behind the farm, then hide in the straw until it was safe to move on again."

As Hanneke imagined such a scene fat drops of rain splattered on her bonnet.

Barlow crawled out and swiped dusty palms against his trousers. "Let's go into the house. Whatever's in that box might be fragile. Besides, Christine left in a hurry. We don't know how much work inside might be needed before you can show the place to a buyer."

Hanneke wasn't keen to go inside the house again, but since she could offer no good alternative, she followed Barlow across the yard. He had a key, and they stepped inside just as the splatters turned into a torrent.

The back workroom was chilly. Tin dishpans sat in the big wooden dry sink. Wooden clogs waited by the door. Flies buzzed against the cheesecloth tied over several crocks that probably held preserves. All mine, Hanneke reminded herself, but this latest change of circumstance still didn't seem real.

Hanneke turned her back on the house, set the tin box in the dry sink, and pried open the lid. Inside was a book: *The Critique of Pure Reason*, by Immanuel Kant. "Oh," she whispered. A salty lump formed in her throat. She picked the book up gently and pressed it against her chest. Fridolin did truly value my mind, she thought. He *wanted* me to think for myself.

"A book?" Barlow sounded confused, or unimpressed, or perhaps both.

"Fridolin and I discussed Kant's philosophy before we married," she explained. "Kant believed that we can only understand what we experience, nothing else. Fridolin was surprised that I hadn't read it."

Barlow grunted something noncommittal.

She was grateful for the unexpected bequest. Still, the gift was bittersweet. "I do *so* wish that the men who killed Mr. Loomis, and presumably Fridolin, could be arrested and punished."

"Without proof of their crimes, the best thing you can do at this point is look to the future." Deputy Barlow walked away without waiting for a response.

Rain drummed against the roof and blurred the windowpanes. Hanneke stared across the farmyard blindly. The week's events had been overwhelming. And she was not, she realized, ready to slam a door on everything that had happened. Not when stray thoughts and worries still nagged at her mind like gnats. *Fridolin, if there are answers to be found I need your help*, she thought.

Fridolin didn't answer.

Hanneke tapped one foot in frustration, trying to think of something new. Mr. Rutherford and Mr. Ainsley had used Bible verses to communicate in code. Perhaps Fridolin had marked some special passage for her in this gift volume.

She opened the book and quickly paged through, looking for any ink or pencil mark. There were none.

"I'm going upstairs," Barlow called.

"Fine." She turned back to the beginning of the book. The endpapers were gorgeously marbled with hues of green and blue. Fridolin's work, surely. She ran a finger across the swirled patterns…and felt a tiny *something* near the edge. Something, almost indiscernible, that didn't belong.

Hanneke nibbled her lower lip. Then she found a paring knife in the kitchen and carefully put the tip to the edge of the endpaper. Slowly, carefully, doing as little damage as possible, she opened a slit along the top of the page. She slid the knife into the slit and used the blade to pull out a folded piece of paper.

Dropping the knife, she examined the page. The brown ink and the handwriting were both familiar.

My dear Hanneke,

I hope you never see this. However, bad things happen on this earth. In the event of unexpected tragedy, I hope that a few words from your devoted husband might ease your heart and mind.

I never expected to marry, but upon the occasion of our meeting, I was so swept away that I let my heart rule my head. You know by now, I'm sure, that I have kept too much of my life hidden. It is impossible to justify and difficult to explain, but I will make what feeble effort I can.

By the time we met, I already understood that asking my sister Christine to follow me to Watertown and keep house for me had been a mistake. She wasn't happy here. Although the farm work was harder than I had expected, I came to be content in this place. And as you will likely understand, I had also found a higher calling. I was committed to staying. Still, I felt guilty about my sister's isolation here. I hoped that my wife—you—would make her life easier. I recognized you as a hard worker, someone who would ease Christine's burdens and provide ready company.

In the deepest depths of my heart, however, I must have known that she might not be pleased to learn of our wedding. When I came home to Wisconsin I struggled to find the right time to tell her. I wrote letters to you, explaining the situation, only to throw them in the fire.

You see, my dear, I am a coward. I let myself enjoy our wedding, our correspondence, without complication. I couldn't bear to disappoint either my sister or you. As I write this, I am steeling myself for what will be a painful conversation with Christine.

A conversation that never happened, Hanneke thought. Was Fridolin killed before he had the opportunity, or did his courage fail him in the end?

It remains my fondest hope that in time, the three of us will settle into a quiet, contented life here at the farm. But if my other line of work overcomes me in some manner, I beg you not to remember me with only disgust or anger.

"Oh, Fridolin," Hanneke whispered. How could a man brave enough to defy the law and flout slave catchers be too afraid to tell his sister and his bride the truth about each other?

I have asked two trusted friends to look out for you if need be.

Mr. Loomis and Micah Ainsley. Both had tried.

Please believe that the two weeks we spent together were the happiest of my life. I pray that memories might provide a bit of solace against what will surely be bitter disappointment.
 Your loving husband,
 Fridolin

Hanneke closed her eyes. At least now she understood Fridolin's intentions. Knowing did ease, a bit, the jagged wound in her heart.

And it helped her focus a bit more clearly on everything that had happened since she arrived in Watertown. Stray bits of memory shifted and aligned, like tangled fistfuls of wool being combed straight.

She gazed out the window again, imagining her husband's final moments on the threshing floor. Perhaps he'd never seen his attacker, or perhaps he'd known a moment of fear before the slaver who'd crept up behind him delivered the blow.

And as she stared at the beautiful *Scheune*, she thought of something she hadn't considered before. That thought led to another, and another, twining themselves into a single strand. *"Gott in Himmel,"* she whispered, pressing a hand against her mouth.

John Barlow circled back to join her, and apparently didn't notice her agitation. "It's obvious that Christine packed up quickly," he said. "If she's truly taken all that she wants to keep, you'll need to decide what to do with the rest."

"Deputy Barlow." Hanneke spoke slowly. "On the day Fridolin died, two young men were here working on the summer kitchen. Franz and Joe Rademacher, do you know them?"

Looking puzzled, he shook his head.

"They told me that when they heard Christine screaming in the *Scheune*, they ran to see what was wrong. Fridolin lay on the floor beside the bloody flail. Christine was in hysterics. She shrieked at them to go fetch Dr. Jenkins."

Barlow folded his arms and leaned against the wall. "Why are you telling me this?"

"Why didn't Christine send for Dr. Rausch?"

He spread his hands. "Does it matter?"

"I'd never been to Dr. Rausch's home before today, but I *have* visited Dr. Jenkins. He lives farther away from here. And he's a Yankee."

Barlow's eyebrows had lowered. "Fridolin spoke good English. I think he looked for ways to reach outside of the German community."

"But in an emergency..." Sensing his resistance, Hanneke tried a new approach. "Do you know Dr. Jenkins? I ask because I remember thinking that he looked unwell. Too thin. His cheeks were flushed, with obvious blood vessels here." She touched the sides of her nose. "In my experience, those can be signs of drinking too much liquor on a regular basis. Is Dr. Jenkins a drunkard?"

"I can't speak to that," Barlow said stiffly.

With effort, she bridled her impatience. "Please, I'm not looking for gossip. Only information."

Deputy Barlow's frown deepened, but after a moment he admitted, "I have had to help him home on more than one occasion. He was once a good man, and a good doctor, but the drink has taken a toll. Despite what the nativists would have everyone believe, Yankees are just as likely to drink too much as

Germans and Irishmen."

"So why would Christine send the brothers to him?"

Barlow stared at her, rubbing his chin with one thumb.

Hanneke hated testing the tentative trust and cordiality developing between them, but there was no help for it. "I can only imagine doing so if I wanted someone incompetent to announce the cause of death."

"What are you suggesting?"

"That my husband was murdered, but not by slavers."

"That's absurd." The deputy's tone was as cold and dismissive as it had been the day they met. "Are you actually suggesting that Christine went to the barn that day, grabbed the flail from Fridolin's hands, and managed to strike a deadly blow?"

Hanneke balled her hands in her skirt, struggling to keep her voice even. "I agree that Christine could not have overpowered her brother, but she might have killed him by other means."

"What other means?" he snapped.

"Christine told me she is a bonnet maker." Hanneke chose her words carefully. The deputy had already broken the law by allowing her to keep Leah hidden. She didn't want him to learn that she'd trespassed into Christine's home. "That occupation requires, I believe, the use of certain chemicals as mordants, or to bleach fabrics..." She walked past him into Christine's workroom as if going to explore the notion.

Christine had made it easy for her. The dyestuffs Hanneke had noted on her first visit were gone. Sitting alone on the shelf was the bottle marked *Oxalic Acid*.

Hanneke picked it up and displayed the label. "It appears from the dust marks that a number of bottles were stored on this shelf. Why was this the only one Christine left behind?"

"What is that used for?"

"Oxalic acid is most commonly used by women in mourning. Black crape bleeds quite readily, and can stain the skin. I chose not to wear crape when my parents died for that very reason, but most well-to-do women feel compelled to observe the traditions."

CHAPTER TWENTY-TWO

He made an impatient gesture.

"Back in Pomerania, my brother's wife once scrubbed stains from her skin with a mixture of oxalic acid and cream of tartar. The spots faded, but the area became inflamed. That's when I studied the effects of oxalic acid. It must be used with care. I happened to mention it to Christine after church this morning because her crape was bleeding, and for a moment I thought she might faint."

Barlow took the bottle from her hand, removed the cork, gave a tentative sniff.

"It's odorless, yes?" Hanneke asked. "And I've read that it blends easily in water. I imagine it wouldn't be difficult to mix into some strong-flavored drink. Switchel, for example, served on a hot day." The mixture of water, vinegar, ginger, and molasses was commonly served to laboring men.

"And what would happen if someone did drink this?" Barlow returned the cork.

Hanneke tried to recall what she'd read. "I do know that only a small amount—perhaps five or ten grams—could be fatal. I believe sores might form inside the mouth. The victim might vomit blood. If Christine did poison her brother, a careless or drunk physician would be more likely to explain away the sores, or dismiss them altogether." A new thought made her wince. "Especially if someone struck Fridolin in the head *before* he died, when blood would still flow, to make his death look like a foolish accident. And...why else would the bloodstained flail still be in the barn? It's as if a tableau was carefully set to reinforce the idea that Fridolin accidentally killed himself."

Deputy Barlow began to pace. "No. I can't accept this ridiculous notion. I've known Christine for two years. I do not believe she is physically or emotionally capable of striking such a blow."

"I think she had help. Did you drive her to town this morning?"

He looked startled. "No..."

"Christine had already settled into the Buena Vista by the time church started this morning. I can't imagine her trudging to the city with valises in hand, can you? I believe she has a gentleman friend."

"Anyone could have driven her to town. A neighbor."

Hanneke fought the urge to reveal that the day she'd invaded the farmhouse, she'd seen two dirty breakfast plates in the kitchen. She'd seen a poorly-crocheted silencer on the night jar lid in Christine's bedroom, even though Fridolin had slept upstairs and wouldn't have heard if she'd used the vessel in the middle of the night—only someone sharing her bed. And, she'd seen a man wearing workman's clothing visit Christine.

"Frau Bauer." The deputy's voice and posture were stiff. "Christine Bauer has left her home and passed the deed on to you. Unless you can prove this allegation, I will not add to her distress by accusing her of poisoning her own brother."

You could talk to her! Hanneke wanted to say. Christine had shown signs of emotional distress that morning. With a little pressure from the deputy –

"Are you ready to return to Watertown? I'll drive you back to the tavern."

The air between them had grown so frosty that Hanneke couldn't bear the idea of sharing even the short drive. "I'll walk."

She retrieved her precious letter, leaving the book to be fetched later. They left the house in silence. After securing the lock, the deputy climbed to the wagon seat. With a curt nod, he lifted the lines. "Up, Belle," he called to the horse. A moment later they turned onto the road and disappeared from sight.

That did not go well, Hanneke thought. With a heavy sigh, she pulled her knitting from her pocket and began walking back to Watertown.

She hadn't gone far, though, when something new occurred to her. Once the farm was sold, it would no longer be a safe haven for midnight travelers. Before leaving this place for good, she should gouge the carved star from the beam on the *Scheune's* back wall. She stopped in the road. Could it wait until tomorrow?

No. It could not.

Hanneke plodded back to the farm, back through the empty farmyard. She needed a blade of some kind to disfigure the carving. She hadn't thought to ask John Barlow for the key to the house, but perhaps there was something she could use in the grain barn.

Inside the *Scheune* she found a sickle hanging in the storage room. She lifted it from its peg. That would do nicely.

But before going back outside she paused. Asa Hawkins's attack had increased the revulsion she already felt for this space. Still, maybe there was something she'd missed, something seemingly insignificant that might help her truly understand Fridolin's last moments. It was worth considering, one last time.

Hanneke walked around the corner to the threshing floor. Everything was exactly as she'd left it—bundles of wheat circled on the tarpaulin, a blood-stained flail. She crouched and studied the pale canvas, wiping away bits of straw and chaff. If Fridolin had been poisoned, and he'd been sick, she might be able to find some trace of—

The slow creak of the opening door broke the stillness.

Chapter Twenty-Three

Hanneke shot to her feet, still gripping the sickle. "Hello?"

Footsteps sounded against the floorboards.

She pressed her free hand over her thumping heart. "Deputy Barlow?"

The man who walked around the corner of the granary looked familiar, although she couldn't place him. He was younger than Deputy Barlow, and red-haired, and he carried a heavy wooden paddle with a curved handle in one hand. That she recognized as a legget, used to drive straw into place as thatchers finished each section of new roof.

She instinctively stepped backwards.

Silently, inexorably, he closed the distance between them. His narrowed eyes held a frightening resolve. When she tried to dodge sideways, he countered the move.

"Who are you?" she demanded.

"Not a yeast seller," he growled.

For a moment that flummoxed her. Then she remembered the earnest red-haired yeast peddler who'd knocked on Angela's kitchen door on Thursday. Lorenz Kiessling. "What do you *want*?"

Kiessling walked closer, backing her against the big threshing bay doors. Something metallic pooled on Hanneke's tongue. Her pulse throbbed an alarm as he raised the heavy legget over his head. Her fingers convulsed around the sickle. As he brought the legget down she lunged to the right, swinging the curved blade wildly. Just as the sickle met flesh she felt a shuddering blow glance off her own shoulder, knocking her to the floor.

A bloodstain appeared on the man's shirt sleeve. His surprise darkened to rage. *"Hündin!"*

Hanneke tried to scramble away but the man grabbed her wrist and twisted it, hard. She whimpered against the searing pain and the sickle dropped from her hand. He kicked it across the floor. With a sense of despair, Hanneke watched it disappear into the sheaves piled in the storage bay.

Kiessling jerked her roughly to her feet. The furious determination in his face was terrifying. She thought, I am defenseless.

No, you are not.

Hanneke leaned back and dug in her heels, forcing Kiessling to turn toward her. Her free hand slid into her pocket and clenched her four steel knitting needles. Then she whipped the needles up and stabbed him where she knew it would hurt.

Kiessling screamed and dropped to his knees. She wrenched away but he managed to grab her skirt. She crashed painfully back to the floor.

"Nein!" Hanneke rasped. She had not survived this wretched week only to be killed in Fridolin's barn. All knowledge and sensation pared to the necessity of escaping this man.

She rolled, kicking violently. Kiessling lunged and landed heavily upon her legs.

Suddenly the floorboards vibrated beneath her. Kiessling's weight disappeared. A new pair of muddy boots appeared in Hanneke's sightline. "What in God's name…!"

Hanneke blinked up at Deputy John Barlow, who'd hauled the struggling younger man to his feet. When Kiessling tried to pull away Barlow threw him hard against the door. Kiessling crumpled on the floor.

Barlow quickly bound the other man's hands behind his back. "Frau Bauer?" the deputy asked. "What—"

"Arrest him," Hanneke managed, gasping for breath. "He tried to kill me. With that." She pointed toward the legget on the floor. "And I believe," she added grimly, "that he killed Fridolin."

* * *

Ten minutes later Deputy Barlow dragged Kiessling from the barn to secure him in the wagon. He took the legget too. Hanneke remained inside, sitting on the floor, leaning against a beam.

When Barlow returned he crouched beside her. "Are you all right?"

"Yes. I just—I'm just resting." Seized by a belated bout of trembles, she didn't dare attempt to stand.

He scrutinized her in the dim light, rubbing his jaw between thumb and forefinger. "Who is that man?"

"His name is Lorenz Kiessling. I met him when he came to the tavern kitchen while Angela was sick. He peddles yeast."

"He peddles yeast?" Barlow looked bewildered. "Is he a lunatic? Why did he attack you?"

"I'll tell you what I think." She glanced at him, daring him to rebuke her, but he only made an encouraging gesture. "Deputy Barlow, do you know what that is?" She pointed again at the legget.

He shook his head. "No."

"It's a thatching tool. I believe Lorenz Kiessling is a trained thatcher. I'm sure he did this barn." She waved a hand, indicating the beautifully finished roof far above them. "It's the work of a master. Do remember when Christine had the roof rethatched? Was it before or after Fridolin died?"

"Well…after, I believe. I suppose she thought a new roof would impress potential buyers."

"This farm is only a few years old, and a good thatched roof will last a dozen years or more. Your neighbor Gerda Muehlhauser mentioned that shortly before Fridolin died the roof withstood a bad windstorm. And Christine told me that Fridolin left almost no money in the bank. Why would she go to such expense?"

Deputy Barlow sank back from his crouch and sat on the floor. "Go on."

"I think Kiessling and Christine are courting, and she gave him a chance to show off his skill in hopes of attracting business. I noticed a red-haired thatcher working on a stable in town the other day, but most Germans in this area are putting shingles on their new buildings. I think Kiessling started peddling yeast in desperation because he couldn't find enough thatching work to earn a living."

Barlow's mouth twisted pensively.

"We suspected that slave catchers murdered Fridolin, as we believe they murdered his friend Mr. Loomis." Hanneke rubbed her shoulder, feeling the residual pain of Kiessling's blow. "But if slavers were responsible for Fridolin's death, who stole my papers the day I arrived? I assumed it was someone who'd been in the Buena Vista taproom. Someone who observed my conversation with Herr Wiggenhorn, and with you. But I overlooked something obvious." She frowned, annoyed by her error.

"What?"

"I heard conversation coming through the open kitchen door. If I could hear people in the kitchen, they could hear me." She paused, waiting for Barlow to catch on, but he didn't speak. "A yeast peddler wouldn't knock on the front door. He'd go straight to the kitchen. I think Lorenz Kiessling was at the Buena Vista that day, out of sight, but able to hear me identify myself as Fridolin's wife."

"Well... that's a possibility," Barlow allowed.

"If Kiessling and Christine are courting, selling this farm might have been their strategy for starting a new life together somewhere. If Kiessling was in the house when you came to speak with Christine last night, he knew she'd decided to let me have my legal due. He was likely the person who helped her move to the Buena Vista early this morning."

"So, you think he attacked you because..."

"Because he was furious with Christine's decision. Kiessling probably returned to fetch his tools from the granary." She gestured toward the small storeroom. "I'd seen some odds and ends in there, but took no particular notice. When he realized I was here—"

"Why *were* you here?"

Hanneke toyed absently with a piece of straw. "It occurred to me that someone should obliterate the star carved on the back wall. Runaways need to know that Fridolin isn't here to help them anymore. I needed some kind of blade, and the house was locked, so I came here to look for a tool. Then I decided to look one last time for evidence that Fridolin was murdered." She gave him another sidelong look, daring him to object.

"Did you find anything?" he asked quietly.

"I think so." Hanneke looked toward the workspace. "If Fridolin *was* dosed with oxalic acid, the poison might have made him sick. I found a stain on the tarpaulin. It was covered with straw, and I didn't get a good look before Kiessling appeared, but I think…"

Barlow stood. "Where?"

"To the right of the flail, towards the center." She watched as the deputy kicked more straw aside and examined the tarp. His attention, his willingness to investigate, came as an overwhelming relief.

"There is a stain here," Barlow said. "I can't say what caused it. But it's the only mark of its kind."

"Talk to Christine," Hanneke implored. "Lorenz Kiessling likely won't confess to anything. But as I told you this morning, Christine seems close to hysteria. If you press her firmly, I believe you'll get answers."

"I'll do that." Barlow stepped close and extended a hand. Hanneke grasped it and allowed him to help her to her feet. "However," he continued, "it might be best if you accompanied me."

"Oh no, I—no."

"I won't compel you. But I do think you may be best able to provoke honest responses. I have little experience questioning women, and until this mess…" He raised both palms. "I counted her a friend."

Hanneke felt drained. The day had ready been too full. But this business needs finishing, she told herself, and squared her shoulders. "Very well. All I ask is that you let me meet you in Watertown. I don't wish to ride back in the wagon with Kiessling. I'll walk."

He looked mildly irritated. "That's not wise."

Hanneke almost smiled. "I will be fine."

Barlow frowned, but acquiesced. "All right. I'll take care of Kiessling and meet you at the tavern." He turned toward the door.

"Wait!" Hanneke realized she'd forgotten something important. "*Danke schön*, Deputy Barlow."

He turned back with a snort of something approaching laughter. "You seemed to be managing quite nicely. I bound a rag over the gash in Kiessling's arm where you sliced him with the sickle. But he had a second wound as well." The deputy couldn't hide a wince. "What did you stab him with?"

"My knitting needles." Hanneke's cheeks warmed but she didn't look away. "It slowed him down. I'm quite sure, however, that he would have soon overwhelmed me. I'm exceedingly grateful that you arrived when you did. But...why did you?"

Deputy Barlow was silent for so long that she thought he might not respond. Then he said simply, "I don't know. I was halfway home when... well, the idea just came to me. The thought that I needed to come back." With that, he left her alone in the barn. A few moments later she heard him call to the Morgan and the creaking rumble of wooden wagon wheels driving back across the yard.

The idea just came to me. The thought that I needed to come back.

Hanneke considered the barn where her husband had breathed his last breath. A narrow beam of light slanted through a knothole. The faint scent of dried wheat and rye was familiar. Astonishingly, a sense of comfort rose among the ugliness. When Kiessling had kicked the sickle away, a thought had come to her as well, clear as a whisper in her ear. *You are not defenseless.*

"Thank you, Fridolin," Hanneke said softly. Then she left the barn.

* * *

Since Hanneke did not have good memories of the Buena Vista, a visit to interrogate Christine would not improve that situation. For comfort, and as silent testament to everything she'd lost when Fridolin died, she wore her lacy wedding shawl. She felt a flicker of pride when, after reluctantly following Deputy Barlow into the hotel that afternoon, Josephine Wiggenhorn's admiring gaze lingered again on her finery.

At Barlow's request, Josephine brought Christine into the women's parlor. "Can I fetch refreshments?" Josephine asked, glancing with some concern at Christine. The proprietress evidently wanted to provide her friend moral support during this unexpected visit.

"*Nein, danke schön.*" Barlow walked Josephine out the door and closed it firmly behind her.

"What is this about?" Christine asked as she settled daintily on a settee. She'd removed both the heavy veil and the stains it had left behind, but Fridolin's sister still looked fragile as a porcelain figurine.

Barlow wasted no time on pleasantries. "Christine, I arrested Lorenz Kiessling this afternoon."

Shock seized Christine's features, then quickly gave way to fear. I was right, Hanneke thought. She took no pleasure in it.

"He attacked Frau Bauer," Barlow continued. He was seated awkwardly on a velvet-covered chair that was too small for him, forearms resting on his knees. "Do you know anything about that?"

"Why—no, I—why would I?" Christine stammered. "I don't even know Lorenz Kiessling."

"Isn't he the man who thatched your barn roof this spring?" Hanneke asked.

Christine clasped her hands tightly. "Well, perhaps…" She looked toward the door. "Could you please call Josephine? I'm not feeling well."

"This won't take long." Barlow's level gaze never wavered. "Did you kill Fridolin?"

"No!" She jumped to her feet. "Of course not! I—"

"Sit *down.*"

Christine dropped back to the settee.

"We know about the oxalic acid," Hanneke told her. "You went pale when I mentioned it this morning. Among all your bonnet making supplies, that was the only thing you left behind at the farmhouse. We found evidence in the barn that Fridolin had been sick—evidence that had been concealed with straw." It took supreme effort to keep her voice steady, but raging at Christine would accomplish nothing. "Why did you feel compelled to murder Fridolin?"

"I didn't!" Christine began to weep.

"You did!" Hanneke insisted. "Why, Christine? *Why?* How could a sister do such a thing?"

Christine sucked in a harsh breath. "Why not ask how a *brother* could do such a thing?" she hissed. Her face had hardened, every feature sharp. "I begged him to sell the farm and move back to Milwaukee. But instead of helping me, he only wanted to help *Negroes*." She spat the final word like an oath.

Hanneke blinked, surprised to discover that Christine had known about Fridolin's clandestine activities—and shocked by the vitriol as well. Christine had obviously kept a part of herself, an angry part, hidden from her friends. But not, Hanneke thought, from Fridolin. Gerda had spoken of him needing "someplace peaceful." Perhaps life with Christine Bauer had not been peaceful for Fridolin even before the marriage. For the first time, Hanneke had a hint of why he'd been loathe to confide in Christine.

"I left Pomerania to keep house for my brother!" Christine shrilled. "I left my friends in Milwaukee when he bought the farm. After everything I sacrificed for Fridolin, he didn't even tell me about the marriage until you were on your way to Wisconsin!"

So, Hanneke thought. In the end, Fridolin did tell his sister about the marriage. "He kept secrets from me as well," she reminded Christine. "I had no idea—"

"But you had *him*!" Christine clawed at her skirt, crumpling the silk in her frenzy. "And the legal claim to everything he owned. I scrubbed and hoed and cooked in that horrid *schwartze Küche*—only to learn that I was to be pushed aside!"

"I wouldn't have…" Hanneke began, but let the thought die. It was too late for that.

"Tell us what happened," Barlow said. "The day Fridolin died."

Christine's tone turned pleading. "I didn't kill him, John! He'd told me the night before about *her*." She waved a hand toward Hanneke. "You can surely understand how that made me feel. I just wanted to punish him somehow. I was working with the oxalic acid…and…I must have lost my wits. I did put a few drops of the acid into the jug of switchel he took out to the barn. But Lorenz said…"

"What did Lorenz say?" Barlow prompted.

"I confided in him about Fridolin's marriage."

In the night, Hanneke thought.

"Why did you choose to confide in Lorenz Kiessling?" Barlow asked. Hanneke didn't know if he was truly confused or just wanted her to be thorough.

"Well, in the past few months we've become…friends." Christine noticed the damage she'd done to her skirt and tried to smooth it out. "Life has been terribly hard for him since he arrived last fall. He's a skilled craftsman, but most people don't want thatched roofs anymore. Anyway, Fridolin's news made Lorenz furious. I didn't know how angry he was until—until later."

"When it was too late." Hanneke was gripping the edges of her chair with the effort of keeping her composure. The man she'd married in Pomerania had been pleasant, thoughtful, a good conversationalist. She pictured him assuaging his thirst in the barn, becoming violently ill…and helpless by the time Christine's beau arrived. "After Lorenz Kiessling had killed Fridolin."

"Lorenz left before dawn." Christine's cheeks flushed, but she kept going. "After breakfast, I tainted the switchel and Fridolin carried it out to the barn. Before long I came to my senses, and prayed to God that he would recover quickly from any harm—"

"But you didn't actually go see if Fridolin was suffering," Hanneke observed tartly.

Christine ignored her, keeping her beseeching gaze on Barlow. "When I realized that the farmyard had gone quiet, I went out to the barn and found Lorenz standing over Fridolin." She went to the deputy and clutched his arm. "Lorenz was the one who killed him! You must believe me, John! *Please!*"

The door burst open and Josephine appeared with a starched rustle. "Is everything all right?" Her gaze swept the room.

"Leave us," Barlow snapped. After a stunned moment, Josephine retreated.

"I didn't know that Lorenz had come back to confront Fridolin," Christine insisted, tears running down her cheeks. "He told me that he'd found Fridolin ill but still alive. And that he…" she shuddered prettily, as if she couldn't bear to form the words.

Barlow drew a deep breath. "If Kiessling told you he'd killed Fridolin, why didn't you come to me at once?"

"Because…because he said he'd done it for *us*," she wept. "He said we could sell the farm and make a new start. He told me to scream for help as soon as he'd slipped out the back. He convinced me that there was nothing to be gained by telling the authorities."

"You must not have needed much convincing," Hanneke snapped. "You sent the Rademacher brothers for a Yankee doctor known to overindulge in strong drink, even though he was farther away. You concluded that Dr. Jenkins was less likely to notice any signs of distress beyond evidence of a blow to the head."

"I—I did no such thing."

"And you obviously didn't object whenever Kiessling told you he'd seized the opportunity to steal my papers on the day I arrived in Watertown. You were willing to leave me heartbroken and destitute in a country where I didn't know a soul."

Christine sagged to the floor in a pool of black silk. "I'm sorry," she sobbed. "I didn't know you then! I didn't know you'd be…kind."

For a long moment, no one spoke. Christine hiccupped and wept, shoulders shaking, tears streaming down her cheeks. A burst of laughter drifted from the taproom across the hall. The air smelled faintly of baking bread. Hanneke wondered if Lorenz Kiessling had sold Josephine the needed yeast.

Then John Barlow caught Hanneke's gaze and jerked his head toward the door. "Get Josephine."

The proprietress had retreated only as far as the hall. She looked anxious, uncertain. "What…"

"The deputy asked for you," Hanneke said, and led the older woman back into the parlor. Christine was still on the floor.

"Josephine, please go to Christine's room and pack her things," Deputy Barlow said. "She's coming with me."

* * *

Hanneke wanted nothing more than to go to her room and sink onto her bed. She arrived back at the tavern at suppertime, though. She went upstairs to check on Leah, who was fussing. Hanneke changed her diaper and sang her to sleep with a German lullaby. Then she went to work beside Angela and Adolf.

After darkness fell, Hanneke wrapped the child in her warm shawl and carried her to Adam's barbershop. The old man was waiting—and to Hanneke's surprise, the laundress in the blue paisley dress was waiting as well. Hanneke had twice glimpsed her in the past, and the woman's countenance had been demure, with eyes averted. Today she stood straight, chin high. It was she, not Adam, who stepped forward and silently eased the child from Hanneke's arms. She started to pull the shawl away.

"No, please," Hanneke said. "Let her keep it."

The woman hesitated, silently meeting Hanneke's gaze. She was older than Hanneke had originally thought—somewhere in her thirties, perhaps. Her facial features might have been chiseled from stone. But her eyes… oh, her eyes brimmed with stories and knowledge that Hanneke couldn't begin to understand. There was a tension within the older woman, highly suppressed but tangible.

For the first time, Hanneke truly understood why she wasn't prepared to keep the child. "I'm sorry," she whispered. "I hope you can reunite her with her mother."

The woman nodded almost imperceptibly. Then she snugged the shawl around the baby.

Hanneke's heart was a dull ache beneath her ribs. She wanted to linger, to provide instructions, to offer more assistance, to ask what the baby's real name was. Instead, she kissed the child on the forehead. "Be safe and grow strong, little girl," she whispered, squeezing the words past the thickness in her throat. When she slipped back outside, the latch turned behind her at once.

Hanneke walked away slowly, glad for the darkness that hid her tears. She'd lost a husband who had truly cared for her. She'd lost a sister-in-law who might, if things had been different, become a friend. She'd lost Leah, and the dream of a family of her own.

When the tavern came into view she paused, trying to shed her melancholy. I'm much better off than I was a week ago, she reminded herself. If she could just somehow earn enough money to pay the overdue taxes, she could sell the farm on Plum Grove Road. After that, if she managed her affairs wisely, she would never again be at the mercy of strangers or disdainful relatives. When she wore out her welcome at the Red Cockerel, she could make her own new start. Somewhere.

She walked around to the back alley and let herself in the kitchen door. Adolf was stacking clean plates on a shelf. "Angela wasn't feeling well," he reported. "She went up to bed."

Oh please, Lord, nothing more tonight, Hanneke thought. "I'll go see to her."

Upstairs she found Angela still dressed, lying on top of the bed, curled into a ball. A lamp still burned on the bureau. "Are you unwell?" Hanneke asked anxiously.

After a long moment, Angela pushed herself to a sitting position. "I'm fine. Adolf shouldn't have worried you."

Hanneke sat down beside her. "What's troubling you?"

She fretted the quilt with her fingers. "It was hard to send Leah away."

That tender place in Hanneke's chest pulsed. "Yes. It was."

"And I keep thinking…" Angela placed a palm over her belly. "Soon I'll have my own baby. I don't know if I can raise a child well by myself." Her other hand clutched Hanneke's arm in sudden panic. "I have nothing to offer a child!"

"Nonsense," Hanneke said, gently but firmly. "You will shower your infant with love. You have a safe place to live. You have a livelihood. You'll teach your child to work hard and to be kind and everything else that is important."

"I suppose," Angela whispered.

"And you have friends who will help you." Hanneke paused considering her next words with care. "Angela, I'm sure the change coming must feel overwhelming. But instead of dwelling on what you don't have, I hope you will consider instead all that you do."

For a long moment, the room was silent except for a moth fluttering at the lamp. Then Angela managed a small smile. "That is wise advice. I'll do my best."

Hanneke trudged back downstairs. "Angela is all right," she told Adolf. "And I'm going to bed." She wanted to sleep for a week.

"Wait!" Adolf cried. "Deputy Barlow arrived while you were upstairs. He's waiting in the taproom."

What *now?* Hanneke thought wearily. There was, of course, only one way to find out. "Very well."

"Shall I stay up until he's gone?"

Adolf's offer made her smile. "I'll be all right. You go on to bed whenever you're ready."

In the public room, John Barlow sat alone. His hat rested on a table beside an oil lamp. In the shadows, the deputy's expression was difficult to interpret. "You've been out," he said without preamble. "I trust your errand was successful?"

His words were cautious—as they needed to be, but the impersonal question pricked Hanneke's sense of loss. "As successful as the situation permitted."

He nodded, but his mouth was drawn into a tight, unhappy line.

"Would you like a drink?" Hanneke asked quietly.

"I would. Not beer. Whiskey, if you've got it." Barlow fished in his pocket for the coins. "Pour some for yourself as well."

Hanneke did. He tossed his back in a single gulp. She sipped hers, wincing at the fire but relishing its warmth.

The deputy wiped his mouth on his sleeve and put the glass on the table. "I owe you an apology. Again."

"I assure you, I would have preferred being wrong about Christine."

"Christine and Kiessling have turned on each other," Barlow told her. "When I told Kiessling that Christine had accused him of killing Fridolin, he claimed that Fridolin was dead when he arrived, and that he only took steps to hide what *she* had done." He shook his head. "I don't expect we'll ever know exactly what happened that day in the barn. But Christine did say that

Kiessling pushed you into the street the night of that first Know-Nothing parade. I didn't bring it up, so she must have been telling the truth about that."

Hanneke slowly traced the rim of her glass with one finger. "What will happen to them?"

"That's not up to me."

Which was just as well, Hanneke thought. John Barlow had known Fridolin, known Christine. It was best for someone impartial to conduct a trial and pass judgment.

Barlow leaned back in his chair but held her gaze. "After everything that's happened, I wanted to express my sincere condolences. I remain willing to assist you in selling the farm or any other legal matters that need sorting."

"Well, I could use some advice," Hanneke admitted. "I won't be able to pay my tax bill until the farm is sold. Do you think the tax assessor might be willing to wait?"

"I'll find out if that can be arranged," Barlow promised.

"I'd be grateful."

A long moment passed before he spoke again. "You've had a difficult time."

That was such an understatement that she almost laughed. "Wisconsin is not at all as I'd expected. But in truth, I didn't imagine much beyond the farm on Plum Grove Road. I grew up in the country in Pomerania, but the property was sold. I always dreamed of helping to manage a thriving farm."

"Like the Forty-Eighters?" John Barlow's question was sardonic, but not unkind.

"No." Hanneke considered what she'd heard about Latin farmers—those idealistic and often impractical men who could translate poetry but didn't know hay from straw. "I do know how difficult agriculture is. Still, when I thought of joining Fridolin on his farm, I knew I could do my share. I knew I could tend the place."

"I don't doubt it."

Hanneke drained her glass. John Barlow was the last person she'd expected to confide in, but something about his mood, the dim light, the quiet, made her want to try. "I also didn't expect to find Wisconsin in such turmoil. Runaway slaves, the Know-Nothings… Many Germans leave the Old Country to escape violence. It's sad to find it here as well." She shrugged, wincing at the lingering ache in her shoulder.

"May I help myself?" The deputy got up, placed another coin on the bar, and poured himself another whiskey. When he sat back down, though, he only stared at it. "I came to Wisconsin from Vermont with my family in 1835, when I was ten. Back then, this area was a frontier. Everyone struggled just to survive. Everyone helped each other. I'm not saying no one ever got drunk or argued, but for the most part…people needed neighbors."

She nodded.

"It didn't matter where they were born. All that labor, all the hardships and sacrifices, everyone struggling to make a better life for their children… and *this* is what it's come to. Hatred. Slavers. A near-riot in the street." He shook his head. "Sometimes I think I should just sell my place. Move on. Follow the frontier."

Hanneke wasn't sure how to respond. "I'm sure you'd get a good price, with all the improvements you've made."

Barlow shook his head. "Maybe, but my wife has friends and family here. And I've gotten to know and respect many of the people who rely on constables and deputies in times of trouble. I'm not leaving."

The sound of a cantering horse drifted from the street, then faded. "It seems to me," Hanneke offered, "that you are uniquely poised to help German immigrants and Yankee settlers understand each other. Given the animosity that currently exists between them, I can think of few things more important. Sometimes all you can do is dig in and try to make things better."

"Maybe you're right." He finally drained his glass and set it back down with a thump. "Now, before I go, there's something else." He shifted in his chair, appearing suddenly ill-at-ease. "I considered Fridolin Bauer a friend, but…I hardly know what to think of a man who dared the wrath of slavers but hid from dissent at home. His bravery saved lives and his cowardice ruined lives."

Hanneke knew it would be a long time before she'd truly sorted out her view of Fridolin. "My husband was a dreamer. A flawed and complex soul.

242

CHAPTER TWENTY-THREE

But…aren't we all."

Barlow was silent.

"He was a man who wished the world well, but did not always have the strength of character to make it so." She hesitated, but the moment still seemed ripe for introspection. "And in truth, Fridolin and I were more alike than I even knew. Since coming to Wisconsin I have told lies. I have broken laws. If he'd lived, perhaps we truly would have gotten on."

"I don't think that's quite true," John Barlow said. "You and Fridolin might have gotten on well enough, but only because you have strength of character for two."

Chapter Twenty-Four

After the deputy left the tavern Hanneke sat alone in the taproom, savoring the stillness and considering her future. Knowing the truth about Fridolin's death helped, but she still had decisions to make.

She had no idea how to sort out the question of where to start her new life, but the solution to one problem did present itself. She fetched her bridal shawl, wrapped it around her shoulders, and walked to the Buena Vista.

She found a hired girl clearing away dishes in the dining room. "Could you please tell Frau Wiggenhorn that Hanneke Bauer wants to see her? I'll wait in the hall." She had no wish to return to the ladies' parlor.

A few minutes later Josephine Wiggenhorn appeared. *"Guten Abend,"* she said with wary courtesy. "May I help you?"

Hanneke didn't know how much Josephine knew about Christine's actions, and she didn't care. The story would travel through the German community soon enough. "Actually, I'm here to help you. I've decided to sell my shawl after all."

Clearly, Josephine had not been expecting that news. "Why…that's wonderful! It truly is perfect for my daughter's wedding. I haven't found anything else so fine. What is the cost?"

Hanneke put the shawl in Josephine's hands. Then she named her price.

Josephine's eyes went wide. "That's exorbitant!"

"Nonetheless, that is my price." Hanneke smiled demurely.

The other woman held the shawl high, fingering the fine strands of silky yarn, examining the lace. Hanneke waited. This was her best work.

Josephine would not be able to find fault.

Finally, Josephine nodded. "Very well. Let me get my purse." She lingered, though, biting her lip before saying simply, "I'm sorry." Then she hurried from the room.

Hanneke left the Buena Vista with the money in her pocket—enough to pay back taxes on the farm, and to buy Angela a new bonnet as well.

* * *

Instead of returning to the tavern, Hanneke walked from town, heading northwest to the farm on Plum Grove Road. What she needed to do most of all was what she did best. She needed to think.

The sky had cleared. The dirt roads were clear pale ribbons in the starlight. The shadows didn't seem spooky, as they had before. She liked the solitude, the sound of leaves riffling in the breeze. Already she recognized landmarks along the way…but absently, for she had much to ponder.

She was still thinking when she rounded the final curve in Plum Grove Road and the shadowed buildings of Fridolin's farm came into view. No, she reminded herself, not Fridolin's farm anymore. This was *her* farm. Beneath the night sky, she leaned on the woven-branch fence and took it in—the small *fachwerk* house, the barns, and fields beyond.

I can sell the farm, she thought, and move on. It would surely be best to leave this place, which held so many bad memories. Wisconsin was not a perfect refuge. She'd imagined a peaceful, bucolic existence. She hadn't expected Know-Nothings who hated her simply because she'd been born somewhere else. She hadn't expected to stumble into slave catchers and a lost baby.

Fridolin's farm was not perfect either. She'd imagined a hearth of her own, a home combining the latest Yankee innovations and the best German practices. She hadn't expected a black kitchen in an old-fashioned house that would be impossible to heat in the winter.

Unbidden, the advice she'd given Angela echoed in her mind. *Instead of dwelling on what you don't have, I hope you will consider instead all that you do.*

245

I do have friends here, Hanneke allowed. Angela and Adolf. Clara Steckelberg. Gerda Muehlhauser. Franz and Joe Rademacher had offered to help with any building repairs. Even Deputy John Barlow was assisting with legal matters.

"And I could tend this place," Hanneke whispered, picturing the property as she'd seen it in daylight. She could move the compost pile farther from the porch, and take a scuffle-hoe to the weeds, and mulch the strawberry patch with marsh hay. She could set out rows of lettuces, tomatoes, eggplants. She could plant more squash. Move the asparagus so the plants would get more sun. Set out bee skeps. Add a cheery marigold border to help keep beetles from the broccoli. In time she could buy a few Merino sheep, and do more of the spinning and knitting that brought her such pleasure.

Sometimes all you can do is dig in and try to make things better. So she'd advised John Barlow last night.

There is good I can do here, Hanneke thought. She could stay at the tavern until Angela's baby was born. Afterwards, if she settled here, she could still walk into Watertown to help Angela and Adolf.

"I could leave the star on the barn," she whispered, a sign for any terrified souls desperate to find a signal of safety. She could defy the Know-Nothings' contempt by being industrious, and generous, and kind to anyone in need.

Hanneke nibbled her lower lip. If she stayed at the farm, she'd be confronted with the memory of Fridolin Bauer every day. She turned that over in her mind, trying to gauge how painful that would be. His memory would forever represent a shattered dream.

"But I would be free," she whispered. For in truth, she was as contradictory a soul as Fridolin had been. She hadn't dared acknowledge a secret desire for independence, not beholden to father or brother or husband, until suspended between old life and new on the Atlantic voyage. Wisconsin was not a utopia, but she did own a fertile farm where she could plant dahlias wherever she wished. She could read books and think as much as she pleased.

Holding on to the fence, she tipped her head back and gazed at the expanse of glittering stars. "I think I will stay," she told Fridolin, and smiled.

A Note from the Author

In 1982, I accepted an interpretive position at Old World Wisconsin, an outdoor ethnic museum with a strong living history program. My first assignment was in the German area, which included two farms originally owned by Pomeranian immigrants. My favorite was the Schulz Farm, a fascinating remnant of Old World architecture transported to Wisconsin and restored at the historic site to its 1860 appearance. This farmstead was the model for Hanneke's fictional farm. You can see it for yourself! Visit https://oldworldwisconsin.wisconsinhistory.org to learn more.

I chose to set *Lies of Omission* in 1855 so I could spotlight the height of the nativist movement in Wisconsin. Members were alarmed by growing populations of Irish and German Catholic immigrants, and hoped their American Party could grow to dominate state and national politics. Originally organized in secret, adherents often denied their involvement by claiming to "know nothing." The Know-Nothings were good at agitating, whipping proponents to a sometimes-violent frenzy with fiery speeches and torchlit parades. Although the specific marches described here are fictional, political processions and mob actions were not unknown in Watertown during this period. In 1851, "Latin Farmers" agitating for German rights in the face of growing anti-immigrant sentiment organized a convention in Watertown to discuss founding a state intended to provide Germanic immigrants a place to preserve their language, laws, and cultural traditions.

In 1850, passage of the Fugitive Slave Act compelled citizens to help return any enslaved people to their enslavers. Historians have documented more than a hundred people escaping bondage who passed through Wisconsin while traveling north. The numbers are likely higher, since the extreme danger involved in the journey required utmost secrecy.

Acknowledgements

I'm indebted to the visionaries who managed to save and restore some of Wisconsin's fast-disappearing architectural treasures in the 1970s and 1980s. I'm also grateful to the Watertown Historical Society and the Trinity Freistadt Historical Society for making rich historical materials accessible. Thanks to Marilyn Koepsell for sharing her knowledge, and to Laurie Rosengren, Amy Glaser, and Barbara Ernst for editorial assistance.

I couldn't be more pleased to have found Hanneke a home with Level Best Books/Historia and the Dames of Detection—Verena Rose, Shawn Reilly Simmons, and Harriette Sackler.

I'm grateful to all my wonderful reader-friends! And as always, heartfelt thanks to my husband Scott. When I text him to say I'll get home late because I'm searching rural roads for old Pomeranian barns to photograph, he simply reminds me to use the flashers when I pull over. I'm a fortunate author.

About the Author

Kathleen Ernst is a social historian, educator, and bestselling author. Kathleen's forty-one published books encompass mysteries, historical fiction, poetry, and non-fiction. The Chloe Ellefson Mysteries feature a museum curator whose knowledge of the past helps solve contemporary crimes. Her children's books include twenty titles for American Girl.

Honors for Kathleen's work include multiple Agatha nominations, an Edgar nomination, a Lovey Award for Best Traditional Mystery, the American Heritage Women in the Arts Recognition Award for Literature from the National Society of the Daughters of the American Revolution, a Major Achievement Award from the Council for Wisconsin Writers, the Sterling North Legacy Award for Children's Literature, and an Emmy Award for Children's Instructional Programming.

Kathleen lives in Middleton, Wisconsin, with her husband Scott (AKA "Mr. Ernst") and feline muse Eliza.

SOCIAL MEDIA HANDLES:
 https://www.facebook.com/kathleenernst.author/
 https://sitesandstories.wordpress.com
AUTHOR WEBSITE:
 https://www.kathleenernst.com

Also by Kathleen Ernst

Balancing: Poems of the Female Immigrant Experience in the Upper Midwest, 1830-1930

The Chloe Ellefson Mysteries
Old World Murder
The Heirloom Murders
The Lightkeeper's Legacy
Heritage of Darkness
Tradition of Deceit
Death on the Prairie
A Memory of Muskets
Mining for Justice
The Lacemaker's Secret
Fiddling With Fate
The Weaver's Revenge

Nonfiction
A Settler's Year: Pioneer Life Through the Seasons
Too Afraid to Cry: Maryland Civilians in the Antietam Campaign

Young Readers
Twenty mysteries and historical novels for American Girl, five novels about the Civil War, and more.

CPSIA information can be obtained
at www.ICGtesting.com
Printed in the USA
LVHW012123240222
711932LV00002B/290